SPECIAL DELIVERY

Hansen barked, "Gatch, how's our fuel?"

"Sir, are you—"

"GATCH, HOW'S OUR GODDAMNED FUEL?"

"Sir, we got nearly three quarters of a tank. Sir!"

"I have a target," Mignola said evenly. "Moving BRDM. He's on the south side of the pass, about one-two hundred."

Hansen caught his breath, backhanded drool from his lips. "I see the bastard. He's trespassing on my battlefield, so let's shoot his ass."

"Yes, sir. Identified."

"Up!"

"Fire!"

"On the way!"

The BRDM surrendered to the forces of physics and American firepower, which was to say they blew the hell out of it.

ARMORED CORPS

ATTACK BY FIRE

PETE CALLAHAN

J

JOVE BOOKS, NEW YORK

THE BERKLEY PUBLISHING GROUP
Published by the Penguin Group
Penguin Group (USA) Inc.
375 Hudson Street, New York, New York 10014, USA
Penguin Group (Canada), 90 Eglinton Avenue East, Suite 700, Toronto, Ontario M4P 2Y3, Canada
(a division of Pearson Penguin Canada Inc.)
Penguin Books Ltd., 80 Strand, London WC2R 0RL, England
Penguin Group Ireland, 25 St. Stephen's Green, Dublin 2, Ireland (a division of Penguin Books Ltd.)
Penguin Group (Australia), 250 Camberwell Road, Camberwell, Victoria 3124, Australia
(a division of Pearson Australia Group Pty. Ltd.)
Penguin Books India Pvt. Ltd., 11 Community Centre, Panchsheel Park, New Delhi—110 017, India
Penguin Group (NZ), Cnr. Airborne and Rosedale Roads, Albany, Auckland 1310, New Zealand
(a division of Pearson New Zealand Ltd.)
Penguin Books (South Africa) (Pty.) Ltd., 24 Sturdee Avenue, Rosebank, Johannesburg 2196, South
Africa

Penguin Books Ltd., Registered Offices: 80 Strand, London WC2R 0RL, England

This is a work of fiction. Names, characters, places, and incidents either are the product of the author's
imagination or are used fictitiously, and any resemblance to actual persons, living or dead, business establishments, events, or locales is entirely coincidental. The publisher does not have any control over
and does not assume any responsibility for author or third-party websites or their content.

ARMORED CORPS: ATTACK BY FIRE

A Jove Book / published by arrangement with the author.

PRINTING HISTORY
Jove mass market edition / April 2006

ISBN: 0-515-14119-4

JOVE®
Jove Books are published by The Berkley Publishing Group,
a division of Penguin Group (USA) Inc.,
375 Hudson Street, New York, New York 10014.
JOVE is a registered trademark of Penguin Group (USA) Inc.
The "J" design is a trademark belonging to Penguin Group (USA) Inc.

PRINTED IN THE UNITED STATES OF AMERICA

10 9 8 7 6 5 4 3 2 1

ACKNOWLEDGMENTS

I OWE A heartfelt thank you to Tom Colgan and Sandra Harding at Berkley for their patience. This novel was written in Central Florida during the 2004 hurricane season. We braved three of the four major storms and spent a few months picking up the pieces. Despite the water damage and power outages, we forged on—but not without the assistance of some great technical advisors.

Major William R. Reeves, U.S. Army, worked closely with me from the outline to the last sentence of this manuscript. Along the way he created maps, updated the book's glossary, helped me with the logistics of battle scenes via extensive and insightful e-mails, made suggestions to improve details within the manuscript, and even wrote dialogue for key scenes that required his experience and expertise. I am honored and proud to call him a friend.

Lieutenant Colonel Jack Sherman, AR, USAR, Operations Officer 5th Joint Task Force, read and critiqued chapters within hours after I e-mailed them. In fact, Jack pored over all three books in this series—over 1,200 manuscript pages—just because he enjoys reading and wants to see me "get it right." This time around he provided me with character insights and battle details that helped shape the climax of this novel. His generosity is extraordinary and deeply appreciated.

Major Mark Aitken, U.S. Army, was serving in Iraq during the writing of this book, yet he remained in touch from the front lines, providing me with anecdotes and advice that touched me more than he knows. Mark's contributions to this series have awed and inspired me. His selflessness is a model for all those who work and serve with him.

Mr. Bennie McRae, who was a tank platoon leader during Operation Desert Storm, volunteered to help with this third novel, and boy did he provide me with some clever plot details ("the bitch plate" scene), as well as some hilarious—and harrowing—stories of combat that influenced what you'll read here. He reminded me of the difference between "by the book" fighting and what happens when the bullets really fly.

Shawn T.O. Priest was the first tanker who assisted me with this series and deserves the title of co-creator. Moreover, he represented the tanker community at a time when I wasn't sure anyone had the time and patience to help. I cannot thank him enough for his service to our country and his encouragement.

Lieutenant Colonel Tom O'Sullivan, U.S. Army (Ret.), who now works for BlackHawk Products Group, provided me with samples of the real gear mentioned in the text and helped me to better describe its use. While he couldn't mail me a functioning M1A1 Main Battle Tank, he did the next best thing. Tom is yet another tanker who worked with me from book one, page one, and his keen eye helped keep the series much more accurate and believable.

Major Phil Corbo, CFC, C1 Plans Officer, Korea, once again helped me hone my outline and kept me honest with story ideas. Just mentioning Phil's name around those in the know raises my credibility, which is to say, he is The Man when it comes to armor in Korea.

These folks offered technical assistance or helped me reach those who could:

Captain Keith W. Wilson

Major Jeffery Price, S3, Support Squadron, 2ACR

Lieutenant Colonel Steven A. Boylan, Public Affairs, 8th U.S. Army, Korea

Bruce E. Zielsdorf, Dir., Army Public Affairs, New York Branch

Charlotte Bourgeois, Managing Editor, *Armor* magazine

David Manning, editor, *Armor* magazine

Joseph S. Bermudez Jr., author of *Shield of the Great Leader, The Armed Forces of North Korea*

Nathaniel T. Robertson, Regimental Historian, 185th Armor Regiment, California Army National Guard

The listing of these individuals is my humble way of saying thank you. None of them were paid. The fact that their names appear here does not constitute an "official" endorsement of this book by them or the United States Army.

"Tanks are easily identified, easily engaged, much-feared targets which attract all the fire on the battle-field. When all is said and done, a tank is a small steel box crammed with inflammable or explosive sub-stances which is easily converted into a mobile cre-matorium for its highly skilled crew."

— BRIGADIER SHELFORD BIDWELL

"In the absence of orders, go find something and kill it."

— FIELD MARSHAL ERWIN ROMMEL

CHAPTER
ONE

SECOND LIEUTENANT JACK Hansen studied his tank commander's extension with aching eyes. His M1A1 Abrams was rumbling toward the Imjin River west of the smoldering ruins of Tongduch'on (TDC). Snowy mountains tinted green by the thermal sight broke across the night sky, their image flickering as the subzero wind howled and the tank hit another ditch.

What time was it? 0220. *Shit.* Was it too late to fight? Or too early? What did the North Koreans think?

A tremor ripped through Hansen's arm. *Damn it.* He made a fist against his nerves, cleared his throat, then called into the boom mike near his lips. "Mingola, you got anything?"

Sergeant Jason Mingola, the tank's new gunner, sat rigid at his station, his face seemingly glued to his primary sight, his CVC helmet too big for his narrow head.

"Mingola, did you hear me?"

"Sir, I'm seeing some gnarly shit, but there's magic I'm looking for, and I can't find it in the thermals."

"Aw, man," groaned Deac from the loader's station.

Private First Class Victor Deacon, the big hillbilly from North Carolina, had about as much tolerance for Mingola's rap as Hansen did.

On the other hand, Specialist Rick Gatch, the NASCAR fan from Daytona Beach who drove the tank, repeatedly bought into Mingola's weirdness by reinterpreting it: "The magic you're looking for is Jesus. And He is out there. Trust me, Mingola." During their last horrific battle in TDC, Gatch had turned over a new leaf, under which he had found God. His recent fanaticism made Hansen long for the old Gatch, a lifer who loved boobs and booze, with the tattoos to prove it.

"All of you shut up," Hansen snapped. He glanced at Mingola positioned below and booted the skinny gunner in the shoulder. "Hey, man, when I ask a question, I expect a straight answer. No weird shit. No funny shit. No bullshit. Got it?"

The sergeant turned back, his face a Halloween mask of bones and dark circles. "Yes, sir."

Time for the test. "Gunner, report."

"Sir, no targets yet, sir."

"Keep looking."

When the young sergeant wasn't blurting out bizarre crap or acting, in a word, twitchy, he would whisper in a strange lilt to Dix, Carey, and Goosey, the members of his former crew. Mingola had been with Second Tank, and his crew's loader had been killed during an engagement with dismounts somewhere in the hills north of Munsan. The sergeant had manned the loader's M240 machine gun, but then the tank had struck a mine, blasting him twenty feet into the sky. Mingola had picked himself up off the snow and foolishly gone back to the smoking tank, despite the danger of more mines or ammo igniting and cooking off. His tank commander and driver had been ground into hamburger and pink viscera. Those images alone could've messed him up for life.

But the real kicker was that he had lost his helmet during the explosion and may have suffered some head trauma; however, Hansen's requests to examine Mingola's medical records had twice been met by the same reply from Army doctors: "There is nothing wrong with Sergeant Mingola. We have examined him and given him a clean bill of health."

Hansen wasn't sure which was worse: having a gunner like Mingola or having to live with the memory of what had happened to his last gunner, Sergeant Lee Yong Sung, a Korean Augmentee to the United States Army. During waking hours, Hansen was able to suppress the events leading up to Sergeant Lee's death, but when it came time to rest, North Korean infantrymen charged through his nightmares, as did the spirits of Lee and all the other men he had lost. Hansen now had a love/hate relationship with sleep, the same one he shared with the war. Sure, he loved the thrills and challenges of combat, but he had grown to hate everything else. He reminded himself that he was only twenty-three, only human, and unable to throw a mental switch on his emotions. Although he had taken the Armor Officer Basic Course, none of his instructors had prepared him for this or had warned him what could happen. He had vowed that it was okay to feel it all, had convinced himself that doing so would make him stronger.

But at the moment, he just felt like shit.

And he couldn't afford that.

As Charlie Company's Red Platoon Leader, the crews of four M1A1 Main Battle Tanks trusted him with their lives. Fifteen other souls needed a leader who wasn't strung-out. Furthermore, as part of the Second Infantry Division, 1st Battalion, 72nd Armor, "First Tank"—the most forward-deployed U.S. Armor unit in all of Korea—he was considered one of the baddest asses on the peninsula. He had sworn to uphold that reputation, whether he felt like shit or not.

So it was back to work. The company's Red and Blue tank platoons, along with the infantrymen of Renegade Platoon (MECH Platoon) and the engineer and mortar platoons, were the muscle and might of Team Cobra, part of Task Force 1-72, operating alongside Task Force 2-9. Presently, the team was moving west to engage in a hasty river crossing via a flotation bridge. Second Brigade was busy doing an air assault into North Korea and all helicopters except MEDEVAC had been dedicated to that event. Thus, without close air support to help secure the area, Cobra would (in theory) seize the far side then attack across with no intentional pause so as not to lose their momentum. After that, they would push on to the Demilitarized Zone and Panmunjom, then ultimately advance farther into North Korea to seize Kaesong.

Like everyone in the task force said, it was about time they were on the offensive. Those godless, gutless bastards to the north had invaded the Republic of Korea on Christmas Eve and had wreaked havoc for long enough. They were overdue for an ass-kicking on their own turf.

While the tank platoons and some engineers secured the near side of the river, grunts from Renegade would raft two Bradleys across to secure the far side, some two hundred meters away. They would take more engineers with them to examine the slope on the far side and prepare the flotation bridge's exit. The water would be moving slowly, so the rafting should be relatively easy, though engineer bridge boats would probably have to break ice along the way. Assembling the flotation bridge and getting the team across should happen in record time—a couple of hours or less— because the engineer bridge company had been practicing all year long with both ROK and U.S. units. Ironically enough, they had been training at the very same location, which, at least for Hansen, made the whole operation seem a bit surreal and just like their last defense of TDC and Camp Casey. Wars weren't usually fought on your own training ground, and while that meant you had the advantage of knowing the terrain much better than your opponent, he came in fast and in huge numbers.

Moreover, the company had to bull through a frozen, mountainous shithole to get near the river, even as they faced the remnants of the Korean Barrier System, which included antitank and antipersonnel mines, as well as concertina wire strung across dirt roads, sometimes eleven rows deep. That wire could get tangled up in a tank's sprockets, where it might eventually cut the wheel seals and make a real mess. In fact, good old Matthew Abbot, Hansen's platoon sergeant and a seasoned veteran of the first Gulf War and Operation Iraqi Freedom, had just thrown a grappling hook over some wire and used his tank to pull it away, clearing their path.

Now, as they trundled a dozen more meters, past a few stands of trees whose branches reached out like gnarled fingers trying to clutch the tank's hull, the river finally scrolled into view, along with the big rock drops prepared on the north and south sides of MSR 3 by ROK forces. When detonated, those massive concrete drops, also part of the barrier system, would successfully block all passage of the road.

The fording site itself lay opposite two hills dubbed 984 to the south and 985 to the north. Engineers would set up observation posts on each hill, since there was little doubt that if enemy forces attempted to move into the area, they would be using the primary mountain passes alongside MSR 3, if not the road itself.

Fire Support Officer Jason Yelas had already pulled off the road and had borrowed an ROK battle position overlooking the river. He and the crew of his BFIST would employ all of their high-tech hardware to scan for enemy targets and field observers while also passing on target refinements to the mortar FDC and situation reports to the task force FSO. However, Hansen had heard that Yelas's modified Bradley was out of SINCGARS range, and the Army hadn't issued his crew HF long range radios because of funding issues. Consequently, the only indirect fire support assets available for the moment would be the mortar platoon, and they would establish their position along MSR 3, behind the engineers, tank platoons, and mechanized infantry.

Hansen's platoon and Blue Platoon—led by his buddy

from West Point, Second Lieutenant Gary Gutterson—
would assume positions on either side of the rock drops
and focus their attention on those mountain passes. Task
Force scouts had already reported at least two enemy reconnaissance platoons moving into the area, which was
why Hansen rode Mingola so hard.

An engagement was imminent.

Once again, Hansen squinted to find North Korean
BRDM-2 armored amphibious vehicles jutting out from
behind icy rocks and ditches. No doubt there were also observers for enemy field artillery, and those bastards would
call in fires the moment they spotted the team.

"Gatch, go left, take us farther down this hill to where it
levels off, then stop," Hansen instructed, seeing that the
next ridgeline would help shield their hull. "Red, this is
Red One. We're stopping here to see what we got, out."

"Whoa," Mingola gasped, leaning closer into his sight.

"Whoa?" asked Deac. "What the fuck does that mean?"

"Whoa!" Mingola repeated.

"Sergeant—" Hansen began.

"Two PCs, fuckin' BRDMs," cried Mingola. "They're
moving fast down the slope. Southern pass."

"Got 'em," Hansen said, having widened his sore eyes
to confirm. "Near one first!"

"Identified," cried Mingola, switching his sight to 10x
magnification.

Deac was already loading the main gun. He threw up
the arming lever and jammed himself into his seat, getting
his ass away from the crushing path of recoil. "Up!"

"Fire!" Hansen ordered.

"On the way!" answered Mingola.

With the potential for enemy PCs in the area, they had,
of course, been battlecarrying a HEAT round, reserved for
destroying thin-skinned armored vehicles. That bad boy
spat from the main gun tube and flew across the river, an-
nouncing to everyone on both sides that the fight was on.

And then, even as the round's aft cap clanged across
the turret floor, flames mushroomed in the distance. The

resulting BRDM's explosion allowed Hansen to breathe again. "Target!"

Now it was time to teach the crew and the half dozen reconnaissance troops aboard that second BRDM how to die for their Dear Leader in Pyongyang.

The lesson would be brief.

"Second PC," Hansen ordered.

Mingola panted into the intercom. "Where'd he go? Where'd he go?"

"Shit." Hansen set his teeth. Mingola should have been tracking that vehicle. Apparently he had shifted his gaze to the explosion. But Hansen was right there himself, scanning. A metallic flash came from the edge of the fireball; then he spotted the silhouette in his thermals. "There he is! Just right!"

Mingola sounded even more breathless. "Whoa."

Deac snorted. "Target the fucking bad guys!"

"I am! I got him!" Mingola said, his voice growing terse, more professional.

"Up!"

"Fire!"

"On the way!"

The familiar rocking of the tank, accompanied by the awe-inspiring boom of the main gun, went nearly unnoticed by Hansen as he concentrated on his extension, on the BRDM, on killing those men. The HEAT round struck the four-wheeled vehicle center of mass. Tires left the ground. Gasoline and ammo ignited. In his mind's eye, Hansen watched ferocious little men grimace as flames crawled up their cheeks before the blast shredded them.

"Target!"

"Hooah!" echoed Deac.

Hansen spied yet another fire about twenty meters west of the two they had created with their good aim and bad intentions.

"Red One, this is Red Four, over."

That was Abbot calling on the platoon radio net. He had probably taken out that third BRDM. "Go ahead, Four."

"We've destroyed one PC. See you got two, over."

"Roger that. Be ready to move forward into the ditch, okay? Red One, out." Hansen switched to the company net. "Black Six, this is Red One. We've engaged and destroyed three BRDMs, over."

Captain Mitchell Van Buren, Charlie Company's CO and Team Cobra's commander, responded quickly, "This is Black Six, roger. Engage and report, out."

Van Buren was a tanker's tanker, a down-to-earth leader who kept his cool and showed his men that he cared about them. He had even helped to find Karen, Hansen's girlfriend, when her bus had been attacked during the evacuation. His rock-solid voice always put Hansen at ease.

"Red, this is Red One. We're moving now to that lower ground in case FOs spotted us. Report when set, out." Hansen then called into the intercom. "Gatch, how's our fuel?"

"Sir, we're still good. You asked like ten minutes ago. We ain't sprung a leak."

"Just report, okay? Now move out!"

"Yes, sir."

"Gunner, any problems?"

"Negative, sir."

"Good. What about you, Deac?"

"Sir, I am a lean, mean, hillbilly killing machine. Ready to get some and bring it home to meet Mother."

"No, Deac, you're deaf. Just report. Do you have any problems back there? The fucking answer is yes or no."

"Uh, fucking no, sir."

"Wiseass."

Deac frowned, his eyes tearing up. "Sorry, sir. Are you okay?"

"No, I'm not, for God's sake! I'm trying to fight my fucking platoon!"

The loader recoiled even more. Hansen had never spoken as harshly to the young man.

"Whoa," Mingola muttered.

Hansen whipped around, jammed his eyes into his extension. "What do you got?"

"Thought I had something. It's gone now. Weird. Guys in 'Nam talked about shit like this. UFO abductions in the jungle. Guys getting taken up in spaceships, then pooped out into rice paddies."

"Gunner, do not speak unless you have identified a target. Do you understand?"

"Whew. Yes, sir."

Hansen leaned back in his seat, massaged his eyes, and wondered if maybe Sergeant Mingola was completely full of shit. The doctors had been right. He was just fine. But for some sick little reason, he had decided to play it strange. Or maybe he was just a nutjob from birth.

Or maybe Hansen was just thinking way too hard.

He was. Blame it on the war. A virus had crawled inside his thoughts, and it was spreading. He kept focusing on the negative, on the what-ifs. He kept telling himself that he needed perfect people working inside a perfect machine in order to stay alive. He could almost feel the obsession gnawing at his head and gut.

And he knew obtaining perfection was impossible. The machine would break. So would the men. Eventually.

So why couldn't he stop obsessing? Why was he beginning to hate the crew? Why did he believe that if he died, it would be their fault? That wasn't fair.

He knew that. But knowing didn't change a goddamned thing.

"Gatch, how's our fuel?"

"Sir, are you—"

"GATCH, HOW'S OUR FUCKING FUEL?"

"Sir, we got nearly three quarters of a tank. Sir!"

"I have a target," Mingola said evenly. "Moving BRDM. He's on the south side of the pass, about one-two hundred."

Hansen caught his breath, backhanded drool from his lips. "I see that motherfucker. He's trespassing on my battlefield, so let's shoot his ass."

"Yes, sir. Identified."

"Up!"

"Fire!"

"On the way!"

The BRDM surrendered to the forces of physics and American firepower, which was to say it got the shit blown out of it.

Hansen yelled, "Target!"

But no one else shared his excitement. He looked over at Deac, a solemn figure in the turret's dim light.

STAFF SERGEANT TIMOTHY Key, Hansen's wingman, ordered his driver to pull slightly ahead of the platoon leader's track. Key, known by many as "Keyman" or "Sergeant" or "that bald motherfucker" believed he could achieve a better view of the sector from his new vantage point. Lieutenant Hansen was hogging all the glory for himself. While that was not surprising, Keyman, like any good (and slightly deranged) warmonger, wanted to get in on the action. You couldn't keep the former Top Tank winner buttoned up for too long before he went insane and let the sabots fly. Blowing shit up was the third essential behind water and oxygen.

"That's looking real good, Boomer. Stop us right here," he urged the driver.

Specialist Tommy Boomer was a big black dude from Atlanta, the kind of guy you wouldn't want to tangle with unless you had serious backup. He sounded like Darth Vader and had come straight from the U.S. Army Armor Center in Fort Knox, Kentucky. After training just one day with the guy, Keyman knew he and Boomer would get along famously. The driver didn't give you lip, and he anticipated the path like a man who had been born to drive tracks. He had the eyes, all right. And you could tell he really enjoyed pouring himself into the driver's hole like pancake batter, grabbing the T-bar, and rocking and rolling.

The tank creaked and jostled to a stop. Private First Class Sean Lamont had already loaded a HEAT round and was seated at his station, scratching his big neck and shaking a leg. "Sarge, this is fuckin' awesome, man. I'm going to be a war veteran. That's awesome. That'll get me laid. And that round in the breach? That'll pop my cherry, you know that? First round I ever loaded in real combat. That's awesome. C'mon, find one of those fuckers. I can't wait anymore."

Lamont was another kid straight from Knox. Prior to enlistment he had spent his young life superglued to the controller of a PlayStation 2, where he had spent six hours a day raising his cholesterol level via junk food and grooming himself for killing. He'd told Keyman that his grandfather had been a tank commander during the Vietnam War, so he was carrying on a proud family tradition.

"There's one tradition that every family's got," Keyman had told the kid. "Know what it is?"

Lamont had wagged his head.

"Dying."

The kid had frowned. And Keyman had dismissed him with a wave. At the moment, Keyman did likewise, then returned to his extension, his cheeks bathed in the emerald glow, sweat gathering on his brow because they had the tank's heater blasting.

"Hey, Zuck, man, I know it's been a long day. But good eyes, eh?"

The gunner snickered and cocked a bushy eyebrow at Keyman. "Like you have to tell me? I'm into staying alive, too. Habit of mine. I'm all about the eyes."

Keyman smiled inwardly.

Sergeant Laurence Zuckerman was way too much like Keyman, despite his thick, black hair and hooked nose. "Zuck the Fuck" as he'd been known by his last crew over in Second Tank was the black sheep of his family, at least according to Lamont, the crew's resident big mouth. He had two older brothers who had become CPAs, while he had flunked out of college and joined the Army. He had a father who, just like Keyman's, thought he was second best, except in Zuck's case it was third best, which sucked even more. Keyman got that. Felt sorry for the guy. But he wouldn't tolerate any shit, either. In fact, since his nightmare MOUT fight in TDC, he had decided that it was time to grow up. Get serious. No more cussing in his turret. No more chip on his shoulder. Just do the job carefully, effectively, and get everyone home.

My God. Why hadn't he adopted that policy sooner?

Maybe it wasn't too late. If he inspired his new crew to do likewise, if he could weld them into a cunning and professional fighting team, then maybe his punishment in the afterlife would be less severe for his failure back in TDC.

Out of nowhere, Lamont blurted out, "All right, I can't take it anymore. I have to ask, Sarge. You know, we've been hearing all the rumors, but we want to hear your side of it. I think that's only fair, don't you?"

Did the kid read minds?

"Lamont, shut the fuck up," ordered Zuck. "This ain't the time or place."

"Hey, watch that," Keyman told the gunner.

"Not cursing is not possible."

"Swallowing teeth is possible. Want me to prove it? Look, clean up your act. That's all I'll say."

Zuck shrugged and made a face.

In the meantime, Lamont hoisted his brows and widened his incredibly naïve eyes. "I heard you left them alone, Sergeant. They say you went off, and the crew got hit by Molotovs, and everyone died."

Keyman lowered his gaze. "That's exactly what happened. The first time we got it, I dismounted to kill those cocksucker motherfuckers. I didn't know more guys were hiding behind some broken walls and shit."

"Nobody could've known that," said Lamont.

"Fuckin' South Korean civilians. Fuckin' people we're fighting for!"

"That's bullshit!" cried Lamont.

"Shut up!" Zuck said.

Keyman went on: "They hit my tank while I was out

searching buildings." He faced Lamont. "I will never do that to you. I'll fuckin' die first. Do you understand?"

Lamont nodded.

"So the ban on swearing's been lifted?" asked Zuck.

Keyman winced. "No." He glanced down at Zuck, turned his gaze over to Lamont, and imagined the keen-eyed Boomer down in his driver's hole. They were good men.

The silence that followed left Keyman feeling tense; he figured they were mulling it over: *Do we believe this guy or what?*

"Okay, okay, we got one," said Zuck. "Moving BRDM, right there, right out in the open. Look at this idiot. You want me to shoot him?"

Keyman snickered. "What do you think?"

"Up!" shouted Lamont.

"Fire!"

"On the way!"

As the main gun recoiled, Lamont was already on his feet, screaming, "Yeah! Yeah! Die you communist mothers! Eat this! Eat this!"

Lamont should have joined the infantry—then he would've received a more up-close-and-personal experience instead of being tucked inside the nice, warm turret, watching it all unfold through his vision blocks the way he watched it happen on his TV and computer screens back home. Even when combat was real, it still looked unreal. Keyman suspected that would change very soon for the FNG, once they got past the DMZ and into dismount country. Fucking New Guys learned the hard way.

The BRDM juked right, but the HEAT round still managed to punch its ass and blast it across the mountainside. "Target!" Keyman announced.

"Sergeant, the engineers and grunts are heading toward the riverbank," reported Boomer. "Could be a few dismounts waiting to ambush 'em."

"Oh, they're out there, Boomer. Freezing their little asses off. Keep watching. You da man."

"That's 'cause I got the boom-boom. And war ain't nothing but a thing."

"Webber? See any movement?"

"Whose Webber?" Zuck asked.

The question struck Keyman like an RPG to the bare chest. He watched himself explode, pieces of bloody flesh darkening into shards of a fractured mirror. Those random, sharp-edged fragments continued to tumble, flashing images of three men:

Sergeant Clark Webber was his former gunner and the only guy with balls enough to stand up to Keyman's bullying. There was no single tanker whom Keyman respected more than that guy, that poor guy who had been struck by a Molotov cocktail and had burned to death while standing in the TC's hatch.

Corporal Segwon "Smiley" Kim had earned his nickname by always keeping his spirits up and smiling when he didn't know the English word for something. He was, of course, a KATUSA, a committed loader, and a young man who had handled himself well around a tyrant like Keyman. Smiley had so much honor that he couldn't keep it all inside, and that, Webber sometimes had said, was the reason for his grin. Either way, the kid had been a great loader who didn't deserve such a gruesome and terrible death, burning beside Webber on the turret.

Specialist Anthony Morabito had been the prophet of doom with no luck at all. He had been short, with just two months left to serve in Korea before the war had broken out. As many combat vets would tell you, you either got whacked your first month in country or your last. Yes, sir, Murphy was dicking with you, applying his laws to your shitty little life. Consequently, the flaming, napalmlike gel of the Molotovs had penetrated the driver's hatch seals, and Morbid had, like the others, lost his life.

All three men wailed each night in Keyman's nightmares, with Webber's voice the loudest.

Even now he could hear his former gunner screaming, "Why did you leave us?"

Zuck was still glancing over his shoulder at Keyman, who blinked and repeated, "Do you see anything?"

The gunner gave him an odd look, then returned to his sight. "Okay. Here we go. I see a bunch of guys running around on the river bank."

Keyman saw them as well, perhaps two squads, probably dismounted from a few BRDMs that the platoon had failed to spot and destroy. Or maybe they were observer teams adjusting position. In the end, though, it didn't matter what their job was, as long as Keyman and his men pink-slipped them into oblivion.

"I'll call the lieutenant," Keyman began. "I bet the FSO already has them."

"I wouldn't waste the time," said Zuck. "We got an AP round. Let's use it right now."

The old Keyman would have agreed and fired the antipersonnel round without notifying Hansen because Zuck was right: time was of the essence. But Keyman wanted to play it by the book. No, he wasn't turning into a hardcore, wannabe West Pointer, but communication—or the lack thereof—too often decided wars.

"Red One, this is Red Two, over."

"Go ahead, Two."

"Looks like two squads of dismounts moving along the riverbank, just north of TRP 01, over."

"Roger, Two. I see 'em. Calling for mortars, out."

"You see?" Keyman asked Zuck. "Better to hit 'em with indirect right now. We lay low, then we pound the shit out of them as we move up. It's a no-brainer."

"But the lieutenant already fired. So did the platoon sergeant. They know our location."

"And I know we can save ammo and let the mortars help out."

Zuck wasn't buying that. "Let me ask you something. Your crew got killed. That's horrible, man. But you ain't lost your nerve, have you? 'Cause they've said you're the baddest motherfucker in this whole company. Now you're handing off the fight to the LT and the mortars, trying to play preacher boy by cutting out the curses, and looking, if I can say it, a little scared."

"Whoa. You don't talk to me like that. Not in my turret. That happens again, I will remove your ability to speak. Do you understand?"

Zuck issued a smug look, then leaned back toward his sight.

Keyman turned to Lamont. "What the fuck you looking at?"

"Language, Sergeant. Language."

At that, the first enemy artillery shell struck the hill just fifty meters ahead, the vibration charging up through the tracks and into the turret. A wall of dirt and snow screened the river, and as it dissipated, the silhouette of a BRDM shone on the northern ridge of hill 984, followed by another.

"Two PCs," Keyman barked. "Near one first!"

"I don't trust the range," cried Zuck. "Wait."

"No time!"

"There it is. Identified."

"Up!"

"Fire!"

"On the way!"

The first track succumbed to the white-hot explosion. Keyman announced the hit, gasped, ordered Zuck to take out the second one.

"Up!"

"Fire!"

"On the way!"

Just as the main gun recoiled, the tank's engine suddenly went dead, and the turret grew strangely quiet.

"Got the second one," said Zuck.

"Boomer, what the hell happened?"

Before the driver could answer, yet another shell dropped sixty or so meters to their left. Then came another. And another, as Keyman screamed, *"Boomer?"*

CHAPTER
TWO

THE INCOMING ARTILLERY fire annoyed Staff Sergeant Richard "Neech" Nelson. Deep down he was scared, too, but he had learned to channel that fear into action.

"Wood, go down farther, right near those trees!"

Specialist Frank Wood, nineteen, who seemingly five minutes ago had been back in the states butting heads with his CO for being a wiseass and a troublemaker, revved the engine and took off. A half-second later, the next shell thundered across the hill behind them.

"Close! Fifty meters!" cried Private First Class "Popeye" Choi Sang-ku from his loader's station.

Sergeant Romeo Rodriguez leaned back from his gunner's sight and frowned. "Fifty? You can't see shit through that vision block. It was closer than that."

"Keep going, Wood," Neech instructed. "Keep going."

"They call me 'Big Wood', if you'd please, Sarge."

"And you can shut up and call me *Sergeant*."

"Okay, Sergeant. But it don't matter. They'll get us. I just know it. Where are those fucking mortars?"

Neech stole a glimpse through his extension. To his left, a ball of orange, red, and white swelled; then he flinched as a shitstorm of rocks, ice chips, and shrapnel pelted the turret and hull. Though their CVC helmets muted some of the pings, the really big pieces hammered hard. Really hard.

"Those motherfuckers are adjusting their fire!" Wood cried.

"Shut up, you goddamned coward," Romeo spat. "Do you know how many times we've been here and done this?"

"You're damned right," Neech said. "Wood, we'll tell you when you have a fuckin' clue. Right now, you are a fuckin' brain-dead dickhead with no opinion, no experience, no nothing. So shut the fuck up and drive!"

Before the platoon had set out for the river, Keyman had casually mentioned to Neech how he was banning cuss words in his turret. Neech had laughed and said that his crew—a Puerto Rican ladies man with an ironically appropriate first name, a KATUSA who loved Popeye's Chicken, and an FNG replacement driver—would last all of ten seconds if they tried that.

As Wood neared the trees, the tank spun out and began sliding. A terrific bang reverberated through the right side of the turret.

"What the fuck was that?" yelled Romeo.

Choi shook his head. "He bad driver! Bad driver!"

Neech checked his vision blocks and gritted his teeth. "Dumbass, you hit the fuckin' tree!"

Choi and Romeo began screaming instructions at Wood, who kept repeating that the collision was not his fault. Meanwhile, Neech, as much as he hated to do so during an artillery strike, popped his hatch and rose for a better look.

Yup, the snot-nose at the T-bar had smashed into the tree and leveled it. He would now get them stuck on a long patch of ice, part of a little stream that during the warmer months flowed to the river.

"I reenlisted for this?" Neech asked under his breath.

Indeed he had. Signed up for a second year in Korea.

Got a nice signing bonus. Did it while standing in his hatch. Figured he'd work his way up to master gunner. He had risen above the death of his first driver, the incredibly young yet legendary Private William Wayne, aka "Batman." The kid had taken a bullet for Neech, and his death had left Neech ready to quit, to die. But then he had been given a second chance and enough time to remember his role, his duty, his honor. When your men depend upon you to get them home, you had best do everything to make that happen. That's what tank commanders did. That's what all great soldiers did.

"Driver, reverse!" Neech ordered, grimacing as the wind bit into his cheeks.

The tank lurched forward, jerked, and then the engine roared as Wood hit the gas and backed up.

"Little more, little more," directed Neech.

"Sergeant, button up, man, come on," said Romeo. "They got observers on us!"

"Okay, Wood, turn right and head up about five meters or so and we'll be out of the streambed," said Neech. "Hey, Romeo, stop pretending you love me and find a fucking target."

"You want to die up there, be my guest," grunted the gunner.

As the tank cleared the bed and rolled on across the snow, Neech lifted his night vision goggles. Since he was already up in the hatch risking his ass, he might as well steal a peek at the hills.

And son of a bitch if he didn't pan a little right and there they were: an enemy observer team, probably the same bastards responsible for calling in all that field artillery. He could even see one guy lifting a microphone to his mouth.

"Wood, stop this tank! Romeo, I got an FO team on the other side of the river."

"Wait, yeah, a little south of us. Yeah, okay, I got 'em. I got 'em. Idiots got cocky and moved in too close. You want to call Abbot?"

"Nope." Neech ducked down into the turret, slamming

the hatch after himself. "All right, boys, we got this one ourselves. Let's make 'em eat heat!"

"FO team identified," reported Romeo.

Choi plopped into his seat. "Up!"

"Fire!"

"On the way!"

Romeo squeezed the triggers on his Cadillacs, and Neech once more felt that surge of adrenaline, the one that had drawn him to the army in the first place, the one that reminded him that he was no longer a fat bastard who had used the military as a diet program. He was a goddamned tank commander, a fire-breathing badass. *You want to fuck with me? I don't think so.*

The small group of North Korean soldiers who were serving as the eyes and ears of the enemy artillery commander disappeared in a ball of roiling flames that lit up the hillside. Neech clenched a fist. "Target!"

Romeo and Choi exchanged a high five.

"Red One, this is Red Three," Neech began over the platoon net. "Identified and destroyed enemy FO team, over."

"Red Three, this is Red One," replied Hansen. "Good work. But let's lean on the mortars now. Keep scanning. Red One, out."

As Neech hung up the mike, he thought of Wood down in the driver's hole. The kid had grown suspiciously silent. "Wood, you still with us?"

SERGEANT FIRST CLASS Matthew Abbot knew better than any man in Red Platoon that you couldn't allow your personal problems or emotions to interfere with your mission. As the wise, old platoon sergeant who considered himself a cliché and a relic around tankers half his age, he still recognized that many looked to him for guidance, encouragement, and support—including the lieutenant himself.

But didn't a platoon daddy deserve a day off once in a while? Couldn't the army cut a man some slack when he had just learned a few days prior that his wife had been killed during the evacuation of Camp Casey? Couldn't he stand on the sidelines until they actually found his wife's body, which was lying out there somewhere in the mountains along MSR 3?

Who was he kidding? He didn't want a day off, slack, or anything else that kept him out of the shit. And he had never asked for such. He knew the army needed everyone right now. He knew he would never walk away from his men, no matter what had happened. He knew his job was to steel himself, get the mission accomplished, then deal with his loss later, in private. That's the way professionals did it. Period. The entire platoon needed a strong sergeant during peacetime. During wartime, they needed someone who went beyond.

So Abbot willed himself to look past Kim's death and beyond to the mission.

All he had to do was focus.

But he hadn't realized it would be so hard.

When he looked in the mirror, all he saw was a sad, wrinkled face. The old Marlboro man with a thick moustache, the cocky guy full of energy, had retreated to the frozen mountains where he dug all night in the snow, his hands bare and frostbitten, his veins clogged with ice.

He still couldn't find her.

"Engineers moving to clear riverbank," said Sergeant Park Kon-sang, craning his head away from his gunner's sight. "This all too slow, right, Sergeant?"

Abbot nodded.

"At least the fuckin' shelling stopped," muttered Specialist Jeff Paskowsky, the loader with a forgettable face and an unforgettable number of superstitions. He rapped three times on his ammo door, his lucky number. "What the fuck is taking those engineers so long?"

"Shit, Paz, we just got here," said Abbot, checking his watch.

Truth be told, Abbot felt just as impatient because he had already heard about the friction between Captain Van

Buren and the engineer platoon leader, a guy named Harris. Van Buren was all about getting the team across the river in as little time as possible. However, Abbot had worked with many engineers before, and he knew Harris would be no different. The guy was tired and scared and remembering little of the stuff he had been taught at Fort Leonard Wood about river crossings and engineer doctrine. Instead, he aimed to do a thorough job of clearing the river bank. The entire riverbank. He was not concerned with speed or with the minimum requirement of just opening a lane wide enough to deploy a tank platoon and allow access to the bridge company trucks and boat/bridge cradle launchers.

In fact, Abbot was monitoring the company net, eavesdropping on communications between the team's platoons and the CO. He turned up the volume, and at that moment, Van Buren and Harris were discussing the matter. While the PL sounded a bit whiny, Van Buren kept his cool—until Harris said it was impossible to speed up the operation. Then Van Buren let him have it with main and machine guns, stating that Red Platoon would be moving in very soon, and if the bank was not cleared, he'd be holding the PL responsible.

Paz laughed. "CO tore him a new one."

"Shouldn't have happened," said Abbot. "If Harris knew what Van Buren wanted, there wouldn't be this delay. But whose fault is that? Brigade's. If they hadn't waited till the last second to dump this on us, we could've avoided these bullshit delays."

Paz looked confused. "So why'd they wait?"

"If I knew that I'd be running this fuckin' war."

The loader smiled, then widened his eyes at Park and made a motion of slitting the guy's throat.

Abbot shook his head and frowned.

Paz no longer trusted the KATUSA, especially after what had happened to the lieutenant's gunner. Sergeant Lee and Sergeant Park had been good friends, and they had both achieved the rare position of gunner aboard U.S.

tanks. Most other KATUSAs served as loaders. Abbot had thought of Lee and Park as the Korean version of Hansen and Keyman, both vying for attention, respect, and to be number one at their positions. Like Lee, Park was a well-known and well-respected soldier with an impeccable record. But maybe that didn't matter anymore. Maybe he, like Lee, had seen enough. When the North Koreans were tying civilians to their vehicles as human shields, what were you supposed to do? Not fire? Allow yourself to be killed because of your guilty conscience?

According to Hansen, Lee had refused the order to fire. He had wanted to leave the turret. Keyman, who had been serving as temporary loader, challenged the gunner. Lee had pointed his sidearm at Keyman, about to kill him. Hansen had fired the main gun, allowing the recoil to crush Lee before the KATUSA could do anything else.

That had been a terrible incident and a terrible way to die. Abbot wondered if his own gunner was having second thoughts. Even more chilling: Abbot wasn't sure how much Park knew. The incident had been kept under wraps. There had been a joint ROK-U.S. investigation, and both parties had agreed that it was a "no-fault" accident and that Sergeant Lee had suffered from a mental illness made worse by the stress of combat.

Park had commented that someone was not telling the truth, that Lee had suffered no mental illness, and that there was no explanation for him being in the path of recoil. Abbot had taken Park by the shoulders and said, "Just let it go. We don't know what happened in that turret. And we never will."

Though he hated lying, Abbot knew that the safety of his entire crew came first. In any event, if history was about to repeat itself, he had best be ready. Talking behind the gunner's back was just rubbing in the salt. No doubt Park knew they were scrutinizing his every move. Paz needed to calm down and do his job.

Abbot waved his hand. Enough was enough. Paz got the message. Then Abbot put a finger to his lips and winked. Paz got that message too.

Paz and Park. A Pollock and a Korean with names that, if you didn't know the soldiers, you could easily mix up.

But there was no mistaking them now. They were worlds apart, growing bitter for different reasons, yet both seated in the very same turret.

Abbot returned to his extension, praying for good news in the thermals. Suddenly, a chill ran up his spine as he once more thought of her. His Kim. And his hands grew cold.

THE ENGINEERS HAD finally finished sweeping the riverbank and had cleared a path for the tank platoons. Hansen gave the order to move out.

But that order fell on Keyman's deaf ears. He was too busy calling out to Boomer, who had climbed out of his driver's hole, gone around to the back deck of the tank, and removed the "bitch plate," a steel plate under the overhang of the turret that was a bitch to get back on. Boomer was jiggling the tank's starter. Before they had left the motor pool, he had gone over the M1A1 with a fine-toothed comb and had had a bad feeling about that starter.

"Boomer, we have to go, man! Come on!"

"Just give me a few more seconds," the driver said calmly. "I'll get her going."

Keyman stood in his open hatch, rocking to and fro against the cold and wishing he could see what was going on back there. Wasn't this his luck? Oh, yeah, the big guy upstairs was dishing it out, trying to see how much Keyman could take before his head cracked open like a walnut.

"Hey, Sergeant, the lieutenant's calling," said Zuck.

Resisting the temptation to curse, Keyman went down into the turret. "Red One, this is Red Two. My piece of crap float tank aborted."

"Oh, yeah?" the lieutenant screamed. "Get that fucking thing going!"

Zuck recoiled. "Whoa, the dude is pissed. He like that all the time?"

Keyman ignored the gunner. "Red One, we got the bitch plate off and we're working on it."

"You got one minute. Do you hear me? One minute! Red One, out!"

"Is he on the rag or what?" asked Lamont.

"Hey, we've been going since the first night," Keyman growled.

Wait a minute. Was he actually defending Hansen?

Had he lost his mind?

No. But maybe the lieutenant had. Hansen was having a serious coronary over there. You could hear the little tremors in his voice. What had happened to Mr. West Point? Mr. Top Tank who had been pretty cool so far?

Keyman returned to his hatch, faced the back deck. "Boomer!"

"Over here," called the driver from the tank's front slope. He was sliding into his hatch. "I feel good!"

"Boomer, it's all about you, man. Fourth down and long. And boom-boom's throwing the bomb. Here we—"

Keyman broke off as the engine spun up and whined. There was no better music in all of Korea.

Zuck and Lamont couldn't help but smile over the ridiculousness of jiggling the starter on a multi-million-dollar tank, just to get it started.

"Okay, Red One, this is Red Two. We're up and running. Ready to move out."

"All right, let's go! Red One, out!"

"Fuckin' Boomer, you are too much, man," said Zuck. "What did you do, spit on it?"

"I was getting ready to, but sometimes if you're nice to these old girls, they can sense it."

Boomer was their disembodied voice, now their disembodied savior. Maybe Keyman was a good judge of character. He had his whole crew pegged, didn't he?

"Uh, Zuck?" he called, remembering the gunner's use of the forbidden word. "You can just call him Boomer."

"Oops," Zuck said. "I said *fuck,* didn't I? And saying *fuck* is not permitted inside this turret. Saying *fuck* is an insult to the good men who work here. To say *fuck* would be inappropriate and might even incite violence. Even if one's name rhymes with *fuck*, or if *fuck* has been added to one's name as, in fact, a nickname, saying *fuck* is still not permitted because by avoiding the word *fuck*, we will all have a much better chance of getting back home, where we will be fucked over by our friends, family, and government."

"Hey, Zuck, you're like a weirdo geek or something, man," Lamont said.

"Yeah, and what's your problem?" Keyman added.

The gunner hesitated as the tank shook hard, then came up and over a rise in the slope. "I just don't get you."

Keyman snickered. "What don't you get?"

"You lose your crew, and now what? You're trying to prove something? And we got stuck for the ride?"

Keyman leaned down to raise an index finger in the man's face. "How 'bout this? I'll prove to you and everybody else that I can get you home. You don't like my rules? Get the fuck out right now."

"Uh, Sergeant?" Lamont called.

Zuck rolled his eyes and smirked.

"All right, you know, maybe I'm being unrealistic."

"Maybe?" Zuck asked, dumbfounded. "This is fuckin' combat, and you want clean language? That's nuts."

"Look, just . . . just keep it to a minimum. We'll say that. We're professionals, and we need to act like it. I don't understand why that's so hard. You know those cocksuckers running around out there? They got fucking duty and honor, and they're ready to die for that asshole up north. They're not talking smack to their PLs and COs. They got the warrior ethos up to here."

"The sergeant is right," said Boomer. "I for one will not use that language. And if I go, I go knowing that I fought with dignity and honor. That's the way it should be."

"Amen," said Keyman. "Amen!" He slapped Zuck on the shoulder. "Are you with us?"

"Whatever."

"I'll try my best, Sergeant," said Lamont. "But it's hard, you know? In some of my PlayStation games, they even have—"

"All right, Lamont. Enough."

Keyman wished he could just tell them the real reason why he didn't want them to curse, why he wanted—needed, really—them to behave like professionals.

But to reveal that kind of weakness would ruin their confidence in him.

And so he remained silent as they muscled toward the river, taking lead, followed by the lieutenant's track, then Abbot's, then Neech's, pulling up the rear.

GATCH FELT RELIEVED that they were moving again. He followed Keyman down the slope, maneuvering directly into the TC's tracks. He kept his focus on driving the tank and tried to forget about the lieutenant's behavior. For the past hour he had been wanting to speak privately with Deac and Mingola, but that, of course, would not happen until they had a chance to dismount. For the time being, they would literally ride out the storm.

If you asked, Gatch would swear that Lieutenant Jack Hansen was incapable of having a meltdown. Hansen was the kind of guy who knew when he could steal time to think, but he also knew how to react quickly and decisively. Some guys couldn't do both. They'd try to create some brilliant tactical plan and get killed while thinking it up. Some guys wouldn't think at all; they'd roll into a situation with guns blazing.

But Hansen, Gatch had liked to believe, was the best of both worlds. A thinker and a quick shot. Now the lieutenant was leaning too far in the wrong direction. And what was with the paranoia? That was pretty scary.

Dear Lord, please protect and guide us during this river crossing. Please give the lieutenant the peace of mind to do a good job and not freak out. Jesus, I'm asking this in your name. You told me to get right with you. And I think I am. At least I hope so. Maybe if I share your good word with the lieutenant, all will be well.

"Gatch, turn left and follow Keyman on up," ordered Hansen.

"Yes, sir."

The tanks fanned out and moved into defensive positions along the riverbank, Red Platoon to the left, Blue to the right. Gatch stopped the tank as ordered, then scanned the area as the bridge company got to work. Those guys were fascinating to watch:

There were two ways to cross a river, either full closure or partial closure. Full, as the name implied, meant that the engineers constructed a complete bridge from one end to the other. If they didn't have enough ramps, they would do a partial closure, with ramps extending out from the bank on both sides. Vehicles would need to be ferried between the gaps. But that wouldn't happen now. The engineers knew this fording site like the backs of their hands. And without further delay, the trucks pulled up, and the first interior ramp slid out of its cradle and into the water with a sudden splash. Then came the others, one by one, some being maneuvered by MK2 bridge erection boats to the other side so that construction would begin simultaneously on both riverbanks. The boats were either pushing or pulling the ramps into position so they could be secured to each other. When all of the ramps were in place, only then would a ratchet be secured to the bridge and stakes driven into the ground, about twenty meters away from the river. The ratchet would then be tightened until enough tension was applied to the cables. At that point, it was time to roll.

The two Bradleys from Renegade Platoon were in position on either side of MSR 3, covering the road and hillsides, their dismounts in position to intercept any creepy crawlies who might stray into the area to call in fires or set up antitank missiles. The other two Bradleys remained on the near side, ready to pounce on any enemy forces that might be waiting to ambush from the north or south.

FSO Yelas was still in his OP and watching the whole

thing, as were the two teams of observers from the engineer platoon who remained on the hills. Although everyone was in position and set, everyone knew that at that moment, they were most vulnerable. If the engineers were able to construct the bridge without taking any fire, well then, you had Jesus to thank.

"Hurry up and wait, hurry up and wait," sighed Mingola. "There's a long line to get into hell. And as usual, we're at the end. . . ."

Although the engineers were now working furiously to construct the bridge, getting the ramp bays and the interior bays into the correct sequence for the whole thing to work, the platoon still had to wait them out.

Gatch was about to lean back in his seat and stretch his arms when Mingola's breathy voice came over the intercom: "Whoa."

And in Mingola-speak, that meant enemy contact.

CHAPTER
THREE

HANSEN JERKED FORWARD toward his extension, squinted, and thought he saw two vehicles moving along the northern slope of Hill 984. A dense fog was rolling in and washing out their thermals. *Shit.* He lost them. *Wait.* There they were. Four vehicles now. A platoon working parallel to MSR 3. "Gunner?"

"Yeah?"

"What do you mean, 'yeah'? Do you see them or not?"

"Whoa. Yeah, yeah. But they're gone again. Something funny about the silhouette."

"Red, this is Red One. We might have some PCs moving just south of the road. Can anyone else confirm, over?"

"Red One, this is Red Two," answered Keyman. "Negative. Negative."

"Red One, this is Red Three. Nada," said Neech.

"And this is Red Four. We didn't see anything," Abbot reported. "Damned fog's getting thicker, though, over."

"Red, we saw something. Let's find 'em, out." Hansen craned his neck at an odd clicking coming from somewhere in the back of the turret. "Deac, you hear that?"

The loader snapped out of a thought. "Hear what?"

"That sound?"

"I didn't hear nothing."

"Gatch?"

"Yes, sir?"

"You hear anything?"

"No."

"Check your gauges."

After a few seconds the driver said, "Everything looks good down here."

"Whoa, here they are again," said Mingola. "But I'm telling you, something ain't right. I know that I know that I know. I can't get a good look at 'em in the thermals."

Hansen widened his eyes until they hurt. For a few seconds, he glimpsed the platoon; then once again, they vanished into the hillside, seemingly consumed by the trees and snow. He got back on the radio, hoping he could get an answer from Captain Van Buren. "Black Six, this is Red One, over."

"Red One, this is Black Six, go ahead."

"Believe we've spotted an enemy recon platoon directly north of engineer OP on Hill 984. Does the FSO have anything on them?"

"Stand by."

"Whoa, we got muzzle flash!" Mingola hollered.

"There he is!" Hansen barked, his gaze riveted upon the vehicle's wedge-shaped bow. "He's engaging us!"

"Wait! That might've been mortar fire," said Mingola.

"Bullshit!" cried Hansen. "Shoot that bastard!"

"Identified!"

"Up!"

"Fire!"

The main gun boomed, recoiled, and belched a HEAT round across the river and into the dense wall of fog. At that very moment, an odd sensation overcame Hansen. He did not breathe. His entire station morphed into a gray blob that crawled up his legs and began to wrap him in suffocating steel.

But just then, the HEAT round slammed into the enemy vehicle, and the subsequent explosions rose like flaming orchids. The aft cap banged onto the floor, jarring Hansen out of the hallucination. He blinked. Took a breath. "Target!"

"Oh my God," Mingola said softly. "I think we—"

"Quiet!" yelled Hansen, spying the next vehicle as it emerged through the fog and smoke. "Second PC! Come on! Come on! He's going to fire!"

"No, he's not!" argued Mingola. "He's not!"

"Shut up, boy, and let the LT fight this tank," grunted Deac as he finished reloading the main gun.

"Mingola, target that PC!"

"But I'm telling you—"

"TARGET THAT GODDAMNED PC RIGHT NOW— OR I WILL!"

As the smoke cleared and the explosion's heat pushed back some of the fog, the next enemy vehicle's profile materialized—along with the familiar image of a CIPS panel glowing in the thermals like a neon sign that read: *Big Mistake.*

"What the fuck?" Hansen gasped. Tremors rose through his gut to clutch his throat.

Those weren't friendly PCs out there. They just couldn't be. They just couldn't—

"Red One, this is Black Six. Hold your fire! Hold your fire!"

"That's a platoon of Strykers up there," said Mingola, his voice breaking up. "Or what's left of them."

Hansen reached for the microphone but wasn't sure he could find his voice. He thought of the driver, the commander, and the nine members of the rifle squad who had been aboard that vehicle. Maybe the squad had dismounted. Maybe he hadn't killed them all. *Oh my God.* "Black Six, this is Red One. Holding fire, over."

"LT, we fucked up bad," said Deac. "Real bad."

Hansen bore his teeth. "We don't know what we did!"

"Yeah, we do," said Mingola.

Brain damage or not, the gunner was probably right. Why did the goddamned Stryker have to look so much like a BRDM? Why was the entire world out to get him? Hansen would either collapse from a heart attack or drag his crew outside and choke each man to death. Then he would do himself. One shot.

On the company net, Captain Van Buren and FSO Yelas spoke tersely about the Stryker platoon. Questions resounded: Why were there no near/far recognition signals, linkup procedures, or shared commo frequencies? If that platoon had been given the mission to help secure the far side of the river for the crossing, then why wasn't anyone in the battalion notified so that word could be passed down to the company team?

That was a mystery, but it hardly mattered with a tragedy lying before them.

And all Hansen could do was sit there, wondering how many men he had killed. Wondering what might happen to him. Wondering why he hadn't listened to Mingola.

Well, he knew the answer to that last one. He no longer trusted the men or the machine. And now he didn't even trust himself. . . .

"Red One, this is Red Four, over."

Hansen was drifting away from the turret, carried on a magic carpet made of fog. He was going someplace where tank commanders were punished for all eternity. It wasn't Hell. It was worse. . . .

"Red One, this is Red Four, over."

"You going to answer that?" Mingola asked.

Realizing that a tear had escaped one eye, Hansen swatted his cheek and grabbed the mike. "Red Four, this is Red One. Go ahead."

"The rest of those Strykers have linked up with Renegade on the far side, over."

Why the hell had Abbot called to report the obvious? "Roger, I see 'em," Hansen answered after peering through his extension.

"That fog was pretty dense, over."

Oh, that was it. The platoon sergeant was feeling him out. "Red Four, remain REDCON-1, out."

"Oh, man, I am so bummed," said Deac. "But how the hell were we supposed to know, right LT?"

Hansen closed his eyes, felt the grip of fear robbing his breath. He snapped his eyes open and screamed, "Gatch, did you hear that?"

"Hear what?"

"The engine made a sound."

"No, LT. I didn't hear anything."

"I'm telling you, I heard something."

Mingola cleared his throat. "Maybe that was your conscience, Lieutenant."

Hansen took the gunner by the rim of his CVC helmet and yanked his head back, ready to breathe fire into the kid's skeletal face. "You're a heartbeat away, motherfucker. A heartbeat away."

"We all are, sir. Just borrowing time here. Trying to pretend we're not. You want to talk to my old crew? They'll tell you all about it."

The guy wasn't even scared. And all Hansen could do was shove him back toward his controls.

It was all unraveling. Big time. He had been striving for perfection, and all he had done was make a perfectly horrible shot. He turned down the volume on the company net. Abbot was monitoring the chatter anyway. But the screams of dying men persisted. Everywhere.

"Don't you want to find out what happened?" asked Deac. "Those guys weren't supposed to be there. So we didn't fuck up. Sorry, LT. It ain't our fault, no matter what."

"Maybe we could've waited until we were sure," said Mingola, his tone growing more somber. "It's my fault, really. But I understand how it is. If you wait till you're sure, then they are too."

"I gave the order," said Hansen.

The gunner shrugged. "I didn't have to obey."

"The hell you didn't."

"Oh, this is all bullshit," said Deac. "You said it your-self, Mingola. That looked like muzzle flash."

"But then I realized it might've been something else."

"Maybe we don't have time for guessing games. Maybe your head's still messed up, right?" Deac rapped a fist on his helmet.

Mingola whirled around. "Fuck you, man."

"Don't talk to me like that, you little scumbag. I'll twist you like a pretzel and shove you—"

"ALL RIGHT! ENOUGH!" Hansen yelled so loudly that his words became harsh static on the intercom.

They all sat there, winded, just looking at each other, Hansen succumbing to the heat of their gazes and lowering his own to the turret floor. "I need to breathe. . . ."

He popped his hatch, went up top, and filled his lungs until the stinging grew unbearable. About twenty meters southwest of his position lay Keyman's tank, he, too, standing tall in his hatch, staring through his NVGs. For a moment he glanced over, then reached into his pocket. Hansen turned away and lifted his own NVGs, then sud-denly his cell phone rang.

Was it Karen calling from Japan or Hawaii? He kept the pocket watch she had given him in his breast pocket, and from time to time he held it tightly and imagined Christ-mas Eve: the cold, crisp air; the smell of her still-wet hair; the light in her eyes when she told him that being home was being with him.

But she wasn't calling. He recognized the number, pushed back his CVC helmet, and reluctantly thumbed a button. "Yeah?"

"Welcome to my world, Lieutenant. Sucks, don't it?" asked Keyman.

He was barely listening to the man. "My fuckin' crew. I need to square them away." Why was he trying to blame them now? It wasn't their fault, and he knew it. What the hell was wrong with him? "Are you having any engine problems?"

"No, I'm good. Brigade HQ fucked up again. Not our fault, right?"

"I have to go." Hansen ended the call, looked over at his wingman, who gave a slight wave.

Though Keyman would never retire from his career as an asshole, he had made an effort, and Hansen should appreciate that. He should appreciate a lot more than he did.

And he had to take responsibility for everything. Though he might try, he could not blame his mistakes on the crew. There were no excuses. Maybe the army would call it an unavoidable error, but he never would. A few seconds could have made the difference. He wanted to cry one second, go on a rampage the next, then stop everything and perform preventive maintenance checks and services on the tank once again. They should boresight too. The main gun barrel on the tank was only good for about a thousand rounds before it needed replacing, and their tank was pretty damned old. Gatch should go out and recheck the wedge bolts and make sure no wire had gotten tangled up in the treads. The engine sounded good outside. *Wait a minute.* What was that creaking?

He shivered as the wind needled across his cheek. *I'm losing my mind. I'm letting it beat me. I can't do that. But how do I stop? Why is this happening to me?*

Abruptly, his lip twisted and he began to sob. Thank God he was still in his hatch. He cursed himself for his weakness, for his inability to cope. *You call yourself a man?*

When guys talked about battlefield stress, he grinned and said that he got more stressed out when he *wasn't* in the hatch and servicing targets, letting steel fly. He commanded an M1A1 Abrams Main Battle Tank, for God's sake. His mind screamed *stop it!*

Yet he knew now what those guys had been talking about. Combat was another reality that sometimes tricked you into thinking everything was okay and that people would behave as expected. But they never did. And when they died, you hardened yourself and let it go. You pretended there was no cost in doing that. But the longer you remained, the harder it got to prioritize your thoughts. Each day you lost a little more of yourself. And deep down, you knew you had become a bomb just waiting to explode.

"Lieutenant? The CO's calling," said Mingola. "You'd better get this. He don't sound happy."

A long breath. One more. Okay. Hansen braced himself and went down into the turret, fixing Mingola with his blackest look. "So, he don't sound happy, huh? How the fuck should he sound? Happy that there's a Stryker full of dead guys out there?" Hansen snorted. "Fuckin' idiot." He took up the mike. "Black Six, this is Red One, go ahead."

"Red One, be advised there was a communications failure between brigade HQs because of all the attention being placed on that air assault up north, and that's why we didn't hear about those Strykers. They were tasked with securing the far side. Rest assured it wasn't your fault, son. The XO's passing up the SIR, and we will continue the mission."

A Serious Incident Report now had Hansen's name on it. How could that be possible? He was the guy who had won Top Tank. He wondered what would've happened if Sergeant Lee were still alive. Would he have listened to the KATUSA? Maybe Lee would've confirmed that a friendly platoon was out there before that mortar fire had gone off. However, all the what-ifs in the world meant jack shit at the moment.

How bad was the damage?

"Black Six, had that rifle squad dismounted, over?"

"Negative. I believe they were still mounted. But again, it wasn't your fault. Stand by REDCON-1. Black Six, out."

KEYMAN WOULD NOT have bet that the engineers would complete the flotation bridge in less than two hours. But those frozen and waterlogged sons of bitches had done the job in a mere seventy minutes. Hooah for the engineers.

And Keyman would never, ever have bet that Lieutenant Jack Hansen would be involved in a fratricide incident. Keyman empathized with the LT, yet he was secretly glad that Mr. West Point now knew the kind of pain that he had experienced. In fact, Hansen's was probably worse, since he was directly responsible for the deaths of those infantrymen, while Keyman's actions had been more indirect. Then again, the LT had been forced to kill Sergeant Lee to save Keyman's life. So . . . how could he be wishing pain on the guy?

Ah, it was fucked up. All his thoughts, hopes, and dreams were floating in a toilet and being stirred by a golf club–wielding midget. And that's what the war did to you. Made you think of screwy images like that. Took you by the neck and slowly squeezed the sanity out your ears. All you had left was the desire to survive the day. Just one more day. Going completely nuts was always on the calendar for tomorrow.

The order came in for Red Platoon to move out and prepare to cross the bridge. Hansen relayed the order, and not two seconds afterward, the river whipped up into fire-lit fountains accompanied by a soundtrack of hissing and booming.

"Some little cocksucker is phoning home," Zuck observed.

An enemy forward observer had spotted the river-crossing operation and was calling in long range artillery on all of their heads—except his own (although that happened more often than both sides would admit). The bridge crews down at the riverbank were already scrambling to take cover, while FSO Yelas was probably going insane himself, trying to find those pesky bastards as the thundering continued.

"Red, this is Red One. Fall back to the rock drops until this fire stops," ordered Hansen. "Move out!"

"Okay, Boomer, let's do it," Keyman cried.

The engine revved, and the turret shook a little as they started forward across the snow, then made a sharp right turn toward the rock drop. Zuck traversed the turret, swinging the gun tube toward the left side of the hull, pointed at the river. The images coming in through Keyman's extension left him shaking his head in disgust. That enemy artillery was ripping the shit out of the area and coming dangerously close to the bridge itself. Some of those fragments could be punching holes in their only route north. One solid hit, and Team Cobra would be in for another major delay while engineers hauled extreme ass to repair and/or replace damaged sections. If enough sections got hit, then it would be time to break out the booze, cigars, and fishing rods.

A pair of rounds fell long of the bridge, which in their case meant practically on top of them. Though no debris ricocheted off the turret, the impacts came through the hull and right up Keyman's spine.

He glanced over his shoulder. Loader Sean Lamont had vanished. In his place sat a deathly pale kid with eyes turned ceilingward. "Hey, Lamont?"

"Yeah, Sergeant?"

"What's the matter?"

"Nothing."

"Ain't no video game."

"Nope." The kid's legs shook harder.

"You ain't seen nothing yet. But I'm not trying to scare you. You know, the chances of a shell actually—" Keyman cut himself off as the tank jostled to a sudden halt and a grinding noise came from the left side, while the treads on the right spun more quietly. "Boomer?"

"How do you like that shit, man? Almost got us high-centered," answered the driver. "It's cool. I'll get us out."

"Red Two, this is Red One, over."

"Red One, this is Red Two. We're a little stuck. Move around us. We'll catch up, over."

"Hey, asshole, what the fuck does 'a little stuck' mean? Do we need to tow you out of there or call an M88 or what?"

Keyman's ears melted off—or at least they felt like they did. The lieutenant rarely swore like that over the radio.

But even more surprising was his lack of patience. "Red One, my driver assures me we'll be right there."

"I hope so. Red One, out."

"I knew he'd lose it," Keyman muttered to himself. "But I didn't think I'd care." He sighed in frustration, then climbed into his hatch.

"Okay, everyone. Pucker up," instructed Boomer. "Here we go." He threw the tank into reverse, gave her the gas, then tried to roll back. Nothing. He threw it into gear once more, then, riding a wave of momentum, pushed forward on one tread.

Yes, they were high-centered, but, judging from the angle, not by very much, and if they could just edge forward a little more, they might tip off the snow-covered rock holding the right tread in the air.

Were it not for the incoming FA fire, Keyman would've dismounted for a better look. In fact, a sudden rush of wind had him ducking into the hatch and buttoning up, just as a wicked boom shook the whole slope. The vibration kicked them forward, off the rock.

"Sergeant, we're free, compliments of the those North Korean artillerymen," sang Boomer, his words flowing through the intercom like cool jazz. "Have to call up the Dear Leader in Pyongyang and put in a good word for them."

"Oh, he'd love that," joked Keyman as he returned to his hatch to inspect the tank for damage. Aside from some minor scarring of the hull's forward slope, the track looked good to go, everything secure in the bustle rack, weapons ready to fire.

Behind them, on the far side of the river, mortars detonated, making a fiery incision up the hillside.

"Lamont, come up top. I want you to see this."

After a moment's hesitation, the loader's hatch popped, and the kid stood, his shoulders rising toward his neck in fear. He rested gloved hands on his machine gun's handles, then craned his neck around, confused.

"See that mortar fire over there?"

"It's theirs?"

"No, you idiot. It's ours. That's our FSO, calling it on the enemy observer team. Now if he's done his job right, the shelling will either stop or keep missing."

"Boy, it really smells out here, huh?"

Keyman had grown used to the battlefield's stench. In fact, if the kid hadn't pointed it out, Keyman wouldn't have noticed. Mud, snow, sulfur, cordite, and the jet fuel used to power their armored beast all mixed with a foul, sewage-like odor emanating from the river.

"Is this the smell of victory, just like Robert Duvall said?" Lamont asked.

Keyman grinned. "Nah. Just the smell of shit."

"I thought so."

"Hey, you hear that?"

The kid looked around. "What?"

Keyman nodded to himself. "They stopped shelling."

You couldn't hear the difference with the CVC helmet on, but you could plainly see that while fires continued to rage along contained points on both sides of the river, the rest of the valley had fallen into a sleepy darkness.

Keyman predicted that by the time they reached the rock drop for cover, the call would come to head back for the river. Coming? Going? You never knew until you got there. Sometimes you didn't know where "there" was until the last second. And none of it really mattered, as long as you could shoot, move, and communicate.

"Hey, Sergeant? You know the lieutenant much better than we do. Is he okay?"

Keyman considered his reply, then crossed mental fingers behind his back. "We've all had some really long days, and firing at the Stryker is just . . . bad. What can I say? But he'll be okay."

The kid looked at Keyman. He wasn't buying.

Neither of them were.

ABBOT HAD ONLY two things on his mind, which, for a man in his position, was quite remarkable.

Unfortunately, the two things were giving him so much stress and heartache that they made up for all those other thoughts that usually clogged his airwaves.

Would they ever find his wife?

Would his gunner remain loyal?

He had watched Park's expression as reports had crackled over the company net. The KATUSA had winced when he had learned that Lieutenant Hansen had fired upon a friendly PC. And then he had uttered something to himself. Abbot was itching to ask the gunner what he had said.

And maybe there was third thing on Abbot's mind: would the talented but highly impressionable young Lieutenant Hansen finally crack?

Abbot had been worried about Hansen from the beginning, and between the death of Sergeant Lee and now the fratricide incident, the likable guy who had graduated near the bottom of his class at West Point seemed destined for the loony bin.

Old man Abbot couldn't take it anymore. Didn't want to. He just wanted to take a nap, then wake up next to his wife. He wasn't asking for much.

"Hey, Sergeant?"

"What now, Paz?"

The loader came forward and put a hand on Abbot's shoulder. "We shouldn't cross that bridge."

Abbot rolled his eyes then nearly smiled as a bad pun found his lips. "Paz, we'll cross that bridge when we come to it."

"I'm fuckin' serious."

"Okay, you've convinced me. I'll call the LT and tell 'em that we've decided to make a swim for it."

Paz sighed. "What I'm saying is—"

"I know what you're saying. We'll be all right. The CO won't send us across if it ain't safe."

"I don't know about that. Hey, Park? What do you think? You think we'll be all right?"

The gunner slowly turned back, his lips tight. "For a

soldier, you worry too much. I always say that. But you never listen. You must be brave."

Abbot stared more emphatically at the loader. "He's right. And you know it."

"Red, this is Red One. We're swinging back down to the bridge, getting ready to cross. Move out!"

"Sparrow?" Abbot called to his driver. "We're blowing this popsicle stand. Fall in behind Neech."

"Hooah," Sparrow replied through a sigh. "It's about time we got this show on the road."

Paz shook his head and returned to his seat as they hit a rut, then rebounded with a jolt.

"Get in your hatch," Abbot urged the loader as he climbed into his own. Paz would man his M240 machine gun, while Abbot helped Sparrow navigate toward the river.

The fact that Abbot even had to ask the loader to get up top disturbed him. As a matter of fact, actions that had become second nature were beginning to falter. Blame it on the long hours and lack of sleep, but they were pushing toward enemy territory, and a combination of instincts, skill, and pure audacity would keep them alive. A stressed-out, overtired crew would make mistakes. And Abbot considered himself too good a tanker to let that happen.

They drew closer to the water, and as they did, several engineers were waving frantically at Keyman and Hansen.

"Red," Hansen began. "Several sections of the bridge are taking on water. They want us to haul ass right now!"

Keyman's tank throttled up and raced ahead while Hansen came up hard behind him, both bounding into the area along the shoreline that had been cleared by the engineers.

Sparrow kept tight on the lieutenant's tail, and Abbot repeatedly glanced over his shoulder to Neech, who stared at the bobbing flotation bridge the way a timid kid stares at a monster roller coaster. Sure, all of them had practiced river-crossing operations before—but not when the bridge had sustained an unknown amount of damage.

Under the careful scrutiny of the engineers, Keyman's track hit the entrance ramp and began to roll across. Hansen followed, then came Abbot.

Sparrow already had his driver's hatch open. If they began to sink, he would bail out immediately, as would everyone else.

"I knew I should've gone on that diet last year," Abbot joked to his crew.

Paz's worried expression did not falter. Park did not remove his gaze from his sight.

Ten meters. Twenty. Thirty. So far so good. But they had nearly 170 meters to go. Abbot split his attention between the path ahead and the sections to his immediate right and left, monitoring the water line as it rose swiftly under their weight but did not spill over the top.

The air whooshed, then an artillery shell exploded on the opposite riverbank, just twenty meters north of the exit ramp.

Captain Van Buren began barking orders to the FSO over the company net.

As debris flew, small-arms fire erupted from the two stands of trees along the southern hill, followed by an RPG that streaked up the riverbank to broadside one of the Bradleys positioned north of MSR 3. Abbot couldn't assess the damage to that vehicle through all the smoke, but Lieutenant Ryback from the MECH platoon was now on the radio and hollering his ass off, reporting the fire, requesting that the FSO pinpoint yet another observer team, and requesting that mortars be placed on the trees.

"Didn't they secure this fuckin' area?" cried Paz.

No battlefield was ever truly secure. Old timers like Abbot understood that.

Up ahead, Keyman's coax thrummed as he returned fire toward the trees. Two seconds later, Hansen's coax painted a second, laserlike line of crimson tracers out to the forest.

Abbot was about to have Park lay down some coax fire, too, but the lieutenant's track dipped suddenly, drawing a huge wave over the bridge.

"Oh, shit," Abbot grunted.

"No, no, no!" yelled Sparrow.

The nose of their tank plunged into the water, and then, as they leveled off, an ice-cold wave rushed over the forward slope, sending torrents into Sparrow's hole.

"Driver, don't slow! Give her the gas!"

Sparrow shivered audibly into the intercom. "Aw, shit! Aw, shit! It's cold!"

"Red Three, this is Red Four," Abbot called back to Neech. "Tell your driver to shut his hatch!"

Before Neech answered, another shell dropped south of the river, striking about midway across. The impact sent a four-foot-high swell rising toward the bridge.

Three heartbeats later, every section bobbed violently on the waves, lifting the tanks.

Abbot glanced back and realized that if he widened the gap between himself and Neech's track, less weight would be placed on that obviously damaged section. He ordered Sparrow to speed up while calling for Neech to slow.

Neech's track hit the section and sank, but hardly as far as Abbot's had, despite the added weight of his mine plow. The water washed up to his road wheels but never cleared the tank's front slope.

Much farther back, Hansen's buddy Lieutenant Gary Gutterson was bringing his tank platoon onto the bridge. *Poor sucker,* Abbot thought. *I hope they're wearing their lifejackets.*

"Red, this is Red One! Hold fire. We have to move faster! Come on! Let's move! Let's move!"

More shelling. Abbot had no choice but to lower his hatch into the open-protected position, where he could peer out through the crack. "Sparrow, you all right?"

"Still here, Sergeant! Freezing my goddamned ass off!"

"We'll get you changed on the other side. Don't you worry, homey."

"Red One, this is Red Two," came Keyman's terse voice over the platoon net. "Stop the platoon. My tank's aborted again!"

"Oh, that's just great," Abbot said, his shoulders slumping hard. "Just great."

"Told you, Sergeant. We shouldn't have crossed this bridge."

Abbot smirked at Paz. "Just shut up."

CHAPTER
FOUR

KEYMAN'S TANK WAS holding up the entire river-crossing operation—which made him a very popular guy at the moment.

Engineers on the other side were waving for him to get moving, as were the guys aboard the boats. Hansen was screaming at him over the platoon net, and no doubt the CO was demanding a report as well. Meanwhile, Gutter-son's platoon was already en route across the bridge, and though Keyman was no engineer, he wasn't even sure if the bridge—especially one that had been torn to Swiss cheese—could support that much weight.

The shelling had stopped momentarily, replaced by the cracking and rumbling of mortars dropping heavily on those dismounts in the trees. That fire gave Boomer enough time to get out of his hatch and head to the back, where he would play around with the starter. Again. The tank had aborted for some other reason that Boomer was still working on; its failure to restart was due to, at least in part, that bad starter. So, after a little jiggling, the driver returned to his station. Tried to restart.

Two miracles in one night was too much to ask.

"I don't believe this shit," Keyman groaned. "Can anything else go wrong?"

Lamont came into his hatch. "Sergeant, the water's rising! We're sinking!"

"And just so you know," Zuck called out. "The TC always goes down with the ship."

"I'll be taking you with me!" Keyman retorted. "Boomer, do we need to get towed across?"

"Give me a second."

The engine started, the hum drawing shouts from Lamont and Boomer.

"Our luck won't last," groaned Zuck.

Keyman shoved the gunner. "Kill that negative attitude, will you? Driver, move out!"

They rocked forward, creating a decent wake as they came up and onto the next bridge section, one that had not been punctured and easily took their weight.

A couple more shells tore up the slopes just north of the FSO's location; otherwise, the skies remained silent as Boomer took them past the middle of the bridge and toward the river bank. So near yet so far.

The wind picked up and put a slight bow in the bridge. Keyman grimaced as the track dipped once more, catching a seam in the connections where one section met another. He lifted his night vision goggles. MSR 3 pushed straight through the hills ahead. If dismounts had made it down to the riverbank, there could be more in the pockets lining both sides of the road. And worse, there could be antitank teams setting up their nasty little fireworks.

"Zuck, keep a close eye on those pockets along the road," Keyman ordered, though he could assume Zuck was already on that. Having a new crew had awakened a whole new set of nerves, and they were talking for him.

Thankfully, the gunner kept his smartass reply to himself. "Thermals are clear so far. But the fog's still washing them out here and there."

Abruptly, they dropped, water flooding over the bridge

about a foot, maybe more. Even the section itself grew unsteady, the tank listing to the right, then left. Boomer rolled his wrist, and, with a roaring and grinding, they nearly leapt off that section. Keyman issued a warning to Hansen about the path ahead. The LT snapped, "Don't tell me what I can already see. Red One, out."

Keyman frowned, but the expression turned quickly into an ironic grin. I'm *supposed to be the asshole!*

Whatever. They only had fifty meters to go, and that was all Keyman really cared about right now. The bridge ahead looked pretty good, though holes from artillery fragments were nearly impossible to see in the dark.

A glance back revealed that the other three tanks were forging on and that Gutterson's TCs had yet to become U-boat commanders. Keyman could not say the same of the crews aboard the company wheels/trains vehicles that would follow them. Nor could he be as confident about the grunts aboard the Bradleys, which had limited swim capability; however, the vehicles' up-armored kits would probably make them sink like rocks. Finally, if there were any bridge left, the mortar platoon tracks would pull up the rear, moving from good section to bad like drunken lumberjacks wobbling across rolling logs.

All of which meant that going first had its benefits if you could forget that point men usually died first.

"Sergeant, we're sinking again!" Lamont was leaning out of his hatch, pointing to the bridge.

"We're almost there, Boomer!" cried Keyman. "Give me a little more gas, bro!"

"I'm trying, but you might want to break out the oars, anyway."

Keyman held his breath. They traversed the section, then came up once again. Twenty meters. Ten. Five.

"Well, here we are," said Boomer. "Dry land. My favorite kind."

Heaving a huge sigh of relief, Keyman looked back as the tank rolled up the exit ramp, the treads spitting water, Lamont flashing him a broad smile.

"Red, this is Red One. Once we clear the bridge, we'll move forward toward the slopes along 984 and assume attack-by-fire positions. Red One, out."

"Be nice if we could get back to an AA and have the mechanics look at this track," said Boomer.

"We don't need 'em," Keyman answered. "We got you."

"Yeah, but I think Zuckerman's right. We're pushing our luck. I don't like that."

"We'll get her looked at next chance we get."

They steered around one of the Bradleys and rode along the ditches and potholes beside MSR 3. Just off to their right, about sixty meters away, lay the Stryker that Hansen had targeted, smoke still wafting from its hatches and shattered hull. Keyman peered through his NVGs and wished that metal carcass were out of sight. He glanced back, saw Hansen looking through his own goggles, and wondered with the LT was thinking.

HANSEN WASN'T SURE how to feel as he observed the Stryker. Or maybe he wasn't sure how *much* to feel. The crew didn't say a word. He had intimidated them into silence. There was but one consolation: they had made a perfect shot on the vehicle. There was no way anyone could've survived. If you were going to kill your own men, you might as well do it quickly and efficiently, leaving no survivors.

That was a grotesque thought. He was not that cold, not that callous. He cursed himself for even thinking it. Was he just groping for anything to make himself feel better?

His cell phone rang again. Fucking Keyman. "What do you want now?"

"Can I borrow five bucks?"

"Fuck you."

"Hey, man. You good?"

"What do you think?" Hansen thumbed off the phone. What was the idiot offering? Therapy on the battlefield? *Give me a break.*

The phone rang again. It was Abbot. What was this? A fucking intervention? "Sergeant, if you don't have something important to tell me about this mission—"

"LT, they found her."

Hansen thought a moment. "They just called you now?"

"About an hour ago. Left a text message. They got her body. They're bringing her to Uijongbu."

"Sergeant, I'm sorry, I, uh—"

"It's okay, LT. I just wanted to let you know. Maybe you can pass word on to Karen the next time you talk to her. I know she wanted to hear too."

"Yeah, okay. I will. Thanks."

Hansen went down into his hatch, took a seat at his station. He felt terrible for Abbot, and the platoon sergeant's situation made him realize how lucky he was that Karen had survived her ordeal. His situation was hardly as bad. So why was he so strung out, so obsessed, so miserable? Why couldn't he appreciate what he already had?

Maybe he wasn't cut out for this. Maybe he just didn't have what it took. . . .

"Whoa. I think we got some dismounted movement way up the road, maybe fifteen hundred meters," said Mingola.

Hansen checked his extension, confirmed, then grabbed the mike. "Black Six, this is Red One, over."

"Red One, this is Black Six, go ahead."

"Dismounts directly north of our position, approximately fifteen hundred meters. Are any of our people out there, over?"

"Stand by."

Mingola gave him a look.

"What? You think I'm fuckin' paranoid?"

"No, sir. I'm glad you want to be sure."

"Red One, this is Black Six. We're unaware of friendly forces operating in that area, over."

"Roger, Black Six. Will relay grid to the FSO and make call for fires, over."

"Mortars are unavailable right now. Engineers are getting ready to close the bridge after the Bradleys make it

across. Those mortar tracks are going to swim across on
their own. But they can't fire until they're on the other side.
Assume attack-by-fire positions and engage those dismounts. I'll get back to you when the mortars come on
line. Black Six, out."

"Red, this is Red One. Dismounts spotted approximately fifteen hundred meters ahead. Could be some antitank teams as well. We've been ordered to assume our
attack-by-fire positions but we'll engage those bastards
too. Report when set. Red One, out."

Keyman led the platoon along a stretch of hillside
daubed in snow and broken by outcroppings of rock glistening with ice. The hill overlooked the road and the smaller
hills beyond where they had picked up the movement.

"That looks good right there," Hansen told the TC over
the radio. "Take us up that hill a little more, then we'll
spread out where it slopes into those berms that the ROKs
built. Perfect hull-down positions."

"That's the plan. And if you hang up on me again, I
won't find you such good BPs, deal?"

"Deal."

Within five minutes all four tanks had maneuvered into
spots along the berms, with about fifteen meters between
each track. Gusts blasted into the hillside, replacing the fog
with swirls of ice and snow. Hansen, along with Keyman,
Abbot, and Neech, stood in their hatches, poring over the
terrain with NVGs while their gunners kept vigil at the thermals. Hansen considered dispatching an LP/OP team ahead
of the tanks, but the platoon already had a good position and
he wasn't sure that setting up an OP would buy them any
real reaction time. Besides, those dismounts were already
pretty close. Deac and Lamont, Keyman's loader, were no
doubt happy that they would remain warm for the moment.

The engine idled steadily, but then a strange popping, as
though Mingola were making some Jiffy Pop popcorn on
the back deck, caught his attention.

"Does anybody hear that?"

"Hear what?" asked Deac.

"That popping noise."

"LT, uh, all of us, we're kind of worried about you, man," confessed Deac. "The tank's okay. The fuel is still good. We don't hear anything wrong with the engine. You have to sleep. That's what it is. You ain't slept in forever."

Hansen was about to scream at the top of his lungs. But then his eyes welled up. He lowered the NVGs and was about to break down when Mingola yelled, "Troops! RPG!"

THE FIRST SQUAD of North Korean infantrymen moving up on the platoon were now within fifty meters, and Neech figured they had been close all along and waiting for orders to engage. Their commander was probably sitting in the rear with the rest of the dismounts that the lieutenant had spotted. While Keyman and Hansen had agreed that using the old ROK position was a good idea, Neech had thought it too obvious, though he had kept his reservations to himself. He wished he had been wrong, but now the presence of enemy troops breathing down their necks confirmed his suspicions.

Although the platoon hadn't been ambushed—not exactly, anyway—they had done exactly what the North Koreans had anticipated. Now the enemy commander had carefully placed his infantrymen to intercept. It seemed that both Keyman and the LT were getting tired and sloppy, their tactical edge dulled. Neech had no tolerance for that. You didn't make fast track to master gunner by overlooking the mistakes of your colleagues. In fact, as the RPG raced toward Hansen's tank, the first thought Neech had was, *I should've said something.*

Neech ducked into his hatch and immediately manned his big fifty cal, even as Romeo unleashed hell and then some with the coaxial. The RPG caught Hansen's forward slope and exploded. Thank God the grenade had struck the strongest part of the tank's armor and had probably inflicted only minor damage.

Meanwhile, Keyman, too, was on his fifty, and his

gunner was dipping heavily into coax ammo. If Abbot was firing—and he probably was—Neech didn't notice. He was too damned busy chewing up the landscape with his own weapon.

Amazingly, Romeo, Choi, and Wood were all business, sounding like soft-spoken librarians given a day to vent their stress aboard an M1A1 Abrams. And vent they did.

"Two more guys coming up the hill," Wood said.

"Got them," answered Romeo, and he punctuated his words with a burst from the coax that tore ragged holes in the enemy troops and kicked them onto their asses.

"There's another guy with an RPG," said Romeo. "He went behind the trees! Wood? Anything? He come out?"

"I'm looking."

Neech checked his own sight, but it was hard to see anything out past the berms.

"Wait. There he is," Wood said, his voice remarkably calm even given the circumstances. "To the right. The right!"

Romeo apparently spotted the little North Korean rocket boy, nixing any cry of confirmation in favor of a burst of coax fire. The tracers reached out and touched someone, the right someone, and rocket boy got his.

"Nice shot," said Wood.

Neech permitted himself a grin. The troublemaker/driver was earning his keep, redeeming himself in the heat of battle. Good for him.

Two more troops crested the berm, both shouldering RPGs. One swung toward Abbot's track, the other taking aim at Neech. Now it was Choi's turn to get in the fight. He had manned his loader's machine gun and sent forth a sweeping volley of 7.62 mm fire that drummed across the berm, intercepting both RPG guys, even as they fired.

The flashes sent Neech ducking reflexively, and by the time he returned his gaze to his sight, only smoke trails remained, along with evidence that the RPGs had missed, while Choi's rounds hadn't.

"Red Three, this is Red Four," called Abbot. "Scratch my back!"

Neech traversed the turret, bringing Romeo's coax to bear on the platoon sergeant's tank. Even as he did, Choi was already firing at the four North Korean infantrymen attempting to mount Abbot's hull. Romeo added his gun to the fray, and amid sparks and ricocheting rounds, the enemy soldiers fell away, one clutching his wounds, the others dead before they hit the snow.

Neech was about to congratulate his men when Wood's calm demeanor finally broke: "Troops! Troops! All over the place! Here they come!"

Choi dropped into his hatch, slammed it shut, as AK-47 fire echoed like a kettle drum throughout the turret.

At least four guys were running up the berm. Two more were advancing from the right, another two from the left. Who knew how many from the rear. Neech went up into his hatch—yes, a stupid thing to do, but he figured he'd steal a glimpse to the rear. He withdrew his pistol, fired at two of the four men ahead, missed both, then whirled back. *Aw, shit.* Maybe six more guys were dashing to the next ditch for cover. He dropped hard into the hatch, barely got it shut before incoming rounds clinked and his arm jerked from a hot pinch. "Ow." He glanced at his arm, saw a tear in his Nomex. Reached for the wound. Damn, it stung. *Fuck it. No time.*

Choi's mouth fell open. "Sarge, you hit! You okay?"

"Yeah. Romeo, kill these assholes!" Neech reached for the mike, winced as he flexed his wounded arm. "Red One, this is Red Three. I'm crawling with dismounts, over!"

Neech didn't wait for a response. He manned his fifty, began firing, thought he heard boots clattering on the hull.

He was about to call Hansen again when a troop outside took the butt of his AK and banged repeatedly on one of the vision blocks below the hatch, believing he could break the thick lens.

"Sergeant, I can't get 'em all!" Romeo cried.

Neech ceased firing and grimaced again as he reached for the mike. The lieutenant wasn't replying, so he figured he'd call Abbot for a little help.

Suddenly, the guy on Neech's hatch tumbled off as salvo after salvo of coax fire rapped on the hull and turret.

"Platoon sergeant to the rescue," reported Romeo.

Yes, Abbot had read Neech's mind and was returning the favor. "Red Three, I'm cleaning you off good now!"

"Roger that, thanks. Wood? Move back. Let's grease these mothers to the rear!"

Wood threw the tank in reverse and hit the gas so hard that Neech nearly went face-first into his extension. Choi fell out of his seat and cursed in Korean. Romeo issued his protest in Spanish.

Neech wasn't sure how many wounded or dead troops they ran over, but he didn't care, as long as his men were safe. He withdrew his sidearm, then went back up top, ignoring the blood trickling down his arm.

LAMONT'S FACE WAS twisted into a sinister grin, yet tears were flowing down his cheeks as he jammed his chest forward into his gun's controls and let the bad guys have it. Keyman was proud of the little gaming nerd, despite those tears. Lamont had already killed a half-dozen men and still hadn't puked. He was a getting a real taste of combat and spitting out the seeds. Oh, yeah, he was one PlayStation puppy who saw firsthand the difference between a "first-person shooter" game and the real deal. Part of Keyman was glad for the troop attack. His loader would become more seasoned before they actually crossed the DMZ into North Korea. Experience could pay off big time. However, while the attack did present the opportunity for lessons learned, the possibility of death was still there, always there.

"Loader, hold your fire! Hold your fire!"

Another burst leapt from Lamont's muzzle before he finally relaxed his hands. There was no movement in the woods out past the berms. Well off to their north, MSR 3 looked dark and empty, although Keyman suspected that the company trains might be moving out about now. He returned his gaze to Lamont, who had just been firing into the trees. The loader had found his rage while still being wary enough to keep his bursts in check so that he didn't melt off his gun's barrel.

At least ten troops now lay dead on the berm, and just as one of them stirred, Keyman withdrew his sidearm and put a bullet in the guy's head. Bang. Just like that. Action. Reaction. All in one fluid motion. No remorse. Done.

The kid needed to see that too.

"We outgunned them," Lamont finally said. "But they just kept coming."

"Yup."

"Why?"

" 'Cause they're nuts."

"I forgot about this."

"About what?"

"I just thought it'd be more tank on tank. I guess I was thinking Middle East. I couldn't even find Korea on a map before I came here."

"I still can't. Don't matter. This place sucks. And it'll be like this all the way up to Kaesong. Probably worse."

"How do you know?"

Keyman gave the kid a look that made him shrink a little.

"How many guys you kill so far?"

"I don't know. But there's three I won't forget." With that, Keyman ducked back into the turret. He regretted those words almost immediately, but they had leaked out, like shit and bile, while the ghosts named Webber, Smiley, and Morbid cursed in his ears.

Shaking off the memories, he got on the horn to Hansen. The LT should've been asking for SITREPs. Instead, he was playing hermit inside his sixty-eight-ton cave. Time to wake up his ass. "Red One, this is Red Two, over."

A VERY DISTURBING thing had happened inside Hansen's turret, and he didn't learn about it until after they had engaged the troops.

He was seated at his station, CVC helmet off, with Deac holding a water bottle near his lips. "Take a sip, LT. I think maybe you're dehydrated."

He bolted forward. "What the hell happened?"

"Don't worry about it," Deac said. "We took care of everything."

"What're you talking about?"

Slowly, perhaps for effect, Mingola turned back toward Hansen and scowled.

In the meantime, Keyman called for a second time on the platoon net. "Red Two, this is Red One. I'll get back to you," Hansen told his wingman, then he stared emphatically at Deac. "What's going on here? Did I—"

"LT, uh, I think you fainted."

"No way."

"Yes, way," Mingola said tersely. "You passed out. Without your helmet, you would've gotten a concussion. Then I would've had to call the army docs to find out if you belong in this turret."

Hansen recoiled. Somehow the gunner had discovered that Hansen had been doing some digging on him.

"That's right," Mingola continued. "You didn't think I knew?"

"Actually, I didn't care whether you knew or not." That was a lie, of course; Hansen had not wanted to stir up any more trouble. Now he had it in spades.

Mingola bore his crooked teeth. "Ain't this ironic? You're worried about me. I didn't faint."

"We didn't tell anybody," Deac assured Hansen, then he reached around and grabbed Mingola by the throat. "And we won't."

The gunner yanked off Deac's hand. "I think we need to report this. I think we should. I don't want a TC who's going to hit the floor every time we engage."

Hansen massaged his sore eyes, dragged a hand across his stubbly chin, then sat there, trying to think. He remembered when Keyman's former gunner, Webber, had passed out. He had never really understood that and figured it was a sign of weak stomach or personality or something. "I passed out in the middle of an attack," he thought aloud. "Jesus Christ!"

"No, you didn't, LT," Deac said, lowering his voice as though someone could overhear them.

"Red One, this is Black Six, over."

After exchanging a hard look with Mingola, Hansen answered the CO's call. "Black Six, this is Red One, go ahead."

"Mortars have crossed the river and are in position. Go ahead and relay the grid for those dismounts. The FSO's standing by, over."

"Roger, Black Six. Will relay grid."

"Good work. Black Six, out."

"Red Four, this is Red One, over," he called to Abbot.

"One, this is Four, go ahead."

"Relay that grid to the FSO. And, uh, did you update the CO already, over?"

Abbot hesitated, and Hansen could almost see the frown on the old tanker's face. "Roger that. Task force scouts are having a hard time pinning down those guys ahead. Terrain ain't helping, but I got a good idea where they are. I'll take care of it, over."

"Thanks. Red One, out."

"Now you got everybody covering for you," said Mingola.

"What do you want, asshole?"

The gunner narrowed his eyes. "Seems we got something in common. So, from here on out, you trust me, I trust you. That's the way it's supposed to be in here, isn't it? Ever since I got here, you've been laying into me and the rest of this crew. Back off."

"So you want a truce?" asked Hansen.

"I want more credit. I think we all do."

Hansen didn't know what to say. Mingola's argument sounded logical.

But then he lost all credibility when he blurted out, "I'm trying to listen to spirits between worlds. They can tell us when we're too close to death."

"Dude, you're just nuts."

"No, I'm serious. You have to close your eyes. The guys that came here before us, back in the first war? Even the ones that have just died, like my old crew? They haven't left. They can help us. If we'll listen."

"All I can say is, I'm glad someone's watching the fort while you guys have your little talk," said Gatch from his driver's station. "And it's not the spooks that'll help us. It's our lord and savior Jesus Christ. He is the way, the truth, and the light."

"Shut up," Deac said with a moan.

"Before we leave Korea, you're going to be saved, Deac. I've been praying for you. Don't turn your back on God."

"Don't ram him down my throat."

Shushing his men, Hansen looked through his extension, surveying the carnage across the berm. He gasped. "Holy . . ."

"That's right," said Mingola. "Look at all these guys just dying to meet us."

"Aw, that's bad," said Deac. "Stick to being weird. Your jokes suck."

A distant booming filtered down through Hansen's hatch, and he observed the mortar flashes in his sight.

Just then Neech called on the radio and said that he had been shot, clean entry and exit, and that he was remaining in the fight. He didn't need the medics at this time.

"Good work, Red Three. If that wound gives you any more problems, let me know. Red One, out."

Neech had been shot before, and he was the kind of guy who took pain in stride. Most of them were.

But the kind of pain Hansen experienced was not as easily shrugged off.

He had killed Sergeant Lee. He was a murderer.

He had passed out during an engagement. He was a failure.

He kept obsessing about the tank and his crew. He was going insane.

All while heading north, directly into enemy territory.

He glanced over at Deac. "You don't hear that popping sound?"

The loader looked afraid to answer. "No, LT. I don't."

Hansen bit his lip. "Gatch? How's our fuel?"

"Uh, let me see . . ."

"I wouldn't worry about our gas," Mingola interrupted. "We got hit by an RPG. I'm good here, but you might want to go up top and check that out."

Panic seized Hansen's gut. He rushed into his hatch, his hands trembling so violently that he could barely pull himself up. The tank's forward slope looked scorched and dented but intact. He didn't sigh in relief. He suddenly feared that some internal damage had occurred. He couldn't suppress the thought and started out of the hatch.

"LT? Where you going?" called Deac. "Could be more dismounts!"

Nothing else was important other than the tank. If he could control the machine, he might regain control of the men. Of the situation. Of everything.

CHAPTER
FIVE

PLATOON SERGEANT ABBOT felt completely happy and completely miserable at the same time. What did you call that emotion? If he knew, he'd be a shrink instead of a tanker. Admittedly, it was a huge relief to know that they had found his beloved Kim and that her body would be returned to him for a proper burial. There would be closure.

Yet the call had taken him back to that fateful night. Hansen had come to him, had agonized over what to say, and had finally mustered the courage to tell him that Kim was dead. Abbot had tried to bury his feelings and focus instead on how the lieutenant had matured as a leader. But then it had hit him, the same way it hit him now. He could no longer imagine that Kim was waiting for him, like she had year after year. When he returned to Texas, the house would be empty.

Was there any reason to go back? Deep down he knew that question would haunt him for the rest of the war.

For now, though, he needed to do his job. He was a professional. Always. He would embrace the mission with all of its shortcomings. He welcomed the stress, knowing he would be too busy to grieve.

All right. He sifted through the information he had gathered during the past few minutes. Captain Van Buren had informed him that the bridge would probably take a few days to repair and that remaining resupply operations to the company would be conducted by air because of the emergency situation. The fuelers could keep them rolling with five-minute shots of gas until they were empty. If the team came across any enemy vehicles that still had fuel in their tanks, or found any fuel drums at abandoned ROK camps, a capture pump could be used to transfer it into their own fuelers' tanks. The company would keep moving and fighting while helos would land and refill the fuelers with FARP gear. There was also a chance that the aviation unit could be tasked to simply airlift a FARP forward and use it to refuel the tanks. The distance between the crossing site and the complex at Panmunjom was about ten kilometers, and, moving deliberately and carefully, the team could reach the complex in about two hours—in a perfect world of no obstacles and no enemy resistance.

Because the terrain beside MSR 3 grew more rocky and more heavily wooded, the platoon had no choice but to use the main road itself. After a long delay from Hansen, who said he was investigating an engine noise, Red finally moved out. The bumps and drone of the tracks were comforting, as were the images in his thermals: no hot spots.

All four tanks rose up and onto the main road, then started forward. Behind them came the engineers, followed by the three remaining Bradley's of MECH platoon, then the tanks of Blue Platoon, then the company trains, and finally the mortars. The Strykers and their crews had remained behind to help provide security for the engineers repairing the bridge. While no one aboard that damaged Bradley had been killed, that RPG had wreaked havoc with the vehicle's engine, so Ryback had squeezed his men aboard three tracks instead of four. The FSO took the two-man FO team aboard his track, since they belonged to the FIST anyway, and that would help out with the passenger load.

Abbot glanced back from his hatch to check on Neech. Because Neech's track was equipped with that mine plow, the platoon's speed needed to be carefully measured. If they moved too fast, Neech would struggle to keep up and possibly damage his plow and track—especially in rough terrain. Moreover, his new driver couldn't see very well to the right side of the tank because the plow's power cable entered through the driver's right periscope opening. Keyman, who was well aware of these issues, had set the platoon's pace accordingly, and Neech was doing a fine job of remaining in formation. But you could never be too careful when on the road, and Abbot always kept that third eye in the back of his head focused on Neech.

Once they reached the area occupied by the enemy dismounts, who had hopefully succumbed to the team's mortar fire, Keyman reported back to Hansen: "We got some surface-laid mines ahead, over."

Hansen called for a halt, then he got on the company net and told the CO about the obstacle. Van Buren guessed that the TF scouts had kept to the high ground and had missed the mines.

"All right, boys, be ready," Abbot warned his crew. "They're in the hills and waiting to drop the hammer."

"Sergeant, I don't think we should breach this obstacle," said Paz, his voice low and shivery. He held up his cell phone. A few minutes prior he had gone up top, accessed the Web, and had checked his horoscope. He read from the tiny screen: "Avoid unnecessary risks."

"Why you always negative?" Park screamed. "Always worried? Be a soldier!"

Park's outburst left Abbot and Paz speechless. Like most KATUSAs, Park had a firm grip on his emotions and rarely let his irritation be known. But you had to take into account their schedule, their lack of sleep, all of it. Park might be a highly disciplined soldier from a culture that embraced order, but in the end he was still a human being.

A pissed off one to be sure.

After lowering himself back into the turret, Abbot nudged Park and asked, "You all right?"

"He always complain. Too much!"

"I know. It's just how he deals with it. You've been around him long enough to know. Just take it easy, all right?"

"Yes, Sergeant."

"And you," Abbot began, pointing at the loader. "Just think happy thoughts, okay? Happy fucking thoughts." Abbot grinned sarcastically.

Paz mirrored the look. "I just feel—and I don't know if you do—but I just feel that we won't make it home. Once we cross the DMZ, none of us are coming back."

"No more," Park said, whirling to glower at Paz. "No more. Horoscope is bullshit!"

"All right, everybody calm down. Paz, we don't need your bad juju right now. Just keep all that shit to yourself." Abbot hoisted himself back up top, into the bitter cold.

During the next few minutes, the LT called for the engineer company to bring up their mine-clearing line charge, which sat on a tracked trailer and was towed by an M113. The MICLIC would be fired over the path to detonate most of the mines. While the team waited for those guys to come forward, Abbot and the rest of the TCs lit smoke pots and tossed them to the side of the road to help obscure the area, while the CO put in a request for some artillery-delivered smoke to further blanket their operation. Grunts from the MECH platoon dismounted and dispersed to provide security and hunt for enemy troops and antitank teams. In the meantime, Keyman and Hansen were visually inspecting the edge of the minefield with their NVGs to be sure they hadn't missed anything.

"We're stopped," said Paz, now manning his machine gun. "Why aren't they attacking?"

"Maybe they're not here," answered Sparrow, who was keeping a sharp eye from his driver's station.

"Or maybe they're trying to lure us into a false sense of

security," Abbot said. He shivered and spied the hills as chatter between LT Ryback of the MECH platoon and the CO broke over the net. So far, Ryback's people had not picked up any signs of dismounts, but that could change in a nanosecond.

Within a few minutes, the MICLIC rocket hissed away, dragging with it a rope lined with charges that smacked across the snow and ice. A few moments later, multiple explosions rocked the neighborhood as the charges attached to the rope detonated any mines within an eight-by-one-hundred-meter path.

"Red Three, this is Red One. I need your plow forward, over."

Neech's reply was immediate, his tone more than a little eager. "Roger that, Red One. I'm coming up."

"Red Three, this is Red Four," Abbot began. "Make sure you don't have too much spoil in front of that blade. That ground's pretty damned hard, over."

"I hear that."

Neech's mine-clearing blade lifted and pushed mines that were surface-laid or buried up to twelve inches to the side of the track. If he didn't have enough spoil, he would detonate any remaining mines and probably disable his track. If he had too much, the blade could get jammed or break. During Abbot's time at the National Training Center, the average number of operational mine plows was only two out of a possible six, meaning that most broke easily and were constantly under repair. Even worse, the wait time for replacement parts was forever and a day. It wouldn't take much to remove Neech from the fight. He had best be careful.

NEECH AND HIS men had already pulled the travel-lock hitch pins, attached the main electrical harness to the slave receptacle, and moved to the beginning of the lane. Captain Van Buren had managed to get more smoke put on the area, but the rockets had fallen a little wide. The damned wind was blowing the wrong way, driving the smoke ahead instead of directly over Neech's path. Between his throbbing arm and the thoughts of everything that could go wrong, it was a wonder his pulse hadn't leapt off the charts.

Oddly enough, he felt calm and completely in control. He wasn't going to argue about it. He, Romeo, and Choi had trained extensively with the plow, and even Wood had had some experience with it, back at Knox. If something did go wrong, it was usually one of the big three problems: broken lifting straps, a broken lifting motor, or a sheared travel-lock spindle and brackets. However, Neech had checked the straps, which were worn but, he believed, would not break. The motor had been recently repaired, and they had been careful not to accidentally drop the blade while moving at higher speeds. Doing so always spelled disaster for the 7,560-pound blade kit. Neech had also reminded Wood to make sure that he hadn't inadvertently left the ON/OFF power switch on the control box in the ON position. If he did that, he could inadvertantly sit or step on the RAISE/LOWER switch while the plow was in travel lock. The motor would try to lift the locked plow and burn out. Other preparations included using hundred-mile-an-hour tape to secure the emergency release cable handle near Wood's hatch so he wouldn't have to climb out to lower the plow.

With everything set, Neech made sure they were lined up straight with the path and positioned approximately one hundred meters from the estimated leading edge of the minefield, just like the field manual instructed. Romeo traversed the main gun tube to the side so it wouldn't be damaged should a mine detonate under the blade. Neech would plow through the field and continue on for another hundred meters to be sure; that was, if he didn't spot more mines. In that case, the MICLIC would move up, and the process would begin again.

"Red Three, this is Red One," called Hansen. "Move out."

They sealed all their hatches, lowered the blade, and started slowly down the road.

"Hey, Wood, you scared?" Romeo asked.

"Don't fuck with him," said Neech. "Now's not the time."

"Sergeant, do you really think we're safe here?" the driver asked.

Neech gave a little snort. "Wood, this thing's built like a tank."

"Yeah, and built by the lowest bidder," added Romeo. "I hope they can bring up a floater. If we make it through here without tripping a mine, it'll be a miracle."

"That's pretty pessimistic," said Neech. "I think we'll be okay. The LT and Keyman didn't spot too many mines. Maybe this was a hasty operation, and their engineers got caught in the middle of it. Who knows?"

Admittedly, Neech and his crew were having a casual conversation while proofing a lane through a minefield. Some TCs would've maintained utter silence, with sweat dripping off everyone's brows as they crept farther, deeper into hell, their every sense trained on the course, their concentration so impenetrable that if you detonated a nuclear bomb behind their backs, they wouldn't have flinched before being disintegrated.

But not Neech. He would rather they move with their heads low, ready to react but not fixating on the muffled roar of an explosion that could come at any time. There was a certain peace obtained in leaving it all to fate. And on the Korean peninsula, peace was a rare commodity.

In answer to Romeo's question, yes, Wood was no doubt scared. They all were. But so what? Being scared hardly made you a coward. Fear heightened your senses and could even make you a better warrior—if you knew how to control it. Neech had finally come to terms with that, though he was still working on the control part.

"Hey, Sergeant, you know what I'm thinking?" asked Romeo. "This minefield wasn't placed by our friends up north. I think it belongs to the ROKs."

"No shit."

"Yeah. It ain't genius work to figure out. Look at all them track marks to the left."

Neech checked his extension and confirmed. "Either the North Koreans took a chance and bypassed the mines, or the ROKs fell back past this area, and we're seeing their bypass lane around the obstacle."

"I still say the ROKs did it."

"I'll run your theory by the LT, see if he can find out anything from higher." Neech conveyed Romeo's suspicions to Hansen, who said he would share them with the Captain.

"Hey, hey, we got a mine ahead," said Romeo, even as they approached the surface-laid device and the plow shoved it aside. Either the mine was a dud or they had just been the recipients of Romeo's aforementioned miracle, because no explosion followed. They reached the area where the last of the MICLIC's charges had torn up the ground, then slowed to a stop. Neech popped his hatch and scrutinized the mountain pass before him. An unsettling feeling overcame him. The area looked clear. It couldn't be that easy. He ordered Wood to move a few more meters into the area, then they stopped again. He took another look. Nada. Weird. He expected FA, antitank missiles, mortars, infantry, something. He got back on the horn, reported his findings, then, not three seconds afterward, Romeo screamed, "Incoming!"

Neech actually laughed. "It's about fucking time they attacked!"

KEYMAN WAS JUST stuffing some chewing tobacco between his cheek and gum when he saw the flash from the hillside. Whether the light had come from an RPG or a Sagger missile, he didn't care. All he knew was that Neech was out there, alone and in trouble. The fact that he should've waited for orders from Hansen was a real consideration—for the better part of a second—before he leapt into the fight.

"Boomer, haul fuckin' ass!"

The tank slammed into gear, the engine wailing, as Keyman added, "Zuck?"

"I'm on 'em," barked the gunner, opening fire with his coax, raking the area opposite Neech's tank. Meanwhile, a terrible explosion rose in front of Neech, and Keyman wasn't sure if the missile had struck the plow or the turret. He shook with the desire to find out.

With Zuck leaning hard on the coax, Keyman joined the party himself by manning his fifty and adding more suppressing fire along the slope from where the rocket had come. The tracers looked just beautiful, arcing across the glistening snow and punching farther out, into the shadows.

"Why did these cocksuckers wait until Neech proofed the lane?" asked Zuck between bursts. "How fuckin' dumb is that?"

"All I care about is making them die!" Keyman hollered, then grit his teeth and fired again. "Lamont, you going to sit there and shiver? Or are you going up top to give 'em hell!"

"I'm going, Sergeant!"

"Good man!"

"Red Three, this is Red One, SITREP, over." Hansen repeated the call.

"Neech ain't answering," said Lamont as he climbed into his hatch. "You think they got him?"

"Boomer, get us up front to shield Neech," Keyman ordered, then he got off his fifty and stood for a better look. Sporadic gunfire echoed from the hills. That could be Ryback's people trading fire with the North Koreans. Keyman was glad he wasn't up there, fighting those bastards in the miserable cold. He whirled as they drew up on Neech's track, then finally remembered to spit some chew.

"Some fuckin' luck, eh?" yelled the other TC, lifting his chin at the big, smoking ditch lying a few meters in front of his plow. The RPG or Sagger had somehow missed.

"Damn, you got nine lives," Keyman answered, lifting his voice above the engines.

"Yeah, but I think I only got seven left. Could use 'em all before this thing's over."

"All but one." Keyman grinned, then turned back, his smile fading fast.

Hansen's tank came rolling toward them, with Deac looking like a real badass mother at the loader's gun. He was pissed off all right, but his anger was clearly directed at Hansen.

Just then, the hills lit up like a carnival after a power failure. Mortars were there again, giving no quarter to the enemy. Brilliant red-and-orange light outlined the trees, then secondary bursts flickered whiter and much higher, like lightning. The explosions' heat swept down the hills, washing over Keyman's face. For a moment, he bathed in the sensation—until Hansen screamed into the radio, "Sergeant?"

"Yes, sir?" Keyman answered softly.

"I won't even get into it." Hansen removed his protective goggles, then blinked hard and tugged nervously at his helmet's chin strap. He acted as though he were strapped with explosives, and that, along with his pale face and sunken eyes, took Keyman aback.

"I'm okay, LT," Neech broke in, his tone nearly jovial. "They missed me by a mile."

"Some good news at least," Hansen said, sounding more distracted than sincere. "Ryback only found one antitank team."

Neech drew his brows together. "That's fucked up. They set up an obstacle and left one team? What's up with that?"

"This ain't their obstacle. It's the ROKs'. That team was part of the recon squad we intercepted. Guess they were the only ones left. We whacked the rest."

"Hey, Romeo, you were right," Neech called down to his gunner. "And I thought you were a dumb shit. Nope. You're a tactical genius. You ought to be running this fuckin' war!"

"This totally sucks," Keyman said, then spat chew once more. "We risked our fuckin' lives to breach an ROK obstacle? Be nice if they told us where these goddamned things are."

"What do you mean 'we risked our lives'?" Neech asked. "Who's lugging around this plow?"

"And who came to save your ass?"

"Shut up, assholes," Hansen said with a moan. "The only real problem we had was with the dismounts. According to the engineers, the ROKs forgot to put fuses in the mines, so firing the MICLIC and proofing the lane was one big waste of time."

"I don't believe this shit," grunted Keyman.

"Oh, it gets better," Hansen assured the man. "The captain says that the engineer PL's got a book full of ROK minefield charts. He had it in his track the whole time. He could've told us all about this obstacle."

"Those motherfuckers need to sit down and talk," said Neech.

"Oh, they will. That Harris guy is already on the top of the captain's shit list. At least now we'll be able to use the passage lanes in the ROK belts. Let's get back in formation."

Keyman instructed Boomer to pull their tank out front, where they would lead the company team once more. Before they left, the fuelers came up and gave each tank a shot of gas, then, once the trucks had fallen back with the rest of the trains, Hansen relayed the order to roll.

"Hold on a second," Boomer called from his station. "I think we're about to—"

The driver broke off his sentence as the tank aborted.

"Darn it," cried Boomer.

"'Darn it'?" asked Zuck. "Are you kidding me, Boomer? We're fuckin' stuck again!"

"And as usual, we got perfect fucking timing," Keyman said through clenched teeth.

"Hey, Sergeant? That F-word thing?" Lamont began. "I thought we were beyond that. But now I'm confused. Can we curse or not?"

"Hey, you know what?" Keyman asked, heading into his hatch. "At this point, I don't give a fuck."

* * *

"GATCH, PULL UP right behind that asshole right now," Hansen barked.

How many more delays could they stand? He wanted to tell Keyman that he was embarrassing the entire the platoon by not being able to address his track's mechanical problems. After all, Hansen's tank was making weird noises too, but he was on top of the situation, pushing his crew to the extreme, while Keyman was screwing up, playing hero, and back to his old antics. "Red Two, what's your goddamned problem now?"

"She aborted again. We're working on it."

"Move your asses!" Hansen closed his eyes and called Captain Van Buren to report yet another delay. First the mines and now this.

As he finished notifying the CO, Keyman broke in excitedly to say that he was up and running.

With a blast of heat that reached Hansen's nose, Keyman's tank took off. Hansen returned to the warm turret as Gatch fell in behind. "Driver, keep your distance. That asshole could break down again."

"Yes, sir."

"How you feeling?" Deac asked.

Hansen took the question as a dig and a reminder that he was anything but all right. He stared hard at Deac.

The loader shrugged. "Just asking."

"No one feels good any more," said Mingola. "Our childhood's been educated away. There's no hope in magic. Somebody killed Santa Claus. There's no reason to dream. Why are we even here, in this place, at this time?"

"You know what this is?" Hansen asked. "This is like being on a road trip with people you just—"

"What? Hate?" Deac asked.

Hansen winced; he hadn't meant to be that cruel.

"I thought we all loved each other," sang Mingola in a dark lilt. "I thought we had established a bond of trust."

"Hey, y'all, the reason we're not getting along is because we don't have our eyes on the prize. We have to keep our eyes on the prize, and the prize is our lord and savior Jesus Christ."

"You see, they ruined our childhoods, so we invented God to cope with this pathetic existence," explained Mingola. "And Gatch, you're right. He's the only dream left. But he is . . . only a dream."

"I can prove that God exists," said Gatch. "You ready?"

Their debate went on, and instead of ordering them to be quiet, Hansen just tuned them out, keeping his gaze in the extension, anticipating their next attack.

They came up on some frozen streambeds running alongside the road where the ROKs had erected "dragon's teeth," cement spikes firmly planted in the ground. It seemed that invading NKPA forces had blown off the spikes at ground level and had created a bypass lane around what was yet another minefield. However, that field had already been breached and further destroyed by FA fire, which had churned up the course into a nightmare of ruts and ditches.

Several BRDM-2s and VTTs lay off to the side, their shells blackened. They had probably been taken out during the first day of the war. Upon closer inspection, Hansen noticed a few twisted and charred corpses lying across the turrets. As the road made a lazy turn northward, they came upon nearly an entire company of NKPA vehicles—tanks, PCs, engineer tracks, you name it—all blown to smithereens, frozen bodies lying literally everywhere.

"What? No one's going to say 'holy shit'?" Hansen asked.

In fact, no one said anything as they advanced into the graveyard. Hansen and Deac kept in their hatches, surveying the flanks and the area out past Keyman's track. Hansen got on the net and told his wingman to be wary of mines and to avoid enemy vehicles that might've been destroyed by depleted uranium (DU) rounds because breathing in the dust could come back to haunt you. He also reminded him to avoid running over anything that wasn't made of snow and rock. The North Koreans liked to booby-trap piles of dead bodies because they knew American tankers liked to crush whatever lay in their path.

In truth, Hansen didn't need to issue all of those reminders. He was compelled to do so, driven by his fear. And while he expected Keyman to snap at him for stating the painfully obvious, the TC simply acknowledged. Then, after two, perhaps three minutes of silence, Hansen's wingman was back on the net, his tone incredulous: "Red One, this is Red Two. Check this out."

Hansen squinted into the distance at two people standing at the roadside near a demolished T-52 tank that had probably taken a direct hit from FA fire. The two were bundled in parkas, one holding a large camera on his shoulder, the other snapping digital pictures with a tiny one. Hansen searched for their vehicle but found none.

Keyman pulled up beside the improbable paparazzi, his loader bringing the M240 to bear.

"Red Two, stay in your turret. Do not dismount. Do you hear me?" Hansen asked.

"I hear you. Did you think I was going to hop out and ask for directions? Over."

"Yeah, right. Which way to the whorehouse? . . ."

Hansen pulled up behind Keyman's track and removed his CVC helmet, his ears immediately stinging from the cold. Lifting his voice above the howling wind, he cried, "Hey, this is a restricted area! What the hell are you doing out here?"

The figure with the camera slid his hood down, revealing himself as an Asian man in his twenties with streaks of blond running through his shoulder-length hair. The other guy lowered his hood, he too in his twenties, Asian, with spiked hair dyed a brownish red. They didn't look like Koreans, though Hansen couldn't place their nationality. "Not Korean!" said the redhead, waving his little camera.

"What the fuck are you doing out here?"

"Press! Press!" said the other guy, holding out a white card with Asian characters that Hansen recognized as Japanese, along with an English word: PRESS.

"This is illegal," Hansen said. "Don't you get that? Illegal."

"Some shit," said Mingola. "Here we are, out in the middle of fuckin' nowhere, and these assholes sneak all the way in to get some pictures and video. Fuckin' Geraldo would be proud."

"Hey, man, you have to talk to my CO," Hansen told the redhead.

The guy shook his head, either not understanding or disagreeing. He turned to his buddy, muttered something, then they resumed their work—completely ignoring Hansen and the four 7.62 mm machine guns pointed at their backs, the nearest operated by Lamont, the others by Deac, Paz, and Choi, all good shots, even the FNG Lamont.

Hansen was about to call back to Captain Van Buren but held his hand inches from the mike. He saw himself leaping from the turret, jumping down onto the snow, and beating the living shit out of these two punks. It was clear that all of his fear and frustration needed to come out.

Deac and Zuck called after him as he threw down his helmet and bolted out of the turret. He came down onto the hull, jumped to the ground, then charged up to the redhead, who was taking close-ups of corpses.

Hansen grabbed the man by the shoulder, wrenched him around then seized his arms and literally shook him. "This is fucking illegal, you dumb motherfucker!"

The camera guy started screaming in Japanese.

That's when Hansen realized he was choking the redhead, the guy's face turning blue.

"Oh my God," cried a disgusted Mingola.

But Hansen hardly heard him, hardly saw Keyman rushing up behind the camera guy, who had dropped his camera and was reaching into his parka.

HOW FAR SOUTH *can this go?* Keyman thought as he twisted the camera guy's arm behind his back, then tripped the scrawny knucklehead to the ground.

With one more shove, he had the kid's face buried in the snow. Then, reaching with his free hand, he fished out a .45 caliber pistol from the guy's pocket and tossed it a few feet away. "LT, this guy's armed!"

Meanwhile, Hansen had pinned the redheaded guy and was continuing to choke the life out of him. *Shit.* The lieutenant would kill that civilian if someone didn't stop him.

Keyman was about to release his victim when Abbot came running over. "LT! Let him go!"

Again, the lieutenant was in his own world, screaming into the redhead's face: "Who's in charge here, motherfucker, huh? Tell me! Are you in charge?"

Neech came circling around behind Abbot, and Keyman called him to retrieve the camera guy's weapon. Just then, Abbot seized Hansen's shoulders and ripped him off the redhead.

But then Hansen grabbed Abbot's collar, drew back a fist, and was about to do something very, very bad.

Striking Abbot, the senior NCO, the most experienced and level-headed guy in the entire platoon, would be insane for two reasons (beyond the obvious legal ramifications): one, it would ruin everyone's morale, and two, a rough-and-tumble NCO like Abbot would kick the living shit out of Hansen.

Perhaps there was enough sanity left in the lieutenant's brain, because he lowered the fist and slowly, ever so slowly, released the sergeant.

However, judging from Abbot's expression, the damage had already been done.

CHAPTER
SIX

WITH HIS CHEST heaving and drool dripping off his chin, Hansen faced Abbot and shuddered so hard that it hurt. He had nearly struck the platoon sergeant, a man he greatly admired, a man who represented everything that was good and decent and honorable about service in the military.

How had it come to this?

Hansen's mouth fell open, and words just spilled out. "Aw, Jesus, Sergeant. I didn't realize it was you, man."

The redhead was shouting something, probably expletives, when Hansen faced him and screamed, "SHUT UP! RIGHT NOW! I WILL KILL YOU, YOU MOTHER-FUCKER!"

Again, he took out his anger on the kid, at once hating himself but determined that the kid would pay if he didn't keep quiet. Lucky for him that he shut up.

With the redhead momentarily controlled, Hansen regarded Abbot, pleading with his eyes.

Abbot raised a palm, then spoke calmly, his rage right there on the surface, waiting to be unleashed. "Lieutenant. What's going on here?"

"These guys say they're reporters," Neech jumped in. "Look at them. They got cameras and shit. They must've hiked up here . . . crazy bastards."

"I'll get the CO to come up, figure out what he wants to do with them," said Abbot. "Neech, you and Keyman hold these guys until he arrives."

Hansen just sat there, knowing that he was supposed to be giving the orders, but he let the sergeant take over because he felt terrible about his behavior, so terrible, in fact, that he wasn't sure he could go on. This thing inside was growing out of control.

Abbot hustled off to make the call. Meanwhile, Mingola had dismounted and stood over Hansen, proffering a bony hand. "Come on, LT."

Hansen accepted the help, stood, brushed off the snow, then flexed his gloved hand, the one he had almost used on Abbot. He stared at someone else's hand. Had to be.

"You're way over the top, and you know it," Mingola said.

Hansen stiffened. "You're out of line."

Mingola nodded, bit his lip, obviously holding back his *fuck you* before he replied, "Yes, sir."

"Get back in the turret."

The gunner held his ground. "You need help."

"I said, get back in the fucking turret." Hansen's blood boiled again. If Mingola failed to obey, he would wind up flat on his back, and Hansen would then drag the black-eyed bastard up across the hull and onto the turret, where he'd dump him like so much garbage into the hatch.

A chill struck hard as that scene played out in his head. *Holy shit.* What was he thinking? Was this the way to build morale?

Mingola finally made a dramatic turn and hiked toward the tank, lifting his arms to the heavens. "Aw, come on, guys. Don't laugh. I didn't ask for this shit! And Dix? You were right about him all along."

"Lieutenant, can we have a word?" Abbot called from his track, his tone indicating that some serious shit was about to hit the fan.

Hansen dragged his boots toward the platoon sergeant, every step an excruciating effort. Where would the conversation lead? What would Hansen say? He feared Abbot's retribution. Though the platoon sergeant was a real humanitarian, Hansen may have pushed him too hard.

GATCH WANTED TO climb out of his driver's hole, get into the turret, and shove his fist down Mingola's throat. The guy was having a full-blown conversation with his dead buddies, and that was too weird for even a quasi-sane tanker like himself. But Gatch couldn't resort to violence. That's not what Jesus would do. He would turn the other cheek. Gatch wondered what the lieutenant thought of that philosophy. Probably wouldn't care much for it, at least not now. Gatch still couldn't believe how close Hansen had come to striking the platoon sergeant and that he had actually assaulted one of those reporters.

After a long, slow breath, he closed his eyes and prayed for their safe passage to Panmunjom, prayed for his fellow crew members—especially the LT—and prayed that God would purge the memories of all those hookers he had screwed. He kept returning to their beds, kept seeing them lying on their backs, their ankles perched on his shoulders as they cooed, "You very big man, Joe! Very big man!"

"Guys, while the LT's out there, I want to talk," said Deac. "Because we need a plan."

Gatch opened his eyes, was about to say something, but Mingola responded first: "You want to talk? Good idea. But there's not much to say. The LT's fucked up. And we're stuck with him. But I'll tell you what. If he asks me to recheck anything, I won't do it."

"And that'll help?" asked Gatch. "Deac's right. We need to do something. The LT's paranoid about the tank, he nearly choked that Japanese guy to death, and he almost hit Abbot. What next? What if he faints again? Dudes, this is crazy. This conversation, everything. We're the best platoon in the company. What're we talking about here? The M-word?"

"That's right. Mutiny," answered Mingola. "And boys, I got no problem fighting this tank. No problem at all. If we have to, we'll take him out of the equation."

"Maybe we'll take you out," Deac retorted.

"I ain't the problem."

"You got a big mouth for a skinny little bastard."

"Listen, you insubordinate motherfucker . . . All I need is a trigger finger."

Deac gave a big snort, then said, "The lieutenant might be messed up right now, but bottom line? Gatch and I would die for him. So don't be talking shit about him or anyone else in this platoon."

Mingola sang "la-de-da-de-da" under his breath, even as Deac finished. "Know what? I don't have to say or do anything. The LT will hang himself, but when he does that, he'll be hanging us out to dry. You want to be there when that happens?"

"The LT just needs some time to rest. He'll be all right," Deac argued.

"But it wouldn't hurt to be ready if he does drop the ball," Gatch pointed out.

"Don't worry about that," said Mingola. "I'll be right here, just waiting. But I still say one more slip up, and we turn him in. Hell, this whole conversation might be a waste of time. The platoon sergeant might be going to higher right now. I know I would."

"Abbot wouldn't do that," said Gatch. "And no one will say anything about the LT choking that reporter."

"I don't know. Maybe Abbot would go to the CO," Deac speculated.

"Well, if he doesn't, then I say we talk to the LT. Let him know how we feel. He already knows we're worried about him."

"But what do we say?" asked Deac. "That we're tired of covering his ass and that we're worried that he'll get us killed?"

"Pretty much."

"Oh, that'll go over real well," said Mingola. "In fact, I want you to do that. It'll be one hell of a show."

HANSEN FOLLOWED ABBOT to the rear deck of the sergeant's track, out of sight and earshot from the others. His pulse quickened as he prepared himself for the worst.

But he didn't think he should give up. Not yet. The platoon sergeant was the most reasonable man Hansen knew, and he had no doubt seen other young lieutenants become unraveled. He had probably even counseled a few. Hansen's situation was nothing new to Abbot, and, given the circumstances, it would be in the sergeant's best interest to help his PL get squared away.

So, to make it easier on the sergeant, and, of course, himself, Hansen decided he would apologize again, express his regret, and really open up to Abbot. Hopefully he could gain some insight from a guy who knew all about fatigue.

They would talk man to man, not officer to NCO.

Abbot draped an arm across his tank, stared at the churned-up snow a moment, then looked up, his expression unreadable.

Hansen stammered. "Matt, I . . . I don't know what to say. I want to talk frankly here. I feel really—"

"Sir, I'm glad you want to be honest, because with all due respect, I am this close to talking to the CO. If you can't lead this platoon anymore, then step down, because there's too much at stake. It's all about the mission and the men, and you're having trouble with both. This is war. We can't fuck around one bit. If you don't get your act together, somebody will get killed. You can't blame me for worrying about that."

The truth hurt, and Hansen couldn't help but go on the offensive. "I know how important this is—that's why I'm so stressed out!"

"We all are, but—"

"But what?"

"But most of us aren't snapping at each other."

"I'm not snapping at you."

Abbot glanced away and slowly shook his head. "Man, you don't even realize it."

"I'm just tired. And those fucking guys back there got to me, all right? I know it was wrong. Just lay off."

"Hey, Lieutenant. I lost my wife. But I'm in that turret. And you can count on me. All we're asking for is the same. But we just don't know. What can I do to help?"

Hansen widened his eyes and leaned toward the sergeant. "You can get off my fucking back!"

The sergeant dropped his voice. "Kid, listen to me. I'm not here to bust your balls. But have you looked in the mirror lately? Are you eating? Don't look like it. And you keep scratching your chin. It's an itch that won't go away. I've seen it before."

Hansen was in the middle of doing that when he froze, looked at his fingers, felt his eyelids begin to twitch. "It's just the stress."

Abbot's expression grew dubious. "All I'm sayin', *sir*—"

"Fuck you with the 'sir' crap. Talk to me man to man or not at all."

"You have to be a man first," Abbot growled. "And right now you ain't shit."

Hansen wanted to pull back a fist. This time he would strike the sergeant. Break his jaw.

But then, like the biggest pussy in the world, he broke down and buried his face in his hands. He fell back against the track, slipped on the ice, and almost dropped onto his ass before the sergeant caught him.

"Lieutenant . . ."

"I'm fucked up, man. It's just . . . too much."

Abbot tugged away Hansen's hands, then took him by the shoulders. Hansen looked up through teary eyes, his knees still feeling like rubber.

"When you first came to Korea, I thought, oh, shit, another Fuckin' New Guy officer. And worse, an asswipe from West Point. Then you won Top Tank, and I realized you were the real deal. But like they say, the candle that burns twice as bright only burns half as long."

Hansen nodded. "I'm burned out."

"Not yet. But you're heading there. If you lean on me, I'll take up the slack, like always. But you haven't been leaning. You're taking it all on yourself. Getting help don't make you weak."

"I don't know what's happening. I don't know about anything anymore. I keep wondering, is this me? Am I the guy who fired the gun and killed Lee? I killed my own fuckin' gunner. Killed him. And those guys in the Stryker, I—"

"Look at it another way: you saved your wingman's life. Not many guys can say that. And you couldn't have saved those guys in the Stryker. Not your fault. End of story."

"I guess I'm just scared that I can't do it anymore. I feel like I have to be perfect."

"You got a lot of talent. Just use it. Forget about being perfect; it'll never happen. First thing? Calm down. You are way too wired. Couple times I thought you were Keyman."

Hansen cracked a smile. "Right now I wish I were him. That motherfucker is so squared away that he makes me sick. He's the angel, and I'm the devil."

"He took your lead. Now you have to get back on the horse. I ain't got no deep psychological shit to offer, just that. But remember, we're counting on you to do the right thing so we can strike fast, kick ass, and all go home."

"I'll try."

"Nope. That ain't good enough. You'll do it."

Hansen took a deep breath. "Yeah, I will."

They shook on it. Abbot nodded curtly and stroked his moustache as he scrutinized Hansen once more. Satisfied by whatever conclusion he had come to, he mounted his track.

As Hansen walked back toward his own tank, he knew that his relationship with Abbot would never be the same. He had lost the platoon sergeant's trust; it would take an act of God to regain it. Maybe Hansen should consult Gatch and put in that request.

Van Buren finally arrived and said they needed to leave the Japanese reporters where they were. He would report their position to higher, but if they wanted to freeze their asses off and risk being killed or captured by NK special ops guys, so be it. Of course, the CO confiscated their weapon and camera equipment, and the team moved on, leaving the two men hollering and shaking fists in their wake.

ABBOT AND PAZ were in their hatches, grimacing as the wind cut across their faces. About a quarter-click ahead, the road would get fairly steep, taking them over a string of hills, and Keyman was concerned about any one of them, especially Neech, getting stuck.

In truth, Abbot was only half listening to the chatter over the platoon net. "You have to be a man first," he thought aloud, the intercom picking up his every word.

"What did you say?" asked Paz.

"What?"

"You said something about being a man."

"Oh, I was just thinking about something. Don't worry about it."

"You got some issues with your manhood?"

Abbot made an ugly face, then returned to his introspection.

How many more times would he replay the conversation? Every time he went over it, he winced at some of the things he had said. Sure, the anger and resentment of having to baby-sit Hansen had influenced his words, along with the struggle to accept his wife's death, but he had been worried about the young lieutenant from the start. Still, he had never shared his doubts. Until now. He did regret the "you ain't shit" remark. That had been a cheap shot. Even so, he had gotten a lot off his shoulders, and he should feel better.

He didn't.

He was even more concerned about Second Lieutenant Jack Hansen, who was, when you got down to it, just a twenty-three-year-old kid from Long Island who still had a lot to learn. On a positive note—and there were very few— focusing on Hansen diverted him from the suffocating pain of Kim's loss. He should thank the LT for being so stressed out. The irony of that made him smile bitterly.

Time to check on Neech again. Well, that was odd. Red Three was falling behind. The shrapnel from that RPG or Sagger had left deep gouges in the plow blade, but otherwise the tank had checked out. Was Neech having problems with something they hadn't spotted?

"Red Three, this is Red Four. You need to tighten up, over."

"Roger that, Four."

"Got any other problems, over?"

"Well, that last MRE gave me some real gas, and I've really been letting them rip, stinkin' up the whole turret; otherwise I'm good to go."

"Roger that. Suggest you keep those hatches open! Red Four, out."

Neech was the only TC in the platoon whose sense of humor had remained intact. More irony there, since he had fallen into a deep depression after his driver had been killed. Then he had gone from suicidal to happy-go-lucky, and the crazy bastard had reenlisted. Now he poured jet fuel on his corn flakes, and if he ever had a dog, he would name it "Sabot." He was probably back there, singing how proud he was to be an American, along with the CD. That kind of one hundred-and-eighty-degree turn was exactly what Hansen needed. Maybe Abbot should get those two together for a little talk. The idea intrigued him.

The road turned slightly left as they ascended the first hill. Abbot estimated the grade at only twenty degrees, but when you factored in the snow and ice, molehills could become mountains. Keyman's tank fishtailed slightly, but Boomer did a fine job of recovering. Gatch knew all about Korea's road hazards (winter or summer), and he didn't miss a beat navigating up the slippery terrain. Sparrow needed no help either, following in Gatch's path. So far so good.

But a look back to Neech stole Abbot's breath.

"WOOD, WHAT'RE YOU doing? You're giving her too much gas!" Neech boomed. "Ease off! Ease off!"

They were nearing the crest of the hill, and the kid, in his infinite wisdom, had decided to throttle up and slingshot them over the other side. His ingenious plan caused the tracks to lose their footing, and the tank began to slide backward.

Choi, who was up top with Neech, groaned a string of curses as they now fishtailed, swung completely around, and began rolling straight for an embankment.

"Don't brake so hard," Neech screamed. "Turn! Turn! Turn, you goddamned asshole!"

So much for Neech's jovial mood. The tracks locked up, and the tank drew up on the embankment.

"Aw, fuck! We're going to hit! Hang on!" yelled Neech.

At the last second, Wood somehow managed to turn them away, regain some footing, and bring the tank to a rumbling halt at the bottom of the hill. The engineers were only about a hundred meters back and rolling steadily toward them, so there wasn't much time to get turned around and back on course.

"Wood?" Neech called.

"Yes, Sergeant."

"Pray you didn't break my track."

"I'm praying, Sergeant. But you gotta admit, you ain't never seen anybody recover a tank like that. I mean that shit was like stunt driving or something. I'm going to get me to California and get in the movies. That was fucking awesome!"

"Get us back up the hill first. Move out!"

Choi lifted his chin to get Neech's attention. "Sergeant, this is bad omen."

"Okay, Choi. It's the end of the world, and we're all going to die. I get that. But let's see if we can have a little more fun first. That's the plan."

"You don't take anything serious?"

"Life's too short, brother. We've both seen that."

The lieutenant called for a SITREP, and Neech held up a finger to Choi while he assured the lieutenant that they would catch up. He probably should have checked for damage before doing that, but the LT needed an answer, and it was better to give him good news after fucking up. Even monkeys and guys like Wood understood that.

Fortunately, as the gods would have it, no apparent damage presented itself, and the tank muscled back up the hill, with Wood applying a more conservative amount of gas, guiding the tank in what he called the low-gear boogie. Just as they came over the other side, crackling explosions and small arms fire echoed from somewhere behind them.

No, wait a minute. That's up ahead. Damned helmet constricted his hearing.

Neech grabbed his NVGs and surveyed the road as it grew more narrow until it leveled off and stretched toward the next hill. The other three tanks were in perfect formation and about a hundred meters ahead of him.

And all three had just driven into a deadly gauntlet, with automatic weapon fire lit by tracers and RPGs coming at them from both sides of the road. The NKPA regulars or special forces had set up shop within the heavy cover. And the bastards had been waiting. Why the task force scouts hadn't tipped off the team was anyone's guess. They could've been captured or killed. Or they could be having communication problems, which absolutely sucked if your name was Sergeant Richard "Neech" Nelson.

"Red, this is Red One! We got troops, heavy machine guns, and maybe AT teams on both sides of the road! Fire! Fire!"

"Red One, this is Red Two. I just got hit by an RPG or something. They're pounding us from all sides!"

"Red, this is Red Four. We got a BMP up on the hillside. I have him."

Just then Abbot's main gun boomed, and across the road a huge fire erupted as the personnel carrier showered itself over the snow beneath a growing column of black smoke.

"Jesus, Sergeant, we ain't driving into that shit, are we?" asked Wood.

"No, *we're* not. You are. Romeo? See that muzzle flash along the left ridgeline?"

"I see it."

"Make it go away."

"Roger that!"

As the tank leveled off and Wood throttled up, cursing in fear as he did so, Romeo put the coax to work, specks of red darting off to the beat of *rat-tat-tat, rat-tat-tat*. The ball-and-tracer ammo was simply beautiful, deadly, and on the mark.

"Red Three, this is Red One. You might have a better angle on them. Can you fire an AP round, over?"

Neech grinned over the lieutenant's request. "Roger. You bet your ass I can. Stand by!"

Seemingly hundreds of rounds began gnawing at the turret, and as Neech hung up the mike, he thought, *Damn, this is some pretty serious shit.* "Loader, battlecarry AP round."

Choi was quite familiar with the antipersonnel round and needed no further instruction to set the range for detonation. "Weapon safe, AP set and loaded!"

"Where you want it?" Romeo asked. "The whole friggin' hill looks like the shit!"

"Keep it on the ridge."

"You got it. I'm on."

"Up."

"Fire at those motherfuckers!"

"Bend over!"

The gun's mighty recoil drove Neech back into his seat, and a blink later the rocket detonated at the preset range, releasing thousands of metal flechettes that sprayed the hill, probing for unsuspecting troops huddled in their path.

As proof positive of the round's staggering effects, every muzzle flash and arc of rocket fire grew dark in that region of the woods, leaving only the rocket's smoke plume billowing like a flag of surrender.

"Adios muchachos!" cried Romeo.

The engine's tone abruptly shifted. Neech drew back from his extension and frowned. "Wood, why are you slowing down?"

"You have to ask?"

Neech checked his extension. "Oh, no."

WHAT HAD KEYMAN expected? Murphy's law dictated that if he was driving a heap, then it would continually abort at the most inopportune times. That's the way old Murphy worked when you had spent a lifetime, like Keyman had, pissing him off, flipping him the bird every chance you got.

So there Keyman sat, in the middle of the gauntlet, taking heavy fire and unable to move. Hansen had called for a SITREP, but Keyman had ignored it. He didn't have time to rub salt in the sucking chest wound that was himself and his crew. He was too busy groping for a bandage. But he couldn't find one. Couldn't even let Boomer go work one of his miracles beneath the bitch plate with so much lead knocking at their door. Murphy had seen to that. He always upped the ante, that bastard.

Keyman and Zuck were on their machine guns, dipping much too heavily into their own caches. They walked like a duck, talked like a duck, and, damn it, sat like a duck too.

But suddenly, Hansen came up on the right side, Abbot on the left, both tanks helping to cover Keyman. The lieutenant was screaming some shit on the radio, but Keyman kept tuning him out. What could he add, other than to order Keyman to get his fucking tank moving?

"Come on, Boomer," Lamont pleaded into the intercom. "I've only been laid twice in my life. And the one time didn't really count because she just gave me a hand job.

Isn't there anything you can do up there? Hot-wire the fucker or something?"

Boomer didn't answer at first. But after a few seconds he cried, "Sergeant? Hold your fire a minute. Abbot and the LT got us covered pretty good. I think I can get back there and only get shot a few times. Wish me luck."

Keyman didn't know what to say. Ordering the guy to remain at his station could doom them all. Allowing him to go outside to fix the tank could get him killed. But Boomer knew what he was doing. And suddenly, Keyman's emotions burst out, "You get out there and fix this tank and show these motherfuckers who we are, right Boomer? First Tank!"

"Yes, Sergeant!"

"Hooah!"

The big driver echoed the cry, then Keyman popped his hatch and watched Boomer climb onto the hull, drop onto the ground, then jog alongside the road wheels. Boomer then hauled himself back onto the hull, all while Mingola and Romeo hosed down the hills with coax fire, trying to cover him.

HANSEN HAD JUST finished talking to the FSO, and mortar fire would be raking the hills in a matter of moments.

"Red One, this is Black Six," called Van Buren. "I'm sending up MECH to put some dismounts in those hills. I want that enemy neutralized before the engineers and trains pass through, over."

"Roger that, Black Six. Be advised Red Two has aborted again—right in the middle of this gauntlet. We're covering him, and I see that his driver is initiating repairs, over."

"Red, did you say that Red Two has aborted again, over?"

"Roger, Red Two has aborted, over."

"Jesus Christ. All right, understood. Continue to engage and report. Black Six, out."

Hansen's hatch was in the open-protected position, and as he peered out through the gap, more gunfire sparked across the turret, driving him back into his seat. "God-damn, this is a hot fight!"

"You ain't shitting," said Mingola.

"Lieutenant, there's another BMP heading along the tree line, coming right at us!" reported Zuck. "He's only a klick out!"

"Deac?" Hansen called.

"Weapon safe, HEAT loaded."

"Identified."

"Up."

"WAIT!" Hansen screamed. "Hold your fire!"

"But he's still coming," hollered Mingola. "And he ain't no fucking Stryker!"

Hansen burst into his hatch, stood, and wailed at the top of his lungs, "Boomer! Get back in the hull! We have to fire!"

The guy was hunched over, his face buried in engine components.

"Boomer!"

If they fired their main gun with the driver so close, he could be injured or even killed. "Boomer!"

Nothing.

You idiot. Use the radio!

Hansen ducked into the turret, snatched the mike. "Red Two, this is Red One. Get your fuckin' driver inside! We got a BMP bearing down on us!"

"Roger that, One," Keyman replied.

"Eight hundred meters," yelled Mingola. "He's turning toward us, ready to fire!"

CHAPTER
SEVEN

WITH ROUNDS RINGING his turret like a church bell, Keyman came up into his hatch, and, without so much as flinching, cleared his throat, cupped his hands around his mouth, and proceeded to scream louder than he ever had in his entire life.

Because another man's life depended upon it.

"Boomer, you have to get inside this fucking tank right now! Boomer! Do you hear me?"

The driver didn't.

There was no time for Keyman to climb out and physically grab Boomer to get his attention. And, of course, the man had unplugged his CVC helmet from the intercom.

Thus, Keyman had all of a split-second to make the decision. "Zuck, tell the LT to fire!"

And in the next second, the guilt and agony began.

NEECH HAD BEEN monitoring the platoon net, and the moment that he had heard about the oncoming BMP, he had grabbed the TC override, traversed his main gun, and put Romeo on the target.

"Red, this is Red Three! I'll get him from back here!" he told the lieutenant.

Neech was still about forty meters behind the other tanks and could fire without seriously endangering Boomer. Maybe Wood's screw-up had been a blessing in disguise. "Moving BMP," he announced to his crew.

"Identified!"

"Up!"

"Fire!"

"On the way!"

If they destroyed the BMP and Boomer made it back into the turret, Neech would accept the title of hero. "Come on," he told God, gaping into his extension. "Ain't too much to ask."

THE HEAT ROUND flew over Hansen's head and scared the shit out of him. But he didn't react until after the BMP popped a wheelie and hemorrhaged fire, fuel, and clouds of gray smoke. Then it blew into a thousand pieces.

Then Hansen got scared. "Fucking target," he muttered, then flicked his glance to Neech's track, barreling toward them.

Gunfire ripped across the hill toward the turret, forcing Hansen back inside. He called Keyman and demanded a SITREP, but his wingman was still not answering.

"Whoa," said Mingola. "We really stirred up the hornets."

Hansen checked his extension, spotted a pair of muzzle flashes in the hills. Big flashes from big guns. "Yeah, and I think I found one of your nests." He worked the override, traversed the gun. "See 'em?"

"Whoa, oh yeah, and a whole bunch of dismounts right around him, standing out like sore thumbs."

"Red One, this is Red Two," called Keyman. "My driver has mounted up. We're up and running! I am moving out!"

"Roger that!" Hansen returned the mike. "Hey, Mingola,

let's teach those guys on the hill why you never bring a rifle to a tank fight."

"LT, I think you found your mojo." The gunner concentrated on his sight. "These cocksuckers are identified."

"Up!"

"Fire!"

"On the way!"

For the first time in nearly twenty-four hours, Hansen felt good, really good, about himself. He beat a fist on his hip and yelled, "Target!" as the enemy machine guns went silent and smoke, lit by flickering fires, devoured the hillside. "Gatch, mortars will be here any second. Get in tight behind Red Two, and let's NASCAR our asses out of here."

"Roger that! And we thank you Lord God for keeping us safe and sound, though we drive through the valley of death, which is right here, right now."

"Dude, can you shut up and drive?" asked Mingola.

IT FELT PRETTY good to be a hero. Neech would whole-heartedly accept all the money, fame, and the large-breasted women that accompanied such a title. He wasn't into the gold plaques, and the medals were good for bragging rights, but those bucks, that *Time* magazine cover story, and those vivacious models digging their long nails into his arms at parties would be enough.

Again, he wasn't asking for much. His father might even be proud—not of his lusting after money, fame, and sex, of course, but of his ability to overcome his depression, move forward, and become an asset to his platoon. When Neech's mom was dying of cancer, his father had fallen into a deep depression and had never recovered. He would never look Neech fully in the eyes, maybe because he saw too much of his dead wife in his son. That made Neech feel terrible. Maybe it drove him to overeat? Who knew? One thing was clear: his mom's death created a huge rift between Neech and his father, one that became even worse when Neech joined the army. But now, if he survived this thing, he could go home and share his experiences with his father. Maybe he could teach dad how to feel something again.

Okay, he was asking for a lot now. A whole lot.

Small-arms fire clanged against the hull for a few more seconds until the mortars plunged from the night sky like hungry metal bats that slammed into the hills, one after another, unrelenting, churning up smoke and death as Red Platoon cleared the area and the engineers behind them entered what was left of the gauntlet.

The road widened several meters, though the hills on either side grew much steeper, with small, leafless trees forming the teeth of a great white maw that consumed each tank.

After warming himself for another few minutes, Neech went back into his hatch, yawned, then resumed watch. After a minute or so, he lowered his goggles, glanced around, and experienced a strong sense of déjà vu.

When he had first arrived in country, he had been given a tour of the DMZ and the Joint Security Area (JSA) compound. Company SOP was for all TCs and above, and eventually all soldiers, to go to the demilitarized zone, see the terrain, and look the enemy in the eye. Neech thought back to that routine bus ride. Now he was retracing his steps in wartime. If he knew then that he would be returning to this route as part of a company team on a mission to seize Panmunjom and Kaesong, he might have taken the trip more seriously. Instead, he and the other new TCs had spent most of their time goofing on both the North and South Koreans and their silly rules. For example, the ROKs wouldn't let you wear jeans when visiting the DMZ because they thought doing so would justify North Korean claims that South Korea was an American colony. However, tourists coming down from the north could wear anything they wanted.

When Neech had first been driven into the DMZ, passing through a fortresslike entrance made of stone, he had caught a distant glimpse of a ridiculously large North

Korean flag that some said was the largest flag in the world. The South Koreans had their own massive flag on their side of the line. One of Neech's buddies had joked that "men with small penises need big flags." After facing those men in combat, Neech wasn't laughing anymore. Men with small penises still fired big guns.

The Joint Security Area compound encompassed several large buildings with sweeping roof lines that sat between a collection of smaller, rectangular-shaped meeting facilities. The compound had been maintained by forces from both sides until 1976. During that year, an American Army captain had chopped down a tree that affected the view of the U.S./U.N. checkpoint. For his efforts he had been axed to death by North Korean soldiers. Since then, the JSA was divided in two, and no one was allowed to cross the demarcation line to the other side. In fact, some of the buildings straddled the line, which was also marked on the inside. It all seemed very weird and very silly to a bunch of young tank commanders like Neech and his buddies.

The South Korean soldiers guarding the DMZ were known as the "South Korean puppet regime" by the north. They and the U.S. troops along the line all wore green uniforms and dark sunglasses. Neech guessed that Ray-Ban or Oakley must have won a government contract to make soldiers look cool. The North Koreans, who were all slightly leaner and shorter, wore simple brown uniforms and no fancy eyewear.

About one kilometer from the JSA stood the Armistice Talks Hall, a minimuseum where, as the name not so subtly implied, armistice negotiations had taken place. Neech had seen the axe used to murder that army captain as well as "evidence" proving that the Americans had started the first Korean War. In fact, the were little booklets for sale with titles like *The American Imperialists Started the War* and *America: The Empire of Terrorism.* He also saw walls with pictures featuring the exploits of the Dear Leader and the Great Leader (his father) at military parades. Neech and the others discovered that the North Koreans were taught an alternate history of the war, one in which they won, though teachers handily omitted detailed descriptions of the victory. "These people are just nuts," Neech had remarked.

"Yeah," one of his buddies had agreed. "But that's what makes them so scary."

Because North Korea's economy was so bad and its people so malnourished, Neech wondered what would've happened if the South Koreans had reinforced the DMZ with fast food joints instead of bunkers. They could've offered free Big Macs and fried chicken to all North Korean customers toting rifles. The war might have been over in a matter of hours.

No such luck. And the enemy was still hungry for American and South Korean blood.

Neech looked over at Choi, who was in his hatch, ready on his machine gun. The KATUSA's lips were trembling, but he stood there, stalwart, gaze locked on the gloomy embankments. Choi was a good guy, and Neech had no doubts about his loyalty or abilities. They had both watched one of their brothers die, and while they rarely spoke about that experience, it would link them until they died.

Looking at Choi made Neech feel even colder. "Hey, guys, you know what we need? Some rock 'n' roll to warm us up. Romeo, you got some U2 down there?"

"Oh, yeah. Sergeant. Coming right up. . . ."

"RED ONE, THIS is Black Six. You should be approaching another ROK minefield about a thousand meters north, over."

"Roger that, Black Six."

"Passage lane is on the right. According to our ROK map, we should keep tight to the hill, and if you need to slow down, go ahead, over."

"Okay, we'll keep tight to the hill and slow down if needed. Roger that, Black Six, over."

"All right. Continue to advance. Let me know when you spot the obstacle. Black Six, out."

Hansen conveyed the information to Keyman out front, then returned the mike and shook his head at Deac, who was offering him a candy bar before he went up.

"C'mon, LT. Get a little sugar in you."

"Not hungry."

"You have to eat something."

"I will. Eventually."

Though he felt good about the way he had handled himself at the gauntlet, the thing inside was already leeching away his high spirits. Soon he would be back on the razor's edge, frustrated with the crew and the tank and wondering how long he would last. His heart would tick like a bomb. There were no wires to cut to dismantle his brain, no end in sight—except death. He closed his eyes, half wishing for the end but knowing deep down that killing himself or even allowing himself to die was selfish, not to mention weak. He had worked too hard for it to come down to that.

With a deep sigh, he joined Deac up top, did a cursory inspection with his goggles, then lowered them and took in a few long breaths to clear his head. His cell phone beeped with an incoming text message. He grinned as he read Karen's admonishment to stay safe and to keep loving her. She was in Hawaii and doing just fine. She ended with "that's an order," followed by two exclamation marks and a few smiley faces.

He was the luckiest guy in the world. She made it all worthwhile. If he could remember that every time the jitters came on, every time he wanted to curse the crew for not jumping fast enough at his commands, then maybe he could, somehow, put it all into perspective.

The facts: He had what it took to lead these men, to bring them all home. He just kept forgetting that. Karen loved him. His crew, along with the rest of the platoon and company team, needed him. They were more important than one tired and paranoid tank commander.

"Hey, LT?" Deac called.

"Yeah?"

"You want that candy now?"

Hansen thought a moment. "Yeah. Thanks."

KEYMAN JUST HAPPENED to look over at Lamont. And he was glad he did. The kid wore the infamous thousand-yard stare, and he hadn't said a word since they had left the gauntlet.

Though he had to keep his attention focused on the road ahead, shifting between NVGs and his unaided eyes, Keyman still seized the moment to make sure Lamont was okay. "We got beat up pretty good back there, huh?" he asked.

After a moment, the loader finally said, "Yeah."

"This beast has got some nice scars to prove it."

"Yeah."

"You got the shakes, don't you?"

"I'm sorry, Sergeant."

"It's okay. I get 'em too. It happens."

"When we aborted, I thought we'd—"

"Yeah, me too. But we didn't."

"Almost feels like we did."

"I know. You keep going back over it, seeing yourself die, right?"

"How'd you know?"

"C'mon, bud. Give me a little credit."

Lamont breathed deeply into the intercom. "It's weird. You feel like crying, but it won't come."

"It passes. And then you get used to it. Don't make you a pussy or anything. Just the body reacting to stress."

"Yes, Sergeant."

"Good. You'll be okay. You just load that gun when I tell you, keep shifting that ammo, and you'll make it back home to get laid for a second time. No hand job. Real sex, okay?"

"I guess that was too much information."

"Yeah, it was. We'll forgive you this one time, but if it happens again . . ."

"It won't. Thanks, Sergeant."

"Red Two, this is Red One, over."

Keyman ducked into his hatch to answer the lieutenant's call.

Automatic weapons fire erupted from the hills, clanging loudly off the turret.

Keyman flicked his glance up.

Just for a second.

Just as Lamont caught a round in the cheek, his head twisting at a bizarre angle.

"Lamont!"

The kid collapsed in his hatch.

"Lamont's been hit!" Keyman cried. He wanted to go up top and check the kid's pulse, but more machine gun fire talked him out of it. "Boomer? Get us the fuck out of here! Zuck? Shoot 'em!" Keyman took up the mike, his gaze never leaving the poor kid in his hatch, blood now dripping into the turret. "Red One, we're taking fire from the hills again. My loader's been hit, over."

"Roger that. Coming into your fire. Haul ass, and I'll get some mortars. We're right behind you. Red One, out."

While Zuck viciously hosed down the hillside, Keyman slid into Lamont's station and lowered the kid down into the turret.

The eighteen-year-old was limp, his eyes still open, an ugly hole in his face. Trembling, Keyman gently laid him across the floor, then checked the kid's neck for a carotid pulse. He moved his fingers twice. Nothing. He undid Lamont's chin strap, removed the loader's CVC helmet. Blood and gray matter poured out.

Keyman nearly gagged. "Aw, fuck . . ."

Private First Class Sean Lamont, the PlayStation gamer with the big neck whose grandfather had been a proud tanker in Vietnam, was dead.

Every part of Keyman's being raged against God, the heavens, Murphy, the unfair asshole in charge. *Why again? Damn you! Couldn't you leave this kid alone?*

The tank hit a huge rut, knocking Keyman down, onto the body. Blood spilled everywhere.

"I think we're past them," called Zuck, ceasing fire as they bounded up and over a small hill.

"I don't give a shit," said Keyman. "Keep going. Get us out of here right now!"

"I got no problem with that." They began a much steeper ascent, and Boomer added, "You know, if they had an antitank team, I didn't see them."

"That don't mean they're not there," said Zuck. "Could be setting up for the rest of the platoon."

Keyman picked himself off the turret floor, grabbed a blanket, and placed it over Lamont's body. Then he climbed into his seat. "Boomer! Fuck! Slow down! The mines are right there!"

"Oh, shit," muttered the driver.

"Where are those good eyes?"

"I got 'em. I got 'em."

Though he wouldn't admit it, Boomer's quavering voice gave him away. He was shaken up by Lamont's loss, so much so that he had nearly gotten them killed.

Turning hard right and braking, the big guy guided them alongside the road, their right track lifting slightly as they reached the embankment, the surface-laid mines splayed out before them like little manhole covers dotting the snow.

It seemed highly likely that those squads in the hills were trying to get the platoon to flee their attack and rush headlong into the obstacle. If so, their gambit had almost succeeded. Despite that failure, they had still taken a young man's life.

Keyman glanced once more at Lamont's body. He choked up, realized he couldn't. Too much to do right now. He needed to call Hansen. "Red One, this is Two. We're at the obstacle and maneuvering into the passage lane, over."

"No shit, I'm right behind you, over."

Oh, the lieutenant wanted to be a wiseass? Well, Keyman had a bit of news that would shut him up. "I have one casualty, over."

As expected, the airwaves fell silent for a moment, then

Hansen came back, his tone much softer. "Roger that, Red Two. Continue to advance. I know Black Six doesn't want to stop until we reach Objective Panther. We'll bring up the first sergeant at that time. Red One, out."

Keyman, Zuck, and Boomer would have to ride with Lamont's body until the company first sergeant could receive it from them. Were they in a battle position and not part of a convoy, they might have had the luxury of handing off the dead much sooner. But they didn't. And Keyman felt certain that the road march to Panmunjom would be the longest one of his life. Yes, he had lost his previous crew, but he hadn't been forced to ride along with their bodies.

Another glance to Lamont made him grimace. The kid's leg twitched involuntarily. Keyman blinked hard, went into his hatch, and backhanded away tears that threatened to freeze on his cheeks. He fished out some chew, stuffed it in his mouth, then made a concerted effort to calm down.

"I think we've cleared the field," said Boomer. "Nothing up ahead. Looks good."

"Stick to the embankment," Keyman warned, sweeping his gaze over the road. "Just a little longer."

"Just let me know, Sergeant. And you know what? I rode the bus up here once."

"I think everybody did. Ain't no bus ride now."

"Nope. Sergeant, you mind if I say a prayer for Lamont?"

"I mind," Zuck said.

"What you mean, you mind?" asked Keyman.

"It's a farce."

"Excuse me?"

"The kid lived for nothing and died for nothing. A prayer won't make a fuckin' difference."

"Yes, it will, Zuck," said Boomer.

"No, it just makes you feel better. Doesn't change a thing. And if we die, it's the same shit over and over."

"That's a pretty sad view of the world," Boomer said.

"Look, if we're all going to die here, let's just be fuckin' honest about it. Life's a raw deal. Then you die. Deal with it. Accept it. And maybe you'll get some respect because at least you'll be fuckin' honest."

Keyman could hardly believe his ears. They spear-headed a company team, and Keyman knew that he needed to have every sense reaching out to the road ahead, ever wary of the hidden danger that had already twice revealed itself.

But when you disrespected the dead the way Zuck had, all sense of duty, responsibility, and logic went out the hatch.

So Keyman dropped into the turret and grabbed the godless motherfucker by the neck, the old Keyman suddenly blazing in his genes. "THIS KID GAVE HIS LIFE, AND YOU WILL RESPECT THAT! DO YOU HEAR ME? DO YOU?"

Zuck tried to nod, but that only made Keyman choke him harder.

"Hey, Sergeant?" Boomer called. "Better get up top and look at this. . . ."

Keyman shoved Zuck, then released the gunner. "You say something like that again, I will fuckin' kill you where you sit. I don't give a shit what you believe. You will respect that kid right there. Understood, you cold motherfucker?"

Zuck's lip curled in a nasty grin. "Yes, Sergeant."

After taking a moment to catch his breath, Keyman said, "Boomer, if you want to say your prayer now . . ."

"Yeah, for us."

Keyman didn't understand until he was back in his hatch, gaping at the road ahead. "Holy shit."

PLATOON SERGEANT ABBOT felt a pang in his heart as he thought of PFC Lamont. Hansen might be the platoon leader, but Abbot ran the platoon, meaning replacement crew members like Lamont were his personal business. It was his job to get them acclimated and squared away. Most were young and impressionable, eager to please, and not too difficult to train.

But you also had guys like Mingola, guys who had some combat experience and thought they had unraveled life's mysteries. Those assholes drove Abbot nuts. Every platoon had its own way of doing things, and "veterans" had a much harder time adjusting. They wanted to demonstrate how smart they were and how much they had learned on the field of battle. They would offer you all kinds of tricks for staying alive and believed that because they had lived, their way was best. They would criticize and attempt to change your practices, which also implied that you were wrong and they were right. They were know-it-alls, to be sure.

Abbot could be one of those guys; after all, he had more experience than most guys in the company. But he played it cool, low-key, didn't ram his philosophy down anyone's throat. He did, however, demand that the members of Red Platoon conform to Red's way of doing things. And as always, he was a keen observer, having already reached his own conclusions about the replacements:

Mingola and Zuckerman were his problem children. The former was just a weirdo with the potential for both physical and mental problems, the latter a psych-job with a giant chip on his shoulder. Wood, despite his troublemaker reputation, had calmed down, and Neech's renewed spirit seemed to be infecting the kid. Boomer was an ace driver and model crewmember, which bothered Abbot because he had yet to discover the man's weakness. Abbot had had high hopes for Lamont, who had said that he was here to be molded into a great tanker. He had told Keyman that the PFC had a lot of potential and that he should take the kid under his wing instead of intimidating him. Though shockingly naïve, the boy had a good attitude. Keyman had heeded Abbot's words, and Lamont had been well on his way to becoming a top-notch tanker.

But on this cold, January evening, Red Platoon has lost a man, Abbot thought, already hearing the National Public Radio report in his head.

There was no consolation in the fact that he was the only tank commander who had not lost a crewman. He,

Sparrow, Paz, and Park were the original four musketeers, one for all and (maybe) all for one. Park was the question mark, but other than his flaring temper and impatience, his aim had remained true and unaffected by torn loyalties. Hansen had lost Sergeant Lee. Keyman had lost his entire crew. Neech had lost his driver, Batman. Was it only a matter of time before the reaper paid them a visit? And if so, would he make them pay more dearly for having ducked him for so long?

You've already taken my wife, Abbot told the bastard. *You've been paid with interest. Leave us alone. Got it?*

Too bad there wasn't some way to cure Paz's fear and superstition, other than gagging him with hundred-mile-an-hour tape. He kept saying that once they crossed the DMZ, they weren't coming back. Point of no return or some shit.

And now, with the platoon having lost a man, the petrified Paz felt even more justified in delivering yet another doomsday rap: "There's just too many unanswered questions. That's all I'm saying. We don't know what we're going to find up there. You know, if God intended for us to—"

"What?" Abbot asked. "You don't even know where you're going with that, do you?"

"I'm telling you, Sergeant. I've never felt worse about anything. I'm not full of shit. If we cross the line into North Korea, we won't be coming back."

Abbot snorted. "That shit again?"

Park swung around, opened his mouth, but then thought better of it. He shook his head tightly, then resumed his scanning.

"Why are you so sure we're going to die up there?" Abbot asked the loader. "Did you have a dream? Did God talk to you?"

"It ain't a thought or a voice. It's a feeling. Like it already happened. I can feel the shrapnel digging into my gut. And for a second it hurts real bad, then I'm at peace and it's real dark for a second, then I'm heading toward the light. I know what it feels like to die. Maybe God's showing me that or something. Trying to prepare me. And Sergeant, maybe God took your wife so that you'd be okay with it, too. You'll be with her forever. Couldn't end any better."

Abbot tensed. "Don't talk about my wife. You don't know anything about her. And don't talk about dying. We don't need that shit. Not now. Are we clear?"

"Yes, Sergeant. I understand your denial. Whoa, hey. We're stopping?"

"Sparrow? Slow down, man."

"Hey, do you see that?" asked the driver.

"Damn, yeah," said Abbot. "We should've heard something from the scouts about this."

"You want to talk omens?" asked Paz. "What do you call this?"

Just then, the CO's voice blared over the company net with a report from the scouts, who had already investigated the scene ahead. Their report did nothing to calm Abbot. He briefly discussed the information with Hansen, who acknowledged and gave the order to resume their advance.

"Look at them," Paz said slowly. "It's like they're frozen in time."

Abbot lifted his goggles. "Let's hope so."

CHAPTER
EIGHT

"I DON'T LIKE this," Boomer was saying as they descended the hill, the tracks chewing through snow and ice. "Hold your breath, fellas."

Keyman was, admittedly, as unnerved as Boomer, but the scouts had already done their work, and the team should consider the discovery a stroke of luck rather than a trap. It had happened all the time during the first Gulf War and during Operation Iraqi Freedom.

The trouble was, with equipment in such short supply and considered so valuable by the North Koreans, it was hard to imagine that an entire platoon of three T-52 tanks had been abandoned by their crews to just sit there on the side of the road, waiting to be captured.

But there they were, just a hundred meters away, pulled over like the guys had dismounted to take a leak. Too bad that wasn't the truth.

Keyman caught himself holding his breath. Damn Boomer was getting him all bent out of shape. "Take it easy, guys. We're just driving on by."

"Did the scouts say they ran out fuel?" asked Zuck.

"I didn't hear that," Keyman answered. "Be nice if we could drain their tanks, though."

"Somebody'll be real happy with these trophies," said Boomer. "An entire platoon completely intact. If that's what we're really looking at." He sighed. "This war keeps getting stranger. . . ."

"I hear that. I just can't believe the crews ran off without blowing the breech blocks or something," said Keyman. "These guys ain't insurgents. We all know that. And they don't surrender. We know that too. It just don't add up. They wouldn't have run off."

"Unless something scared them," said Zuck.

Keyman frowned. "Like what?"

"I don't know. The bogeyman. Or they heard we were coming."

"Or maybe these tanks are just bait."

"So you're saying they dismounted to ambush us? Give me a break."

"Here's what I think," offered Boomer. "The crew left. Who knows why. Task force scouts find these tanks, radio back. The CO calls higher, who wants the scouts to be sure the tanks aren't manned. So they check them out."

"It's easy to figure out what Brigade is thinking," said Zuck. "Just think stupid. But what about the Koreans?"

"I think I got it figured," Keyman said as they came within fifty meters of the first tank.

A dozen or so leaflets were lying in the embankment, blowing in the wind, and much farther north, hundreds more littered the hills, making them look more like the steep banks of a landfill. All that was missing were the thousands of seagulls and other birds wheeling overhead, and, of course, the stench. Keyman did one more pass with his goggles, then said, "Yup, I think I know what happened."

"Yeah, me too, now," said Boomer. "Me too."

"Well, I'll be damned," said Zuck. "Maybe that shit actually does work."

"I wouldn't have bet on it," Keyman said, half-astonished

himself. "Not with the Koreans, anyway. Maybe these guys got separated from their company—"

"And when they read the news and weather report—as supplied by the U.S. Air Force—they got second thoughts," Zuck finished.

"I would too," said Boomer. "If the news was telling me my comrades were already dead and that it was going to rain artillery for the next week."

Keyman ducked into the turret and got on the platoon net. "Red One, this is Red Two, over."

"Go ahead, Two."

"We're passing now. I don't know if you can see 'em yet, but it looks like the bonnet boys dropped some leaflets. Psyop shit. Maybe it worked, over."

"Roger that. Continue to advance. Red One, out."

KEYMAN'S REPORT BROUGHT back memories for Abbot. During Operation Desert Storm, U.S. forces had dropped a 10,000-pound HE bomb on some Iraqis, then they had dropped leaflets telling them they had just been attacked by the largest conventional bomb in the world, courtesy of the United States. The leaflets ordered them to surrender—or they would drop more bombs.

And they would drop dead.

It was a no-brainer for most Iraqis, and U.S. forces got a lot of POWs out of that one.

Abbot wished he could dismount and grab one of the leaflets, but the lieutenant had just instructed that no one should do so. Consequently, the platoon would never know exactly what the leaflets said or if those words had truly struck fear in the dark hearts of their enemy.

That bothered Abbot. So much of his world he could not control. You were continually looking for answers, for absolutes, especially during wartime. You couldn't even count on your next breath.

As they started by the tanks, Park said, "Very strange to be so close to enemy tanks. I want to shoot them."

"That's good," said Paz. "Just keep thinking that, okay, buddy? You see a T-52, you shoot it."

"I know why you say that, Paz. You think I want to be traitor and kill you. You think I am like Sergeant Lee. But he was not traitor. And I am not."

Abbot wished he could see the expression on Park's face, but he and Paz were in their hatches, and they only had the KATUSA's voice for cues. While his tone could've been much harsher, he spoke evenly—which for Abbot was even more unsettling. He was about to raise his hand to gain Paz's attention, but the loader's big mouth was already working:

"I never said you were a traitor, Park. Come on. You know me, bro."

"I know you complain about everything. Probably me too. I want to be soldier. That's all."

Abbot finally got Paz to look at him. He glared at the loader, put a finger to his lips, then pounded that finger on his chest, mouthing the words *let me talk.*

Paz nodded.

"You know what, Park?" Abbot asked. "We're all men here. Let's get this out on the table. We know you and Lee were good friends. We know you think something happened in that turret. And you're entitled to your opinion."

"Yes, Sergeant."

"But don't let that mess you up now. We're counting on you to do the right thing."

"Yes, Sergeant."

"We've all been through a lot together. And we're all from different places, be they the U.S., Korea, or that screwed-up planet where Paz came from."

Laughter erupted from the diver's hole. At least Sparrow appreciated Abbot's weak sense of humor.

"We're all different—that's what makes us great," Abbot continued. "I mean, we're getting this on the table, but look what we bring to the table."

"Yes, Sergeant. It is big table."

Abbot smiled. "Bottom line is, you have to trust us, and we have to trust you. Can we?"

After an awkward moment's hesitation, the KATUSA answered, "I don't know."

"You don't know?" Paz asked, flabbergasted.

Abbot waved an index finger across his throat even as the gunner said, "Sergeant, you know what happened to my friend Lee. Tell me. Then we can talk about trust."

Abbot swallowed, exchanged a look with Paz, then contemplated what to do.

If he told the KATUSA the truth, Park might very well abandon his post and run off, just like Lee had intended to do. He would ruin his life, seal his own fate.

However, if Abbot lied to Park, he would actually be saving the young man. The KATUSA was a brilliant gunner who could continue to have a great career with the ROK Army when his stint with U.S. forces was over. If he could just hang in there and forget about all the bullshit, he could have a decent life and not wind up in jail. Or worse.

But like Abbot had said, they had been through a lot together. Didn't he owe Park the truth?

HANSEN TORE OFF his CVC helmet and listened to the purring of the tank's engine. It was there. That noise again. He wasn't losing his mind. Something was definitely wrong.

Then it was gone.

He glanced over at Deac, then Mingola. They hadn't heard a thing. There was no noise. There never had been.

Why couldn't he believe that?

"LT, did you hear something again?" Deac asked.

Hansen felt flush. "No." He slid on his helmet, fastened the chin strap. "Just got a stiff neck." He shifted his head, as though working out the kinks.

Meanwhile, Mingola began whispering something indecipherable, and for a moment, it sounded as though he were speaking in tongues.

"Mingola, what're you saying?" asked Deac.

"What?"

"You're saying something."

"No, man. They're speaking through me."

"Guys, don't talk now," Hansen said. "I can't take any more noise."

They drifted into a long silence. Hansen sat there, gazing through his extension, trying to force away that engine noise. *There's nothing wrong,* he told himself. *Nothing wrong.*

Except with me.

THE HOWITZERS FIRED during the first hours of the war had blasted the hell out of MSR 3, which was just the way the redlegs liked it. Those artillery guys were intent upon destroying anything and everything heading south through the mountains. Collateral damage to the road itself was a necessary evil, and all those shells created a haphazard string of potholes, huge chunks of rock lying in the path, and mounds of shrapnel-laced snow. The platoon had just come upon such an area, and Keyman had called to say that he could not navigate any farther because a big rock blocked him on the left and a long ditch lay on the right. He wasn't about to get stuck in the ditch and hold up the entire company again. Been there, done that.

Neech got the order to move up and plow them a path between the two. He was happy to oblige and once more felt like he was truly contributing to the company team's success.

"See, guys, we go from being the slowest tank, the liability, to being the most valuable. I don't know about you, but this saving-the-day crap is getting old."

"Sergeant, I like your attitude," said Romeo. "It's about time you got cocky. Just be careful, too, eh, *amigo*?"

"Roger that. Hooah!"

Neech guided Wood toward the rock. They lowered the plow and made contact with a slight thud. Wood eased on the gas, and the rock began to slide out of the way with an appreciable creak and grind. Finally, the stone rolled aside.

Neech called back to Hansen, told him it would be a good idea for him to remain forward, since the course looked pretty hairy for the next hundred yards or so. He got the go-ahead.

"All right, Big Wood. Let's see what you got."

"That's what she said," the driver answered.

They rolled through the obstacle course of debris, the plow cutting down mounds and forcing them back into the ditches. Keyman flashed him a thumbs-up. Neech flipped him the bird, then grinned. Keyman returned the finger and smirked. It was fun to fuck with that hardass.

Off to Neech's left, trees had been blown to splinters, others knocked onto their sides by shells that had not struck as close. Yes, indeed, a hurricane of TNT and metal had slammed into the mountainside, its path of devastation evident wherever you looked.

After another five minutes of measured navigation, Neech surveyed the road and gave the order to raise the plow. He radioed back to the LT that they were clear, then shifted to the side of the road, allowing Keyman, the lieutenant, and Abbot to pass so that he could resume his position in the rear. Being the ass end of the platoon wasn't so bad when the platoon was out in front of the company team. They were still one of the first tanks in the fight.

Just a quarter kilometer later, Keyman was on the radio, reporting that they were approaching the JSA complex and that smoke was rising from several buildings.

Neech went up for a look himself and gasped as he took in the devastation. Nearly every structure had sustained some kind of damage, and a few of the one-story buildings had been completely leveled. Six, maybe seven bodies lay strewn in the road—the remains of the ROK/U.S. border guards.

Although Team Cobra had been tasked with seizing the complex, there wasn't much to seize. The platoon moved into battle positions along the embankment of an intersecting service road, while the engineers paused behind them, and the mortars began delivering smoke to blanket the area.

Meanwhile, the Bradleys raced forward and pulled up before the first string of buildings, dismounts leaping from the back and vanishing into the shadows.

"Shit, they really blew through here," said Romeo.

"Looks like it." Neech had an ugly feeling in the pit of his stomach as he reflected once more on his first visit to the complex. War had been the furthest thing from his mind.

Now it lay before him in all its twisted glory.

DURING THE NEXT thirty minutes, the MECH platoon, along with help from the engineers, secured the immediate area. Oddly enough, the North Koreans had left only a few squads at the complex, having diverted forces either north in defense or south to continue the offense. At least that was the rumor, and because of that, Hansen was certain that the team would face massive numbers of dismounts once they moved farther north. The company began scrounging up fuel from the JSA motor pool. There wasn't a lot of the precious liquid but possibly enough to keep them going until their air resupply arrived.

They established an Assembly Area where the tanks and Bradleys could get their meager fills of fuel, and Hansen dismounted to go have a word with Keyman, who was turning over his loader's body to the first sergeant.

Once there, Hansen, Keyman, Boomer, and Zuckerman stood like zombies in the dim light, watching as Lamont was hoisted out of the track and taken away. Hansen went up to Boomer and shook his hand vigorously, but there was nothing left to say. He moved on to Zuck, who offered a weak handshake and wouldn't look up. The two hustled off, leaving Hansen alone with Keyman, who sighed loudly and shook his head. "Can I tell you this ain't fun anymore?"

"You can. You did. I agree."

"He was a good guy."

Hansen nodded.

"I know it ain't fair. None of it. But that don't mean we have to accept it, right?"

"Right."

"I lost three fuckin' men back at TDC. We march north, and I'm the first fuckin' guy to lose a man. What are the goddamned odds of that?"

"I don't know."

"If God's fuckin' with me, I wish he would lay off."

"Yeah."

"You're worse than me, aren't you?"

"What?"

Keyman shifted closer to Hansen, eyes widening. "Are you listening?"

Hansen shuddered, licked his chapped lips. "I have to go."

"You have to go. Okay. Thanks for the pep talk."

It took a moment for Hansen to recognize the sarcasm. Man, he really was out of it. "I'm sorry, buddy. Sorry about your loss."

"Yeah, you sound like it."

"Hey, what the fuck do you want from me?"

Keyman snorted loudly over the outburst. "Sir, I don't want a goddamned thing."

"Good."

Hansen stomped off, cursing the man for picking on his leadership skills, for being sarcastic . . .

For being right.

He suddenly felt guilty, turned around, but Keyman was already gone. Maybe they could talk again later. Maybe he could apologize for being an asshole.

Now he felt even more terrible, but thank God he still had the will, small though it was, to fight. Back to business. He was supposed to meet with the other platoon leaders and the CO, who had established his command post outside the neutral nations' meeting buildings, or, rather, what was left of them.

Hansen had heard that every U.S. and ROK soldier who had worked in the U.N. detachment had been executed. Their hands had been tied behind their backs with commo wire, and they had been shot in the back of the head. The North Koreans had committed the same atrocity during the first Korean War and were repeating history for propaganda effect.

As he hiked past a back alley where some of the executions had occurred, lights flashed and he craned his head, realizing that reporters were present, taking pictures and shooting video. A couple of the company troopers were there too, going off on the reporters for not covering up the remains. The identities of those poor men were supposed to be concealed until the U.S. could officially notify their next of kin.

Hansen stopped dead in his tracks. He was a breath away from going over there, raising his pistol, and capping each news whore. He would do so summarily, effectively, without remorse. Just a few more bodies to drop on the pile. His hands tingled with remembered energy from choking the Japanese guy.

He turned toward the group, took a step. Why couldn't he control his anger? He was suddenly scared of what he might do, scared that was going to melt down. Again.

"Hey, Jack?"

Second Lieutenant Gary Gutterson came jogging over, looking as lean and birdlike as ever, though his eyes seemed much wider than usual. Then again, he was gaping at Hansen.

"Gary?"

Gutterson arrived out of breath, took a moment, then said, "Man, are you all right? You look shittier than shit."

Hansen tugged at his chin, caught himself, then simply answered, "Yeah."

"Jack, I'm serious, man. Are you okay?"

"Look at that," Hansen said, turning toward the reporters, who were being ushered away from the bodies by the company troopers. He scratched his chin. "Fuckin' piranhas. Come on. CO's waiting."

Gutterson shifted into Hansen's path. "Let him wait."

"Come on, Gary. What the fuck is this?"

"This is one hand washing the other. You taught me how to get along with my platoon. I can't thank you enough for that. Let's just say I heard you've been having a few morale problems."

"And you'll teach me how to boost morale? Mr. Fuckin' By-the-book?"

"I threw that shit out the window, Jack. You did too. Is it what happened with Lee? Or the Stryker? I heard Keyman lost his loader."

Hansen stormed away from his former roommate, who immediately raced to catch up with him. "What now? The whole fuckin' company is talking about me?"

"No, Jack."

"Then how did you hear?" Damn it, he was scratching his chin again.

"Doesn't matter. Remember when I was worried about that? Who cares what these assholes think? I know what you're about. I know what it's like."

With that, Hansen stopped, whirled, about to go off big time on the skinny geek whose obsessive-compulsive behavior had once driven him nuts. Did the tables always have to turn?

He stared at Gutterson for a few seconds, seeing real empathy in the guy's eyes. His breath slowed. He suppressed the urge to scratch his face.

And what the fuck? He was crying again. Out of nowhere.

"Aw, shit, Jack."

"Get out of here. I'll catch up with you."

"Nope. We're going together."

Hansen turned away, used gloved hands to brush off the tears. "It's just . . ."

"Fucked up," Gutterson finished. "Yeah, I know."

"You lost, what, like four guys yourself?"

"Five."

"What do you tell yourself?"

"I tell myself that I can be as good as you, even though I'm a skinny runt with a small dick."

That almost woke Hansen's smile. "You know what my problem is, Gary? I've seen so much of this shit, and I was afraid to go cold like a lot of guys. I didn't want to stop feeling. But I've gone the other way, worrying about everything. And I can't take it anymore."

"Just do like they told us: Focus on what you can control. Screw everything else."

"I've been doing that. I can control the tank. I can control the men. But it's like I've been focusing too much. I can't stop thinking about the tank breaking down or the crew fucking up on me. And now it's the worrying I can't control."

"I don't know what to tell you, Jack. We just have to deal with it. Maybe I've gone cold, like you said."

"You think I'm a pussy."

"Funny. The first time I met you, I thought the same thing: 'He thinks I'm a pussy.' "

"But I didn't."

"You're a shitty liar. Come on. CO's waiting."

There they were, Red and Blue Platoon leaders, both twenty-three, bullshitting about life and death like they were old war vets.

Still, there was an air of confidence that surrounded Gutterson. You could just see it. The squeaky-clean nerd had gone from alienating his platoon to working with them to earning their respect to getting them to die for him. He was one book you couldn't judge by its cover.

AFTER GATCH FINISHED supervising the tank's refueling, he, Deac, and Mingola went off to join the other tankers in raiding the JSA's shoppette for sodas, chips, cookies, and whatever other junk food and drinks they could find. They needed to conserve their MREs since who knew when resupply would come, and besides, Meals Ready to Eat had nothing on a nice box of Twinkies, which, according to Deac, covered all of the major food groups.

As was his wont whenever they dismounted or went out for a night on the town, Gatch assumed the role of posse leader. He led "his men" back to the tank, where they sat on the rear deck, enjoying their grub in the morning calm of the lieutenant's absence. Gatch had never felt more on edge around the man, even during the first day they had met. However, the past few hours had gone fairly well, and he wanted to believe that the lieutenant was getting squared away. Though Gatch's doubts wouldn't vanish any time soon, he would without hesitation give his life for that man. He had seen enough of Hansen to know that behind all the stress was a great officer who had already led them through hell and back.

Deac peeled the wrapper off his next Twinkie and spoke in an accent that was somewhere between Carolina hillbilly and South Korean bar girl. "Uh, Dear Leader in Pyongyang, thank you to leave behind good eating shit."

"Oh, I bet they got the munchies, too, but all the sugar and salt made 'em sick," said Mingola, who was noshing on his own bag of chips. "We're more used to poisoning our bodies."

"Hey, not now, asshole. I haven't had a Twinkie in a long time, and I'm trying to enjoy it, okay?" Deac's mouth worked like a cow's as he devoured the cream-filled cake. "Breakfast of champions."

"What time is it? Oh-four-thirty?" Gatch asked. "I hope we can just hang here for the day and not move till dark."

Mingola smiled sarcastically, cheekbones threatening to burst through his face. "That'd make too much sense. Better we push forward in broad daylight so the bad guys can get a real good look at us."

Gatch grinned knowingly, then looked down at the chip in his hand. "Hey, we didn't say a blessing first."

"Dude, don't go there," Mingola said. "It's fuckin' junk food, for God's sake."

Gatch closed his eyes. "Lord God, we thank you for this junk food and for keeping us safe. We ask that you get us all home in one piece."

"All right, all right," Mingola cut in.

"Let him finish," Deac said, his tone promising pain if Mingola disobeyed.

"We ask it all in your name. Amen." At that, Gatch turned to the gunner and said, "You might outrank me, but no one outranks Jesus. If you disrespect him again, you might suffer his wrath."

"And mine," said Deac.

"You fuckin' clowns are ganging up on me?" Mingola asked through a chuckle. "I'm not the problem. Your butter bar is."

"Ours?" Gatch asked. "What? He's not yours too?"

Mingola shrugged. "For now."

"He seems a little better," said Deac. "He rocked back at the gauntlet."

"I'll give you that," conceded Mingola.

"I think God has a hand on the LT," Gatch added. "And I'm thinking our plan now should be to trust in him."

"Yeah, because we can't trust the lieutenant, that's for sure," said Mingola. "And you know what still fuckin' irks me? Once we cross the line, the shit won't stop hitting the fan. And it's like he's either going to be a man, or he'll get us killed. I can't sit there and let that happen."

Deac was about to say something, but Gatch silenced him with a look. Man, it was usually the enemy that went asymmetric on you—not your own crew! The lieutenant could still have a breakdown, and now Mingola could launch a preemptive strike. At that point, it'd be up to Deac to run interference. Gatch would, as always, be trapped in his driver's seat, wishing he could get out and do something.

"So here they are, the three stooges," said Sergeant Timmy Thompson, a pudgy gunner from Blue Platoon who had shambled up, towing his loader, a Puerto Rican guy named Lopez whose terrible acne diverted you from his tough guy expression.

Gatch, who was probably a foot shorter than Thompson, hopped down from the tank and said, "Not this time, Timmy. It's different now."

"No, it ain't," said Deac, arriving at Gatch's side. "He might be turning the other cheek, but I ain't. You guys want a pissing match, bring it. But I think you'll be sorry."

"I doubt that," said Thompson.

"Oh, yeah? Let's talk about the gauntlet," Deac said, stepping back for the tank. "Why don't y'all come over here so I can show you how many rounds we took. Oh, gee, here's like six or seven right here on the rear deck. And here's like, what, a dozen more? Then maybe we'll step over to your track. Uh, did you take any hits? Or were you guys begging to be shot at after we softened 'em up for you?"

"Deac, don't waste your time," said Gatch. "They're not worth it."

"Actually, we didn't come here to fuck with you, man," said Lopez. "But we like it. Hey, who's the skeleton?"

Gatch glanced back at Mingola, who was stuffing a chip into his mouth. "He's our gunner from Second Tank."

"I guess that's fitting," said Thompson. "A second-rate gunner for a second-rate crew."

"Ha!" cried Deac. "Dude, y'all are deaf, dumb, and blind. We're Top Tank in this company."

"But y'all took out that Stryker. A good friend of mine got killed."

"And we came by to let your LT know that," said Lopez. "Where is he?"

"You guys got some fucking balls," Deac cried. "You try to pull that shit, and our LT will tear you a new one!"

Mingola, who had finally decided to come down from the tank, moved up next to Gatch and said, "Our lieutenant is still with the CO, and I'm sure he doesn't give a rat's ass about you or your buddy because what happened out there was Brigade's fuckup, not ours. The last thing he or anyone else needs is cocksuckers like you trying to rub it in our faces. You guys ought to run back to your track before Hansen gets here, because I wouldn't put it past him to cap you motherfuckers."

"Yeah, we heard he was losing it," said Thompson.

"Did you hear about me?"

Before Gatch could blink, Mingola's fist was airborne.

CHAPTER
NINE

ABBOT HAD SEEN it a million times before and would see it a million times again before he retired. Okay, a million might be an exaggeration, but in his career he had broken up more fights than he could remember. Sometimes when guys were off for a little R&R, they got their beer muscles, and a wrong look or word could set off the fires and the fists.

What he witnessed now, though, had nothing to do with alcohol, and while egos may have played a role, they were not the root cause. There was, Abbot believed, a need, especially during wartime, for his men to get their hands on human flesh and squeeze the life out of it. In the days before technology had dehumanized war, men fought the way nature had intended: hand-to-hand. You looked your enemy in the eye and felt his hot breath on your face before you drew blood. You listened to him groan as your blade dug between his ribs. Then he fell away, clutching his wound. You didn't move. You watched him die right there, covered in what you had taken from him. And once the light had gone from his eyes, you rose and banged your fists on your chest, shrieking in victory.

You were an animal. You were the fittest. You had survived.

Being cooped up in a tank denied you of all that. The armor, while protecting you, was a violation of nature, which was why many tankers preferred to be in their hatches and shooting dismounted troops with their pistols. They were in the shit, savoring the adrenaline rush of being so near to death while imagining themselves as gods.

Not to mention that they could see and hear things a hell of a lot better. . . .

The company team had just come through a nasty gauntlet, and no doubt Abbot's men wished they could've drawn blood with their own hands instead of shooting the enemy from afar.

And maybe Abbot was just practicing armchair psychology and was completely wrong, but he believed that because his men had been denied the chance to kill the enemy point-blank, they were like sixteen-year-old boys with blue balls, walking around with the ache because Barbara Boobjob liked getting her titties squeezed but just wouldn't put out. They had been teased with the idea of drawing blood. So, his men were taking out that frustration on each other.

Someone had to pay.

His conclusion seemed logical. Most guys never read that far into it; they attributed fights to other things like personal rivalries, racism, or just all of the physical discomforts and the stress. While those seemed like legitimate causes, Abbot still thought something much more powerful—a need to kill—was behind it all. He remembered the old *Star Trek* episodes, where the aliens always said, "You humans are a warring species." There was that one show where Kirk had to fight the lizard man on the planet and used sulfur to make a weapon. He should've choked that lizard bastard to death, but the guy wearing the cheesy costume must've been stronger.

Men were born to kill. Lots of smart people agreed with that. But you couldn't explain the details to a bunch of monkeys dressed in Nomex. All they knew was how they felt. Abbot jogged toward them. "Gatch! Deac!"

A pudgy guy from Blue Platoon—Abbot forgot his name—was lying on the deck while Mingola held his neck and did a jackhammer number with his bare fist, striking the eyes, the nose, the mouth.

At the same time, Deac was on the deck, wrestling with a short Hispanic guy while Gatch tried to break them up.

Announced by a chorus of shouting, Keyman and Neech, along with their crews, came rushing from behind the row of tanks. Those guys would reach the brawlers first.

"Key? Neech?" Abbot cried, knowing that's all he had to say.

The two TCs rushed into the fray. Guys were screaming, Abbot the loudest of all, and in the next few seconds, the red-faced men were separated and held back from each other.

Once everyone grew quiet and froze, Abbot paraded before the group, all eyes on him, blood dripping from a few faces, the cold wind blowing. The brawlers looked guilt-stricken, all right. As they should. "Aren't you assholes tired? Shouldn't you be getting some sleep instead beating the shit out of each other? Let me see. Get into a fight and risk court martial or get some sleep. Hmmm. That's a hard fuckin' decision."

"Sergeant, your man started it," said the pudgy guy.

"You're Thompson, right?" Abbot asked, his memory not as bad as he had thought. "From Blue Platoon."

"That's right, Sergeant."

"So which one of my men started it?"

"The skeleton right there," said the Hispanic guy, jerking his head in Mingola's direction.

"What's your name?"

"Lopez, Sergeant."

"So what you're saying, Lopez, is that you neither started nor ended this fight. Am I correct?"

"Yes, you are, Sergeant."

Abbot stepped back and exchanged an amused look with the rest of his tankers. "Well, that sucks for you, doesn't it?"

The men chuckled loudly. All of them except Thompson and Lopez, of course.

"Your guy threw the first punch," snapped Lopez. "He started everything. He needs to go down!"

"Mingola, you struck this man?"

The lieutenant's gunner winked. "Not as many times as I would've liked, Sergeant."

Abbot furrowed his brows. "Tell me, Mingola, were you exercising your basic need to kill? Were you frustrated that you couldn't go hand-to-hand with those assholes back along the road? You just needed to get some?"

"Sergeant?"

"Forget it. Why'd you hit this guy?"

"I'm not sure. I guess he's the kind of guy you just want to beat the shit out of. You know the type?"

More chuckles from the group.

Deac stepped forward and lifted his chin. "Sergeant, these two limp dicks came over here because Thompson says the LT killed one of his friends aboard that Stryker. They actually came here because they wanted to make the LT feel bad. Make us feel bad too."

Abbot did an about-face and marched back up to Thompson. "Is that true?"

"It is, Sergeant."

"And you thought it would be appropriate to rub our lieutenant's face in it? You don't think he feels bad enough already? You think he and his crew need fuckups like you reminding him? What, you think they fired at that Stryker on purpose? This is un-fuckin' -believable. What were you thinking?"

Thompson stammered.

Abbot smacked him in the head. "You and your buddy get back to your fuckin' track. I'll let your LT know what happened here. But I don't think he'll be as understanding as I am."

The two men just stood there.

"BACK TO YOUR TRACKS!"

Thompson and Lopez hustled away, across the assembly area, hoots and guffaws from Red Platoon echoing behind them.

"All right, let's break it up," Abbot ordered. "Mingola? Deac? Gatch? Come here . . ."

Abbot's tone turned their complexions an even lighter shade of pale. But then he surprised them by dropping his voice. "I need a favor."

"Anything you want, Sergeant," said Gatch, while Deac and Mingola nodded.

"I need you to support the LT in any way you can. There's a lot of pressure on us right now, and we're all strung out."

"But not as much as him," said Mingola.

"Which is why he needs allies, not enemies. Bitching don't help. Do you read me?"

"Loud and clear, Sergeant," answered Deac. Gatch was right there with his nod, but the tank's scarecrow of a gunner held his dubious expression.

"Hey, Mingola. Why the face?"

"How 'bout this, Sergeant? I'll do whatever I can to support him."

"That's right. You will. We're not negotiating here."

"Okay. But if something happens, I *will* take command of the track. It'll be your platoon, of course, but that tank will be mine."

Abbot's expression now matched the gunner's. "You really want to be a TC?"

"I just want people to listen to me. My old TC didn't. I loved that guy. But he blew me off. And we rode into a fuckin' minefield. He didn't listen to my warning. And they all died." Mingola choked up, caught himself, and then his voice grew harsh. "I can't go through that again. I just can't."

"Okay, I get it. But don't let that interfere. You will support the lieutenant in every way possible."

"Yes, Sergeant." The gunner tossed a look toward Blue Platoon's tanks. "That's why I hit that fat fuck."

Abbot cocked a brow. "You know what I mean. Now finish your snack, and when you're done with maintenance, go over to that blue building over there. They got some heaters and cots set up. Grab some shut-eye."

"You too, Sergeant," said Mingola.

Abbot nodded, muttered a "hooah," then turned to leave.

The night sky was beginning to wash into a dark purple, and pretty soon that familiar sheet of gray would spread over them. A little sunshine wouldn't hurt anyone, but since the war had begun, the sun had barely shown itself. Kim used to love working in their garden, and she got real tan during those Texas summers. When it got cloudy and the storms rolled in, she used to snuggle with him on the sofa. They'd put in a DVD, watch the movie, and listen to the rain hitting the roof, the thunder echoing across the neighborhood. Abbot could taste the wine, and he remembered picking popcorn from his teeth. Life had been good. He should be thankful he had had that much. Becoming a bitter old man would be a terrible conclusion to a life that wasn't half bad. One day at a time. That's all you could do.

He glanced back, watching the lieutenant's crew begin PMCS on their tank. They looked really young. Just yesterday he had been one of them, tear-assing across sand instead of snow.

Abbot grinned to himself and shuffled on, waving to Paz, who stood at the end of the main gun tube, finishing up the boresighting with Park. As he neared the track, Park climbed down from the turret and called to him. Abbot waited for the gunner to hop down from the rear deck.

"I think about what you say," said the KATUSA, lowering his voice and looking toward Paz, who was busy removing the boresight device from the gun tube. "You are the platoon sergeant. You and the lieutenant talk about private matters and such things. He would have told you what happened with Sergeant Lee. He would not lie to you."

Abbot tightened his lips. Was his guilty expression

showing through? "Are you saying you don't believe me?"

"Sergeant, perhaps you fear to tell me. You worry what I might do. That is why you lied when I asked for what happened."

The gunner had seen right through him. Abbot had, in fact, lied to Park in an effort to spare him from his possibly rash reaction. Ignorance was supposed to be bliss, damn it.

But now Abbot worried that his lie had armed the bomb. And worse, maybe the lies themselves would upset the KATUSA even more than the truth of what had happened to Sergeant Lee.

"Park, we have an expression you might know: talk is cheap. It doesn't matter. It won't bring back Lee. He's gone. And we all need to move on."

"I cannot—until I know what really happened. How can I trust you if you are not to trust me?"

Okay. The KATUSA would force the issue, and Abbot could either concoct yet another lie or let him know what had happened. Maybe the lieutenant would be okay with that, despite their orders to remain silent. They would be letting Park have a peek under the rug, and what lay there was pretty ugly to say the least. Park could go to the ROKs and attempt to expose a cover-up. Then again, ROK and U.S. officials had jointly agreed to the official explanation. Park could scream all he wanted, but no one would listen.

And it seemed all the gunner wanted was closure. Moreover, Abbot sure as hell wanted a level-headed man behind the Cadillacs of his tank when they moved into North Korea. Park needed to respect Abbot enough to die for him. At the moment, Abbot wasn't sure he would.

"Park, maybe you and I and the lieutenant can have a word together. Maybe after that, you'll know you can trust us. Okay?"

"But you said talk is cheap."

Abbot grinned with embarrassment. Park was a clever bastard. "That's right. Talk is cheap. It won't raise the dead. But it could make you feel better, okay?"

"Okay. So you did not tell me the whole truth . . ."

"We'll talk. All right, boys. Soon as you're finished, go get some sleep."

He fished out a cigarette, lit it, took a long drag, then leaned back on his track and waited for the lieutenant to return from the OPORD meeting.

NEECH KNEW THAT Romeo and Choi wouldn't have too many problems adapting to the weather, the lack of sleep, and the extreme need for food and water. On the other hand, Wood was the new guy, hadn't been in country for long, and had never been in a combat situation. Neech should expect problems with the specialist, but maybe he would get lucky and the guy would pull through okay. Neech would just need to stay on him.

Most people never think about how the body adapts to change because they spend most of their lives in controlled environments. You set the thermostat to seventy-five degrees and forget about it. But if you were like Neech, standing in the TC's hatch of an M1A1 Abrams for long periods of time, you noticed the changes. Even with all your cold-weather gear and the heater blasting below you, Korea's ice would still get under your skin. However, after spending twenty-four hours or more in the cold, you wouldn't feel the temperature as much as you first did. The body would adapt. Still, your need for calories would increase dramatically. You would be okay if you didn't stop eating. If you did, you would feel frozen, shake like a leaf, and for the most part be known as a miserable fuck by the rest of the crew. If you didn't hydrate every few hours, you'd get a severe headache, as though you had sucked down a half dozen kettles from some liquor vendor in TDC because you were new and didn't realize how bad that shit was. So yes, you needed liquids, just the right kind.

Consequently, raiding the JSA shoppette was a good thing, and now, with their bellies full, Neech and his crew were settling down to some much-needed sleep. Wood lay on the cot beside his, staring wide-eyed at the ceiling.

"Wood, close your eyes, man."

"I can't, Sergeant."

"That's an order."

The kid frowned, shut his eyes, took a deep breath. He began to toss and turn.

"Shit, Wood, come on. . . ."

"I'm sorry. My damned ears are still ringing. Friggin' Romeo on the coax. Like a drum on my head."

Neech understood. When they employed the coax, there was a lot of concussion, and the driver's ears usually paid the price. Add to that Romeo's affinity for blasting the shit out of everything in sight, and you could sympathize with Wood—if you weren't trying to sleep yourself.

"Know what you do? Concentrate on the ringing. Turn it into white noise. Then it'll eventually put you to sleep."

"You read that somewhere, Sergeant?"

"Nope. Done it."

"Okay."

A moment passed, and Neech was just getting comfortable on the cot when Wood blurted out, "Sergeant?"

Neech lifted his voice in a stage-whisper: "Goddamn it, Wood, I'm trying to sleep!"

"Sorry. It ain't working."

"What?"

"You told me to concentrate on the noise."

"I know what I told you. Just shut up and go to sleep. Look at Romeo and Choi. They're fuckin' snoring already. That's where we need to be!"

"It's cold in here."

"They got the heaters going."

"Ain't as good as ours."

Neech rolled over and glared at the young man. "You're not a troublemaker, Wood. You're a whiner. Now just shut up and go to sleep."

The kid returned a wounded look, then rolled over, putting his back to Neech.

Another moment passed, and Neech began to feel bad. He shouldn't be breaking down his driver; he should be building him up, preparing him for the long road ahead. "Wood?"

"Yes, Sergeant?"

Neech hesitated. "Nothing."

"Okay."

"Now I can't sleep, you asshole."

"I'm sorry, Sergeant."

"You know what, I am too, bro. Let's just close our eyes and imagine that we're getting the best sleep ever."

"Yeah. And maybe we will."

CAPTAIN VAN BUREN assembled the orders group inside the JSA briefing theater, the same theater where Hansen and the others had received their tour guide briefing when they had visited the JSA during peacetime. The irony and the déjà vu was clearly felt by everyone.

"Okay team, I'll make this quick," Van Buren began. "A mechanized battalion is defending Kaesong city to our west. The majority of frontline North Korean forces have been destroyed, but they still have scattered companies and battalions along the highways leading north to Pyongyang, some made up of militia. Now that Combined Forces Command has gone on the offensive, these forces are conducting defensive missions to stop our advance. They have been ordered to die in place, so expect heavy resistance.

"The brigade's mission is to seize Kaesong to allow follow-on forces to gain access to major highway networks leading north. Our mission is as follows: on order, Team Cobra attacks west along Highway One to seize the high ground on the outskirts of Kaesong. I say again, on order, Team Cobra attacks west along Highway One to seize the high ground on the outskirts of Kaesong.

"Intent and concept of the operation: We will attack along Highway One at best speed using fire and maneuver. Any obstacles will be reduced using organic equipment and engineers when necessary. We will continue with the same order of march we used coming here to the

JSA, but I might move Blue Platoon behind Red if necessary. Destroy all enemy forces encountered along the route and remove obstacles as you encounter them. Red will conduct hasty breaches to allow the team to keep moving, and engineers will conduct further obstacle reduction after the lead platoons are through. Once we reach the high ground at Kaesong, FIST, FOs, and TACP will again occupy OPs to report and engage enemy forces with CAS and FA fires.

"TF scouts report contact with isolated enemy squads along the route so far but no major obstacles. Expect the route to be heavily damaged from artillery and CAS fires. Highway One was used during the initial North Korean attack and CFC pounded the hell out of it. Report any major road damage that may affect our movement and find a bypass; we have to keep moving. Engineers, conduct an assessment of road damage and prepare a report for me to call up to higher when we reach Kaesong. We are scheduled to receive aerial resupply of fuel, ammo, and food within the next few hours, but it could be late. Report any critical shortages to the XO. He and some guys from the maintenance section are in the JSA motor pool looking for additional parts and POL supplies. Identify any other shortages to him and the first sergeant so we can address them here before we move out.

"Gentlemen, we will be the first major allied ground force to attack into North Korea since CFC went on the offensive. Our battalion fought well during the first Korean War, and we will do so again. Good luck and God bless us all."

Van Buren then fielded a few questions from Lieutenant Ryback, whose mechanized infantry had taken a real beating. Ryback was hoping a few replacements could be airlifted in, but that might not happen. Van Buren told Harris, the engineer platoon leader, that he should be prepared to slice one engineer squad over to the MECH platoon in an emergency situation.

"It's just as well if you don't get replacements," Hansen told Ryback as they, along with Gutterson, left the building.

"The FNGs get whacked first. It's Murphy's Law. Just ask my wingman."

The seasoned grunt nodded. "I just hope we get resupplied sooner than later. I'm low on everything, including morale."

"I heard they actually got Fedex flying in emergency repair parts for us," said Gutterson. "And as they secure airfields in the north, those Fedex guys will be zooming right in."

"So Fedex is sponsoring the war?" Ryback said with a laugh.

"Using them is pretty common," said Hansen.

"Actually, it's a show of American industry's support for the national/global war effort," Gutterson chipped in. "You know, even my favorite general in the whole world, Erwin Rommel, wouldn't have minded commercial support."

"Your favorite general is Rommel?" Ryback asked. "Wasn't he a Nazi?"

"One of his few mistakes. He was a brilliant tactician. They called him the Desert Fox. He kicked ass in North Africa. He relied upon captured supplies for support while Germany ignored him."

"Good thing the Germans didn't have their own Fedex back then—"

"Otherwise, we'd all be speaking German right now," Hansen finished for Ryback.

"I already do," said Gutterson. "Would you like to hear—"

"Nope," said Ryback, breaking off from the group. "Catch you guys later."

"He's a rude bastard," Gutterson said.

"Aw, leave him alone. He's got a lot on his mind. Just like us."

"Yeah, you're right. Hey, I never finished telling you that story about my Uncle Jack. About when he was a tank commander in Germany. I was just reminded of that. Eight guys and two tanks made about a hundred and fifty guys feel like total idiots."

"I remember you saying something. But maybe later, Gary. I just need to need to close my eyes for a little while."

"Yeah, for about a week. And I'll join you."

A sharp crack echoed from the buildings behind them. Hansen flinched and reflexively dropped to his gut. Another crack sounded, kicking snow and ice just an arm's reach to his right. "Gary, we got a fucking sniper!"

No reply.

"Gary? Gary!"

Gutterson lay face-down in the snow, blood pouring from a gunshot wound to the back of his head. Two more rounds punched the ground between them.

Holding his breath, Hansen tugged out his sidearm then crawled around, drawing another shot from somewhere above. The round punched into Gutterson's back. Hansen spotted a muzzle flash from the rooftop to his left and returned fire once.

"He's on the fucking roof!" someone cried in the distance.

Hansen fired two more rounds, then rolled over, arriving breathlessly at Gutterson's side.

Snow puffed just a few inches from his knee. He ducked, flinched, but then reached out, pulled Gutterson onto his back. His friend's head hung limply to one side, his tongue slipping from his lips. Blood continued pooling around his head. Hansen wiped snow from the TC's face, then shook him. "Gary?"

The man was quite obviously dead, but it wasn't clicking with Hansen. "Gary?"

Automatic weapons fire split the air overhead, accompanied by more cries. Ryback's grunts were on the move, and as the platoon leader was fond of saying, Ryback rhymes with payback.

"Medic!" Hansen screamed. "Got a man down over here! I need a medic!"

Two soldiers came bursting from one building, and Hansen spotted one carrying a medical bag. At that he rose and took off running. He slipped around the building to his left, paused, popped out his old magazine and slammed home a fresh one. He was a being of pure muscle, no longer in control, and he had but one thought: kill the motherfucker who . . . oh my God . . . who killed Gary.

Hansen raced on, coming around the corner of the next building. The shooter had been perched directly above him, maybe twelve feet up. Gunfire resounded from the roof, then someone leapt to the ground, nearly knocking him over.

Though long shadows draped across the alley between buildings, Hansen saw enough.

It was him! The sniper! A little guy, probably special forces, dressed in a nondescript black parka and carrying a Russian-made Dragunov sniper rifle. That's all that registered before Hansen lost his breath.

The sniper rolled a couple meters away, brought up the rifle, appearing as startled as Hansen.

A mere second would decide who lived and who died.

Hansen dropped to his knees and fired.

As did the sniper.

CHAPTER
TEN

HANSEN FELL FORWARD onto his elbows, unsure if he had been shot. That didn't matter, though, as long as he still had control of his pistol.

He did.

So he thrust out his arm. The sniper was lying on his back, about to sit up.

BANG! Hansen fired once more, striking the guy somewhere between the arm and chest.

The sniper jerked, cried out, turned to raise the rifle.

Hansen sprang forward, landed on the guy, then with one hand shoved the rifle aside and directed his pistol at the sniper's head. The Korean looked painfully young. Not a line on his narrow face.

"Hey, he's got him!" someone shouted from behind.

"Don't shoot, man," came a deeper voice. "We can take him alive!"

Footfalls grew louder. Hansen breathed heavily into the sniper's face. He couldn't catch his breath. Everything inside raged, told him to fire at this fucking bastard who had killed Gary. Put a bullet this scumbag's head. There was no guilt. Nothing.

Except payback.

And the shouts.

"He's worth more alive!"

Hansen glanced up as one of Ryback's troops snatched up the Dragunov, then stepped back.

"We'll take it from here," said another trooper.

Ryback himself came jogging up. "Fuck, Hansen, secure that weapon."

Slowly, almost imperceptibly, Hansen shook his head.

"I asked you to secure that weapon!"

Hansen didn't move.

"Are you kidding me? Secure that weapon! This is a POW—if he lives."

BANG! Hansen put a bullet in the sniper's head. He turned away from the gore.

The troopers looked shocked.

"Aw, shit," groaned Ryback.

Hansen looked at the lieutenant, and for a moment the whole world went dark, tipped on its axis, then returned to normal. He blinked hard.

Ryback's eyes bulged. "You fuckin' executed him."

"I didn't see anything," said one of the troopers.

"Looked to me like the lieutenant shot this man in self-defense," said the other trooper.

Hansen pulled himself to his feet, shuddered, realized the tremors weren't going away. "Report what you want," he told Ryback. "He killed my friend." Hansen eyed the sniper once more, then holstered his pistol.

The grunts—not a one of them—said a word as Hansen walked away, passing through six or seven more troops rushing toward the scene. As he headed back to where Gutterson still lay in the snow, the two medics standing over him and talking, he grew numb. What he had just done was, in his estimation, completely evil, but his mind wasn't turning those thoughts into pain or guilt or anything. He was just . . . empty.

* * *

KEYMAN WAS ONE of the last guys off his cot when the shots had rung out.

He couldn't blame that on his exhaustion, nor could he say that he was a heavy sleeper and could snooze through an artillery attack.

He had been exhausted, yes, and he had perfected the art of slipping off into la-la land within a matter of minutes, even while seated at his station. Most of your seasoned soldiers could do the same. No big trick. Just a survival skill.

However, since the war had started, he had been unable to recapture those very deep sleeps he had once enjoyed back in his billet at Camp Casey. There was always a clock ticking in the back of his head, a ticking that reminded him that at any time he could be killed.

Thus when the shots had echoed, they should have wrenched him awake. But they hadn't. He had been dreaming. He had been exacting revenge upon those South Korean street thugs who had hurled their Molotovs and had killed his old crew. He had the bastards cornered, and the booming came from his own weapon. The dream was recurring more frequently, and it reminded him that yes, mentally speaking, he was pretty screwed up. After he killed the bad guys, he sat down to a game of poker with Webber, who proceeded to swindle him out of every last buck. Then he, Webber, Smiley, and Morbid went over to Ajima's tent for some coffee and ramen. The old lady leered at them as they discussed how they were going to kick Hansen's ass during the next gunnery. Everything was back to "normal." Ajima used the F-word, and they all laughed.

Then . . . more gunfire. Not a dream. And Keyman had cracked open his eyes.

Now the whole company team was at REDCON-1, with he and the rest of the platoon aboard their tracks while Ryback's people and the engineers continued to scour the complex for more snipers. From his hatch, Keyman lifted his NVGs and swept the complex for a second time, while Zuck sat ready on the coax. A glance over to the loader's machine gun left Keyman feeling hollow again. Lamont's ghost shook his head.

And there it was. If a replacement for the loader failed to arrive, Keyman would be heading into North Korea with a three-man crew. Zuck would serve as loader, and Keyman would fire the main gun from his position. In regard to operations, that wasn't a big deal. They trained all the time for such an event. In regard to emotions . . . shit, they would have to get past the loss. They needed to remain in the here and now. There was no time for yesterday or tomorrow. No one said it would be easy.

Now the whole operation had taken another brutal turn for the worse. They had lost a tank commander, a friend of Hansen's, another butter bar from West Point who had also graduated near the bottom of his class. But Gutterson had dug in and done pretty well for himself. No one was calling him a geek on the day he died.

Rumor had it that Hansen had gone after the sniper, but Keyman hadn't heard much more. Just that they had gotten the bastard. Hansen was still with the CO. Keyman thought of calling the LT, then thought better of it. He might be interrupting some kind of emotional crises or some shit. Hansen wasn't putting out much love as it was.

So Keyman called Abbot, using the cell phone to keep everything on the QT.

Unfortunately, the platoon sergeant answered his phone not with a "hello," but with, "This had better be important, asshole."

"Our boy's not having a good day is he?" Keyman began. "First the Stryker, then Gutterson. I'm getting some bad vibes here. And I'm running out of things to say."

"I want to meet with you and Neech and talk about this, if we get a chance. We need to support him. But we need to be ready if anything happens."

"Oh, we'll be ready. Let's hope it doesn't come to that. Funny thing is, I was starting to respect that man."

"No shit. He saved your life."

"I mean respect his leadership. I didn't think he'd get chipped down so quick."

"That's hard to predict." Abbot paused. "Watching Gutterson get shot . . . it could've tipped the scales. I mean he was right there. He held him."

"Well, that'll fuck him up for life—but we just need him for now." Keyman surprised himself with his icy tone. "I hope the CO's smart enough to realize that Lieutenant Hansen might need replacing."

"Yeah? Who's going to step in?"

"You."

"I don't want it."

"Bullshit. You want it bad. Take it."

"Only if I have to. Of course, that'll make you platoon sergeant, and you'll need one ear glued to that company net, which I know you just love."

Keyman sighed and considered that. Yes, they were both reluctant to take on all that responsibility, but both would rise to the occasion, even if that meant Keyman having to split his attention between fighting his tank and the radio, and Abbot having to do likewise with the platoon. Although Abbot had said he didn't want to be platoon leader, he was being modest. His actions on and off the battlefield had earned him the respect of the entire company, and he was more than capable of leading the platoon. Furthermore, he didn't ram his wisdom down anyone's throat.

"Well, we'll take it as it comes," Keyman told the sergeant. "And hey, this call is costing me a fortune. Talk to you later."

He thumbed off the cell, then stole a moment to duck into the tank, out of the wind. He expected Zuck to glance back at him, but the gunner was leaning into his sight and not moving. "You watching pornos again?"

Keyman shifted his foot, about to nudge Zuck, when he realized that the guy had fallen asleep, his chest rising and falling with a machinelike rhythm.

"Oh, man." Keyman put on his CVC helmet, plugged

himself into the intercom, then whispered, "Hey, Boomer, you with me?"

The burly driver was breathing easily and shit, he was probably fast asleep, too.

Some crew. Sleeping on the job. Keyman yawned and leaned back in his seat. A month ago he would have been tearing these guys new assholes. But not now. Not anymore.

Let the grunts worry about more bad guys. He and his boys needed to rest. They had earned it. He closed his eyes.

Webber was waiting for him at the card table. "I'm a pool shark, a card shark, and a loan shark," the gunner said with a confident grin. "You don't have a prayer, you bald bastard."

"Shut up and deal them cards."

CAPTAIN VAN BUREN spoke somberly with Hansen, but never once did the CO's voice crack. That he controlled his emotions was both a comfort and an inspiration to Hansen. What the CO actually said went by the wayside, but how he said it was everything. He was as broken up about Gutterson's loss as Hansen was, but he knew that men in their position didn't have the luxury of grieving the way civilians did. That would happen much later on. Alcohol would be involved. A lot of alcohol.

Gutterson's platoon sergeant, a guy named McMillan, would take over for his fallen comrade if a replacement didn't arrive. Hansen had never spoken much with the sergeant, though he didn't care for McMillan's arrogant tone, which filtered through even when he said hello. With eyes permanently hidden by deep folds of skin, as though he'd spent a lifetime in the sun, McMillan seemed to be scrutinizing nothing—and everything—all at the same time. Like Abbot, he had been in the first Gulf War. Unlike Abbot, he liked to brag about it. But at the moment, he kept his trap shut. He knew better. And he was probably feeling Gutterson's loss too, though Gary had never said much about his dealings with the man. Hansen wondered if their relationship was as strained as his had been with Keyman. Chances were high.

Van Buren dismissed the platoon sergeant, then draped an arm over Hansen's shoulder and led him closer toward the spot in the snow where Hansen had killed the sniper. "Son, you're going to be okay."

"Yes, sir."

"I know what happened here. You got closure with him and with me. Hooah."

"Hooah. Is there anything else, sir?"

"No, you're dismissed."

Hansen was about to leave, stopped. "Sir? You ever get scared?"

Van Buren grinned, as though he had been asked that question a thousand times and was ready to deliver his stock answer. Then he thought a moment, frowned, and said, "Hansen, no one in his right mind would do what we're doing and not be scared."

"No, I mean scared that you're not good enough. That you tricked yourself into thinking you could do it, when deep down you know you're just faking it. Do you know what I mean?"

"I think so. Everybody has doubts. But I didn't get to where I am—and you didn't get to where you are—by being incapable. We're here because no matter what happens . . . no matter how many guys we lose . . . we don't quit. Ever. That's our motto: everybody fights, nobody quits. And that's why we're the best company in the battalion. That's why we're the best company on this godforsaken peninsula."

"Yes, sir."

"It took a lot for you to do what you did in that turret with Sergeant Lee. And you went on. You took out that Stryker. And you went on. Now we just lost Gutterson."

"And we'll go on," Hansen said.

"Yes, we will. This is not jingoistic bullshit. These are the facts."

"Yes, sir. All right, sir. I won't let you down."

Wishing his tone had been more convincing, Hansen saluted and left. He kept tight to the buildings, feeling as though eyes were everywhere.

When he reached his tank, he found Deac and Mingola sleeping in the turret. "WAKE UP, ASSHOLES! WE'RE AT REDCON-1, FOR GOD'S SAKE!"

They snapped awake. Deac went back up to his hatch and seized his machine gun, while Mingola wiped grit from his eyes and stared through his sight.

Just a few moments later, the order to stand down came over the company net, and Hansen called for a meeting of his TCs. They gathered near his tank's rear deck, while the rest of the crews went back to get some rest.

Abbot cleared his throat, then shifted his weight uneasily from leg to leg. "Uh, sir, before we begin, I think I speak for all of us when I say we're real sorry about Gutterson."

Hansen's eyes grew sore, and he squinted against the burn. "Thank you, Sergeant. He was a geek, but he turned that around. We could've used him."

All three TC's found great interest in their boots. Looking up was too damned awkward.

To spare them, Hansen launched right into a summary of the OPORD, going over every detail while trying to capture the same tone Van Buren had used with him. He sketched a diagram in the snow so that his men could visualize the route. "Any questions?"

Keyman spat some chew, narrowed his gaze on the snow, then glanced up.

Hansen figured his wingman would have some wiseass remark about how they were riding half-cocked into hell and that the mission sucked.

"Sounds good," said Keyman.

Hansen drew back his head. "Excuse me?"

"I said it sounds good."

Hansen chuckled under his breath. "Are you all right?"

"Are you?" Keyman widened his gaze.

"Well, the little green men are still talking to me, but I ain't listening—if that's what you mean."

No one smiled.

"Come on, you fuckers. I'm stressed, but we can do this. No matter what happens we fight. We never quit."

"HOOAH!" they answered in unison.

"Now then, we can thank our theatre commander for this little tactical pause, and we *will* take advantage of it. I order all you assholes to return to your catnaps!"

"Yes, sir!" said Neech.

"I'm right behind you, Neechy," Keyman said.

The two men hustled off, but Abbot lingered behind.

"Something else, Matt?" Hansen asked.

"I wish there were a better time or place, but we got another issue we have to deal with. I don't even want to dump it on you now, but I'm little concerned."

The pit in Hansen's stomach deepened as he ran through the possibilities of more bad news. "Can it wait?"

"I don't know."

"Then fuck it. What do you got?"

"It's Park. He knows something's up."

"We've talked about this. You hold your ground, and if he can't take it, then we'll replace his ass too."

"I think we should tell him."

"What?"

"I've worked with him for nearly a year now. He's a great gunner. I don't want to head up there without him. But he's got his doubts. And I think if we tell him the truth, he can handle it. I think if we're honest with him, he'll respect us more for it."

"Or he'll shoot me."

Abbot shook his head. "If anything, he'd kill himself first. Or go AWOL. But I think all he wants is to know we respect him enough to tell him the truth."

"Matt, I don't know."

"Look, there isn't much he can do to retaliate. Frankly, I don't think he'll say a word."

"You think telling him will smooth things over in your turret?"

"At first, I didn't. But now I think I got him figured

out. Damn KATUSAs are hard to read. So, can I talk to him?"

"No."

Hansen paused just long enough to watch Abbot's expression grow long. Then he added, "I will."

BY FIRST LIGHT Chinook and Black Hawk helicopters had finally begun a continuous air bridge to deliver much-needed fuel, water, pallets of ammo, and major assemblies like engines. Those supplies dangled below the Chinooks' bulky fuselages, while inside their cargo bays smaller parts, chow, sundries packs (with fresh toothpaste, razors, and other stuff), and mail too, including care packages, all waited to be unloaded by eager company personnel. The Chinooks also hauled in completely assembled sections of track for those vehicles that needed them as well as MICLIC reloads and a new mine plow for Neech's track.

Meanwhile, while Team Cobra resupplied, the CAV flew security missions while mortars and field artillery shot Harassment and Interdiction (H&I) fires to keep the enemy guessing. Additionally, the USAF and Army attack helicopters were doing some deep attacks. The tactical pause was similar to the one U.S. ground forces had taken during the race to Baghdad during Operation Iraqi Freedom, and although higher was putting pressure on them to get moving soon, Van Buren wanted to make sure they were loaded for bear.

Unfortunately, the resupply was not without the usual screw-ups. One of the Blackhawk pilots got a little antsy as he was coming in to land and accidentally dropped a slingload of fuel, causing the blivet to burst upon impact. Abbot also reported that the rest of the new fuel airlifted in was contaminated. The tanks and Bradleys would still run, but there could be some problems later on. The challenges didn't stop there. The "loggies" (logisticians) had messed up the loads, sending them way too much tank ammo and not enough for the Bradleys. And worse, they loaded a whole pallet of 30 mm chain gun ammo for Apache helicopters. What the hell was the team supposed to do with attack helicopter chain gun ammo? Hit it with a hammer? To add insult to injury, Ryback reported that when his men opened up their M16/SAW ammo, about a third of their shipment was blanks, and the team's overall shipment of chow was down about a third because the brigade support area troops had stolen and eaten the rest—including *all* of the steaks the DIV CG had ordered delivered hot to Team Cobra.

However, the company's senior KATUSA and the XO saved the day. They took a few trucks down the road to an ROK Army camp and were able to procure some hidden fuel and M16/SAW ammo since the U.S. and ROKs had spent years establishing some common ammunition rules so they could interchange ammo in emergency situations. Also, the ROKs had their own version of the MRE, and because they "loved" them as much as U.S. troops loved their own MREs, the two were able to bring back enough "food" to address some of the loss. Of course, throughout it all, Van Buren was on the A/L net, chewing out the brigade S4 for all of the mistakes, which would delay the team's departure until nightfall.

BY LATE AFTERNOON, after six hours of beautiful, uninterrupted sleep in which Hansen had not had a single dream, he awoke feeling groggy yet still better than he had in the previous twenty-four hours.

Before he had a chance to clean up, his turn came, and he got a chance to log on to the Web and check his e-mail. Karen had written him a really sexy love letter that wasn't X-rated but suggestive enough to raise his pulse. He also had mail from his parents and from a few buddies from high school who said how proud they were of his work and that he should keep his head low. Lastly, he received an e-mail from his grandfather, who at eighty-eight had probably been goaded onto the computer by Hansen's mom. Though Grandpa had never been in the service, he expressed his pride and heartfelt thanks, which left a big lump in Hansen's throat.

A short time later, after a shave, he sat down to chow with the rest of the platoon, grimacing over the smell, a cross between something spoiled and something burned. Keyman introduced him to his replacement loader, Specialist Victor Halitov, a muscular blond guy of about twenty with a distinct Russian accent.

"Nice to meet you," Hansen said, taking the man's hand and wincing over Halitov's gorilla grip.

"Lieutenant, I am Halitov. I am here to fight!"

"That's what I'm talking about," Keyman said. "Got me a Russian asskicker in my turret."

"I became American citizen when I was eighteen," said Halitov. "And when I was nineteen I joined United States Army. The best army."

"Good for you, Specialist," Hansen said. "You keep your ammo moved up, your gun loaded, and your eyes sharp, and you'll do just fine—if you survive Keyman."

The big guy nodded. "I am Halitov. I am here to fight!"

That drew a chuckle from the rest of the table.

Hansen glanced down the row of faces until he came upon Park, who eyed him for a second, then averted his gaze. Abbot, who had been watching, widened his eyes. After chow, Hansen would speak with the KATUSA.

"Hey, know what I got from my mom?" Romeo asked the group. "Got me some pimple cream. Extra strength."

"Aw, dude, can I borrow some?" said Paz.

"Me too?" asked Deac.

"I'm not giving it out. Two bucks each."

"Two bucks? Are you nuts?" Paz asked.

The three tankers began bickering over the price, and all Hansen could do was roll his eyes at their negotiations and at how clearly their age was showing. But you know, he might buy a little pimple cream himself.

The two troopers who had watched Hansen shoot the sniper came by with their trays and nodded curtly. Hansen returned his own uncomfortable nod.

"That was odd," said Keyman, who was seated opposite him. "Those crunchies looked like they were paying you tribute or something."

"They should," Hansen said. "To all of us. Right? When they need saving, we come rolling in."

"Uh, yeah, right." Keyman narrowed his eyes, then resumed shoveling instant mashed potatoes down his throat.

Abbot was staring absently at his plate, and though Hansen noticed, he decided to pretend he hadn't. That was the trouble with down time: You had too much time to think. To stress yourself out. To remember that your wife had been killed. Hansen wondered if his platoon sergeant was, at the moment, back in Texas, having dinner with his wife.

He turned his attention to Neech, who was carefully chewing his food, part of his diet regimen. He said the more slowly you ate and the better you chewed your food, the less you would eat and the more calories you would burn. Hansen admired the TC's discipline.

"Hey, Neech, your plow should be finished by now, right?" Hansen asked.

"Yeah, they're hauling back the old one for repairs."

"And what about you, Key? How's it going with your track?"

Keyman turned to Boomer, who cleared his throat. "Sir, we were going to swap out the engine, but we didn't have to. I'm confident we won't abort again."

"But if we do, I'm going to call in fires on my own head," said Keyman. "I swear to God I will."

"Don't worry, we're in good shape," Boomer assured the man.

Hansen grinned. "Shit, if you abort, we'll just send in Halitov."

"Yes, sir!" cried the Russian. "I am Halitov."

"He's here to fight!" Keyman finished.

They all smiled, but it wasn't as funny the third time.

* * *

HANSEN AND SERGEANT Park retreated to one of the smaller meeting rooms inside the remains of a single-story building whose south side had been sheared off. Though there was no heat, they were at least out of the wind and would have a moment's privacy as the rest of the company prepared to move out. They took seats. Hansen wasn't sure where to begin, and Park's troubled expression—quite remarkable for the man—left Hansen feeling even more awkward.

"Sir—"

"Lee always spoke highly of you," Hansen blurted out. "You guys were like twins."

"Yes, they said that many times. We even became gunners same month. We had competition. But we always helped each other. We made each other better. We were lucky to have that. Very lucky."

"That's the way it should be."

"Yes." The KATUSA closed his eyes for a moment, then asked, "Lieutenant?"

"I know. Lee's death was terrible. And you want to know what happened."

"Please tell me."

"Park, let me present you with a situation. And you tell me how you would react. Okay?"

"Okay."

"The North Koreans have tied innocent civilians to the hood of their vehicle. They are firing at you. They have a chance to disable or destroy your track. Your tank commander has ordered you to fire at the vehicle. You know you will kill those civilians. What do you do?"

"I fire."

"Why?"

"Because I was ordered to do so. Because the enemy is attacking. Because he could kill me and my crew. I am certain that I have already killed civilians back in TDC. Some refuse to leave, even during war. There is nothing we can do to make them go. Some will always die. That is the collateral damage that we have."

"Thank you."

Park mulled over the scenario for a few seconds. "So that is what happened?"

"I don't blame Lee. He had seen too much. I didn't want to fire either. But we had no choice."

"Are you saying he refused the order?"

"He did. He wanted to dismount. Go AWOL. Run away. He couldn't take it anymore. But Keyman wouldn't let him do that. Lee drew his sidearm and pointed it at Keyman."

Hansen had never seen the KATUSA's expression grow so surprised. "He was going to shoot Sergeant Key?"

"At first I wasn't sure. But you know how Keyman has a way of bringing out the worst in people. And he did that with Lee. I'm not trying place blame on him. Maybe Lee would've fired, maybe he wouldn't have. We'll never know. But I couldn't take a chance. Lee was standing in the path of recoil."

"So you fired the main gun."

Hansen slowly nodded. "If you want to blame me, blame me. I killed Sergeant Lee because I thought he was going to shoot Keyman. It was the most difficult decision I've ever made. I may never have a gunner better than him. He helped me win Top Tank. He was the very best. I'll remember him for the rest of my life. And I deeply regret what happened."

Park couldn't hold back the tears. Deeply embarrassed, he looked away, wiped his face, and muttered something in Korean, probably a curse.

"Park, I'm sorry we kept this from you. We were told to keep quiet. But Abbot came to me, said you deserved to know the truth. And so here I am, trying to show you that we respect you enough to tell you now. I am sorry about all of this. More sorry than you'll ever know."

Suddenly, the KATUSA sprang to his feet, grabbed the metal folding chair beneath him, and flung it across the room. "Not fair! Not fair what happened!"

Hansen stood and raised his palms. "Take it easy, bro. Of course it ain't fair. It fucking sucks. But it happened. And we either deal with it, or we get out."

"I don't know what to do."

"Do like that Russian. Just fight. And you do that because this is your country. These are your people. And we want to help." Hansen thrust out his hand. "Are you with us?"

Park eyed the hand, his lip quivering.

"ARE YOU WITH US?"

The KATUSA reached out and accepted the shake, his grip much firmer than the typical Korean handshake. He was in.

"Abbot trusts his life with you. We all do. You can get past this. And I won't stop you from taking out your anger on the enemy. None of us will."

"Yes, sir."

"Now then, I'll let Abbot know we spoke. And what I told you was exactly what happened. Don't believe for a second that it wasn't. There's been too much lying going on. Let's a make a deal: only the truth, no matter what."

"Yes, sir. No matter what."

"All right. Go on back."

Once the KATUSA had left the room, Hansen dropped heavily into the chair, sighed, and threw his head back. "So, tell me, God, did I just make a huge mistake or what?" He tugged out his cell phone, dialed Abbot. "Hey. Okay, he knows."

"Is the shit hitting the fan?"

"Well, he did throw a chair."

"You kidding?"

"No. But I think he'll be all right. I put him in the same situation, and he said he would've fired."

"That was smart."

"I got lucky. It just popped into my head that way."

"All right. I'll keep you updated."

"Hey, Matt? No matter what he does, I think you were right. We owed him the truth."

"Thanks, LT."

ABBOT POCKETED HIS cell phone and watched as Park drew closer to the tank.

"What's the matter with him?" Paz asked while helping Sparrow load ammo into the bustle rack. "He looks more pissed off than usual."

"Nothing guys. Just keep quiet." Abbot dismounted and met up with the gunner, whose face had grown flush. "Hey, Park."

The KATUSA glanced up at Abbot, then turned away. "Sergeant."

"Are you all right?"

"I don't know."

"The lieutenant just called me."

"Everybody lied about Sergeant Lee. I knew that happened. I knew. But it is good that I know truth."

"Are you sure? I mean, if you can't do this, you have to let me know."

"I would have fired at the enemy. I would have killed the civilians. I would do that now, if you ordered it."

"I hate that order."

"Me too. But I will obey it. Lee was wrong. And he died for that." Without another word, Park mounted the tank.

Abbot wished he could stand there, fully assured that when the critical moment occurred, Park would do the right thing. However, it would be foolish to completely trust the man. The truth hurt, and it hadn't worked any miracles. The fact remained that Abbot always had one hand on the tank's TC override so he could take control away from his gunners, but now he was even more conscious of that.

"Hey, Sergeant?" Paz called. "I checked your horoscope. You want to hear it?"

"As a matter of fact, Paz, I don't."

"You might like it. Hard work and sacrifice will earn you rich rewards."

Abbot smirked. "Maybe in the next life."

"And Sergeant, about heading north?"

"Yeah, I know," Abbot said impatiently. "It's a bad idea. But we're going anyway. Let's get this bitch ready to roll!"

CHAPTER
ELEVEN

"GENTLEMEN, WE ARE on the offensive, moving north, ready to strike fast and kick ass!" Keyman cried over the intercom.

He wasn't the type to get overly excited, gung ho, what have you. In fact, intimidation had always been his motivator of choice, and he had never given a shit what the men thought, as long as they obeyed.

Now he wanted them to feel good about him, the mission, everything. Was he getting touchy-feely? God, he hoped not, yet for some reason it now seemed important that the crew like him. Maybe if they did, they would do a better job for him and each other.

Or maybe deep down, he didn't want to be hated anymore. Being liked wasn't a sign of weakness. He recognized that now, and it was one of those things that he had secretly admired about Hansen. In the past, the lieutenant had had it all: looks, talent, and a crew who thought he was a "good guy." Too bad he wasn't able to keep that up. Some guys cracked under the pressure. Keyman wouldn't.

"What's the best company?"

"Charlie Company!" answered Boomer and Halitov.

"And who's the best crew?"

"Uh, the lieutenant's crew?" Zuck asked.

"Come on, Zuck!" Keyman booted the gunner's head. "Who's the best crew?"

"RED TWO!" replied Halitov and Boomer.

"All right. I might agree with that," said Zuck. "But this locker room speech is pretty corny."

"No, it's not," said Boomer. "I'm pumped up!"

"Me too!" added Halitov.

"That's right," Keyman said. "We're ready to get it on, man. All we need is a target."

"You sure you weren't a butter bar in another life?" Zuck asked. " 'Cause you sound like one."

Maybe he's right, Keyman thought. *Maybe I've become Hansen. Or at least the old Hansen.*

Keyman's tank came up and over a hill, then rattled down the back side, the incline much sharper than he had anticipated. Steep hills walled in both sides of the highway, and within a matter of seconds the defile looked like an Olympic bobsled course whose icy twists and turns lay hidden in the gloom.

"Boys, it's good to be on the road again," Keyman said, forcing a calm into his voice. In truth he was seriously puckered up as they slid a little left and Boomer turned out of the slide.

"When I was little boy, I dreamed of such nights," said Halitov. "This is good."

"Shit. This motherfucker is really playing up the Russian bit," said Zuck. "He probably doesn't even have an accent. He's fucking with us. Ain't that right, Halitov?"

"I will fuck later. Right now, I fight."

Keyman's smile hurt. Despite all his headgear, his cheeks were plates of glass. "I like that, Halitov. You're a man who's got his priorities straight. We fight, we fuck, we celebrate. That's what I'm talking about!"

"Red Two, this is Red One, over."

What did the lieutenant want now? "Red One, this is Red Two, go ahead."

"Black Six says we may hit some turns that aren't on the map, over."

Keyman checked his own map, which hung from a clipboard at his station. "Roger that, over."

"Just don't run around turns without being sure. You know the drill, over."

"Roger."

"Anything hot in the thermals?"

"Uh, negative. Cold as a witch's tit and staying that way so far, over."

"Roger, continue to move. Red One, out."

"Sounds like he's back to his paranoia," said Zuck. "Back to meaningless radio calls. For God's sake, if I got something hot in the thermals—"

"Zuck, that's it."

"You want to defend him, that's up to you."

"Well, they said we were going to have weather," Boomer groaned. "They weren't lying. I used to like the snow, but not since coming to Korea."

They were running without headlights, guided by Boomer's night vision and Keyman's NVGs, but the falling snow still shone through, growing dense as another of the country's forsaken fronts blew through the region.

Halitov, who stood ramrod straight, manning his machine gun like a cyborg, suddenly opened his mouth and thrust out his tongue to catch some flakes. Keyman was about to comment on the loader's appetite when the lieutenant chimed in over the net, addressing the entire platoon:

"Red, be advised TF scouts report a shitload of machine gun positions on both sides of the road. Lots of sandbags. They suspect mortar and FA took out most of them, but there will be a few left, over."

"This is Red Two, roger that."

Neech and Abbot also responded, and Keyman glanced over at Halitov and said, "Get ready, dude."

The big Russian took one hand off his weapon, raised his thumb, smiled. "I am—"

"Yeah, we know who you are. Just watch these fuckin' hills."

"Yes, Sergeant!"

They forged on for another ten minutes, with parts of the road to their left blasted apart by FA fires. Fortunately, the gaps on the right permitted safe if not exceedingly bumpy passage. Keyman swept the entire area with his goggles, his heart beginning to race. The road leveled off for about fifty meters, then they ascended the next hill, a dim sheen reflecting off the snow.

"Hey, Boomer?"

"Yeah, I see that ice, Sergeant. And hey, something could happen when we get up the top. If I'm a crunchie, this looks too good to pass on. Know what I'm saying?"

"Yeah, I do." Keyman dropped into the turret. "Zuck, if them fuckers start shooting, I want a HEAT round going right up their asses."

"Do you mean you're requesting a counterattack with direct fire on the enemy's position in order to neutralize his capabilities?"

"You got something better to do than bust my balls?"

"Nope. This keeps me entertained. But don't worry. We'll blow the living shit out of them. One of the few things I do well."

"Hey, man. That chip on your shoulder? One day it'll fall off. Trust me."

"Whatever."

As they neared the top, Keyman set his hatch in the open-protected position and monitored his extension.

The tank was but a second from leveling off when those telltale clangs, like someone banging on the hull with a ball-peen hammer, sent every man into action:

Keyman yelled, "Troops to the right!" and traversed the turret toward them. He had spotted a wall of sandbags about forty meters up the hill, half hidden by trees and snow and illuminated by two large muzzle flashes on each side. He laid the gun on target.

Halitov ducked into the turret and slammed his hatch shut.

Boomer slowed and steadied the tank as the turret swung over him.

"Those assholes are identified," said Zuck.

Halitov yelled, "Up!" a half-second after arming the main gun and rolling into his seat.

"Fire!" ordered Keyman.

Zuck squeezed his triggers. "On the way!"

As Keyman's head jerked back, he thought, *I love this shit!* It was amazing what a little food and rest could do for your spirits. He felt like he had just won Top Tank for the very first time. No one could touch him or the rest of the crew.

The machine gun nest heaved a great wall of fire that licked its way up the trees, melting snow and singeing branches. Somewhere inside that fire were North Korean grunts who had been so cold for so long that they probably welcomed the heat, saw it as a final reward before becoming heroes for all eternity.

Keyman and his crew roared like ogres as a few more trees caught fire. He didn't bother to announce, "Target!" He did slap Zuck on the shoulder and say, "Nice fuckin' shot!" Then he was back at his extension, searching for more troops.

"Red Two, this is Red One. SITREP, over."

"Didn't he see it?" Zuck asked.

"I told you to quit that shit. Red One, this is Two. We have engaged and destroyed one enemy machine gun nest. Continuing to advance, over."

"Roger that. Next time engage them with coax and TC's weapon first, over."

"Uh, okay. Roger that, out."

"He thought firing the main gun was overkill," said Zuck. "I thought that was the point. Maybe give the rest of those idiots something to think about."

"Yeah, but I see what he means. We should clean up quietly, otherwise we'll tip off any more assholes waiting up the road. Damn, that's a no-brainer. Where's my fuckin' noggin?"

"Let them bring more men," said Halitov. "More to kill!"

"Hey, big guy, you won't be wishing that when they're crawling all over us, getting ready to drop a grenade down your hatch," said Zuck.

The tank shifted unsteadily to the left, then Keyman swore as his neck jerked and he got tossed to the right. "Boomer?"

"We're going skiing," the driver cried.

Keyman burst into his hatch and gaped as the tank began sliding down the hill as gracefully as a big metal bull with Keyman sitting atop. All he needed were reins, chaps, and a cowboy hat.

Slowly, almost inevitably, the tank's right side swung out. Snow arced behind them, the tracks whined and sent vibrations through the turret, and the engine revved as their illustrious driver did everything he could to save their beast.

"Boomer, don't you throw a track!" Keyman warned.

And then, with perfectly bad timing, the lieutenant started a frantic radio report, something about the scouts spotting surface-laid mines just ahead.

Keyman turned bug eyes on the ground racing below them and spotted a mine about ten meters off.

They were sliding right toward it.

For a second, he couldn't find his voice. Then he yelled, "Oh, shit. Boomer?"

He was about to call the driver again when a fresh spate of machine gun fire sent him plummeting into his hatch, along with a rush of falling snow. "Boomer, there's a mine right there!"

"I don't see anything!"

"Christ, it's right there!"

"We're taking fire," cried Halitov.

"To hell with that," said Keyman. "We got a mine!"

"Turn, you asshole!" hollered Zuck. "Turn! Turn!"

* * *

HANSEN'S WINGMAN WAS in deep shit. No time to think. Just act. He put Mingola on that second machine gun nest located about a hundred meters up the hill to their left. The coax gnawed into those knuckleheads, hopefully buying Keyman's driver a moment to course-correct.

In the meantime, yet another machine gun nest came alive to the right, about sixty meters up the hill and positioned on the edge of a broad outcropping, making it damned hard to get a clean bead on it from their position.

"Red Four, this is Red One," he called to Abbot as they passed below the nest.

"I see him," Abbot answered.

And not two seconds later, a crimson streak extended across the hill like a gleaming tightrope terminating at Abbot's tank. Sergeant Park was taking out some aggression on those grunts. The coax gnawed into the outcropping, sparks flying, debris hurtling across the hillside.

A low-pitched explosion from the road ahead seized Hansen's attention. *Holy shit!* Had Keyman hit a mine?

Boom! A secondary and higher pitched explosion resounded as the first died. Dense smoke swept through the entire mountain pass, driven by the frigid wind.

"Red Two, this is Red One. You all right? Red Two, this is Red One. Talk to me, buddy!"

KEYMAN'S TANK SLID to a stop no more than two or three meters from a mine lying smack in the middle of the road. They had turned and missed the one farther back by half that distance and had actually shoved it aside without detonating it. That was damned fine luck, but now they were in a minefield, and something had just exploded. Okay, so it wasn't them. But they could be next.

"Boomer, what the fuck was that?" yelled Zuck. "I blinked and missed it."

"RPG, I think. He shot at us, hit the ground, set off a mine! Two bangs for your money."

The lieutenant called again on the net.

"That telemarketer's on the net," said Zuck.

Keyman sighed and took up the mike. "Red One, this is Red Two. We're stopped. No damage yet. Got mines ahead. RPG fire coming in, over."

"Roger that. Red halt! Engage troops!"

"What does he think we're doing?" asked Zuck.

Keyman kicked his gunner. Hard. Then he got on his fifty, probing for more grunts who would pop out from behind a tree and squeeze off a rocket.

But there were so many trees. *Shit.* He decided to hose down the entire hill. Then he thought better of that. Wouldn't be smart to waste ammo, extra fill or not. He went below, grabbed a couple of smoke pots, used his Zippo to light them, then let them roll. In a few seconds the tank was hidden behind curtains of smoke, and the incoming nearest them died, while sporadic fire from the rest of the platoon droned on.

Keyman was about to head back into the turret when, from the corner of his eye, he caught a shifting silhouette. He spun toward the bustle rack.

A Korean carrying an RPG stood not twenty meters from the tank. He was lost for a second in the smoke, then reappeared like a ghost who had glided closer, the launcher now jutting from his shoulder.

Keyman spat chew, drew his pistol, gripped the lip of his open hatch to steady himself, then fired four rounds. The first must have missed, and maybe the second too, but the third and fourth kicked the audacious RPG-toting cocksucker onto his back before he could send the rocket screaming into the tank's engine compartment. The smoke had been a good idea, but it worked both ways.

Swinging around, Keyman realized that the guy he had just shot had inadvertently become the diversion. Two more troops had charged into the center of the road, both carrying RPGs, and they had been the ones who should have kept him busy, while their buddy took a shot at the tank's ass. They had fucked up. Big time. Now they would die for their mistake.

Halitov had spotted them, and as he drilled one with 7.62 mm fire, the other scrambled to the right.

A huge explosion tossed snow, ice, and body parts fifty feet into the air as Keyman turned away from the booming. That dumbass Korean must have stumbled right into a mine.

Talk about blessings in disguise. He would have to drive through minefields more often, especially when enemy troops were stupid enough to wander into them. Well, maybe that wasn't a good enough reason. . . .

"That's the way, uh-huh, uh-huh, I like it, uh-huh, uh-huh," sang Halitov, who was obviously—and unfortunately—a fan of old disco songs.

"Holy fuckin' cow," said an astounded Zuck. "He blew himself up! I like when that shit happens—just not too close to me."

"Hey, Boomer, move us up a little," Keyman ordered. "We're losing our smoke. And I think our friend cleared the next mine for us."

"Okay, but just a little. And you know what? You guys want to be heroes? I bet we can breach this field without calling up the engineers. See all these other ruts? This field was laid real quick, and it's the second one here after their guys bypassed it. I'm pretty sure I can find their bypass lane, then the engineers can lay cones to guide everybody else through."

"Neech and his new mine plow won't be happy. I don't know. Sounds too dangerous. Let me call the LT. See what he thinks."

"You know what he'll say," said Zuck.

"I used to. Let's see."

"Why don't we just give it a try first?" suggested Zuck. "If we blow up, he'll figure it out anyway."

On the one hand, Keyman would be a hero for saving the company team a lot of time. On the other hand, he and his crew could become martyrs for efficiency. Moreover, even if they steered a path through the field, carefully avoiding each mine by sticking to the enemy's bypass lane, that might only mean they had gotten lucky again, narrowly missing a mine that another vehicle might strike. Hasty breach or no, they needed to be sure that the path was wide enough and would be clear for everyone.

When Keyman called back to Hansen, the lieutenant's answer surprised him: "Black Six wants no delays. We have to keep moving. If Boomer thinks he can get us through, then let him try. Red One, out."

"Holy shit, dudes, we're going for it," Keyman said. "Boomer, let's mosey. . . . And I mean mosey. . . ."

"Wow," said the driver. "I didn't think Hansen would give his blessing."

"We're not blessed. We're fucked," said Zuck.

"You forget who's driving. Let's see if we get this old girl to stand on her toes."

Back in his hatch, Keyman did what he could to catch his breath. He kept telling Boomer that the road looked good. He probably said that a half-dozen times before he realized how annoying he sounded.

WHILE CAPTAIN VAN Buren didn't like what Hansen had suggested, the CO had recognized the time they would save, so he had given Hansen the go-ahead as the MECH platoon dismounted and went up into the hills to provide security and hunt down the grunts who were manning that last nest.

With bated breath, Hansen sat in his turret, watching as Keyman's tank rumbled along the jagged line between life and death. They were keeping mostly to the right, and no one was sure how big the field was. "I count six, no seven mines ahead. Moving around two," Keyman suddenly reported.

How the TC managed to speak in such a nonchalant tone was beyond Hansen. He would've been pissing in his pants, driving so close to all of those mines. This was not a tactic recommended at Fort Knox. Some would say it was just plain stupid. But those guys didn't have appointments to keep in North Korea either.

And if there was any man who could find a bypass lane within a minefield in the dark, on an ice-covered highway in North Korea, it was Boomer. Hansen had heard a lot about the guy's sixth sense. He was confident the driver could steer them to victory.

Surprisingly, all that confidence made Hansen grin. For once he wasn't worried. He wasn't thinking about the men, the tank, or the possibility that Keyman and his crew could blow up. He was thinking about what they would do after they breached the field.

And that was a trick: Keep thinking ahead. Assume success, react to failure, but keep focusing on the mission and the next move. All right. He would do it. And maybe the trembling would finally stop.

"They're still looking good," said Mingola, observing Keyman's tank through his sight. "But the road's going to veer a little to the left, and we'll lose them."

"Red Two, this is Red One. Slow a little so we can tighten up, over."

"Roger that."

Hansen called for Abbot and Neech to move up closer, then all four tanks made the turn and began to descend a thirty-degree grade.

The tank hit a rut, and suddenly Mingola's head fell forward, onto his controls, and he began to hyperventilate.

"Sergeant?"

"I'm all right," he snapped.

"No, you're not."

"Just a little déjà vu. That's all."

Hansen leaned down and grabbed the gunner's shoulder. "Hey, man. It's cool. We'll be all right."

Mingola shrugged, began to catch his breath. "Yeah, we hear that all the time, don't we? . . ."

"Red One, this is Red Two. My driver thinks we have cleared the field, over."

"See?" Hansen asked the gunner, who just shrugged. He keyed the mike. "Roger that, Two. Just keep moving and keep looking. Red Four, how're the engineers looking back there?"

"They're coming in right behind us, following our tracks."

"Roger that."

"All right, Red, continue to advance. Red One, out." Hansen switched frequencies to the company net and informed the CO that they had successfully bypassed the minefield.

"Excellent work, Red One. Keep moving. Black Six, out."

"Well, guys, if that don't make you believe in Jesus, then I don't know what will," said Gatch. "What y'all just witnessed was a miracle."

"Hey, Gatch?" Hansen called. "Order us up five or six more of those, okay? We'll need them to get to Kaesong."

"Roger that, sir. But hang tight. God's going to protect us. I just know it. And I feel really good about that. You should too."

"I'm trying, Gatch."

ABOUT FIFTEEN MINUTES later, the platoon came upon several oxcarts abandoned on the side of the road. Upon closer inspection, Hansen spotted a body lying buried under a thin layer of snow, along with the oxen.

"This guy tried to head south when the war broke out," Hansen said.

"He didn't get too far," said Deac.

"The cold probably didn't get him," Mingola said. "He was shot for defecting. They shot his animals too, and left him in the road as a warning to others."

"Maybe he got hit by a shell," said Deac. "The road's all chewed up over here."

"Doubt it," Mingola said. "When your government is running your whole life, even saying that you should cut your hair twice a month, you think they're going to let you go south on a permanent vacation? I don't think so. . . ."

They passed several more bodies farther up the road, all farmers or other peasants who lay like toppled statues, some even groping at the air with fingers that, in the poor light, looked gray and blue.

As horrible as the images were, Hansen welcomed them. They helped put his life into perspective. He was bitching and moaning about "not being good enough." His problems were a joke compared to what these people had gone through. They had toiled all their lives just to wind up frozen dead on the side of the road. His life was a king's compared to theirs. He needed to appreciate what he had, trust himself, and quit whining. Damn it, he would do it!

"Red One, this is Red Two," Keyman called. "Boomer thinks he has something."

THOUGH RELUCTANT TO do so, Keyman shared his driver's findings with the lieutenant, who said he would pass them up to the CO. In the meantime, he ordered Boomer to slow them to a crawl, while he, Zuck, and Halitov searched the mountaintop to their right, trying to confirm the sighting.

"Boomer, I hope you're right about this, because I still got nada," said Keyman.

"Same here," said Zuck.

"Guys, we're coming up on a hairpin turn," said Boomer. "It makes sense. I'm telling you, I saw that OP. Maybe just for a second, but it's there. The road's going to move up a little."

"Stop talking, brother, I got it," said Zuck. "Enemy observation post. Bingo. We have you."

"I see 'em, too," said Keyman, narrowing his gaze through his NVGs and spotting at least two soldiers propped up on their elbows, with binoculars shielding their faces. They had even been foolish enough to start a small cook fire, and that shone brilliantly in Keyman's goggles.

"They're not looking this way," said Zuck. "How could they miss us?"

"I don't know," answered Keyman. "They've probably been up here for a long time, though. Can't see or hear straight anymore. Finally gave in and started a fire."

"Red, this is Red One. Halt. Black Six has ordered us to take out that enemy observation post with an antipersonnel round. Red Two, engage that post and report when complete, out."

"Zuck, give me a range," said Keyman.

"Okay. Lasing . . . eighteen-twenty meters."

"Halitov, you know how to set the range on an AP round?" Keyman asked.

"Yes, Sergeant. I am here to set range and fight!" cried the loader as he kneed open the ammo door and withdrew the round. "I set correct range!" Once he had done so, he slammed the round home into the breach block. "AP round loaded. Loader ready!"

Meanwhile, Zuck had already traversed the turret and put them on the target. "This is going to be sweet," the gunner muttered.

"All right," Keyman said, leaning tighter into his extension. "Let's do this."

"The OP's identified," said Zuck.

"Up!" Halitov cried.

Keyman clenched his teeth. "Fire!"

"On the way!"

As Keyman sucked in a deep breath and the tank rocked back on its tracks, the AP round spat from the gun tube with a thundering promise of death.

The second Keyman's lungs were completely filled with air, the round detonated, and all those razor-sharp, dartlike flechettes inside dispersed in a conical arch, cutting through foliage and flesh with equal and mindless abandon. Before Keyman's heart could beat again and he could exhale, every enemy soldier caught within the round's range was dead, pinned to the mountainside, the blood from their many wounds flash-freezing in the wind. At least that's the way he imagined it, although his thoughts couldn't have been far from the truth.

He breathed, studied his extension. "Looks right on the fucking money."

"Nice work, guys," said Boomer.

"Of course it was," Zuck said, mildly offended.

"Red One, this is Red Two. We have engaged and destroyed enemy OP, over."

"Roger that, Red Two. Advance to where the road begins to turn, then halt. We'll have dismounts move up for a peek around the corner, over."

"Roger. We'll advance to the turn then stop, over."

"Good. Red One, out."

A few minutes later, the road began to hook sharply to the right, and the hills on both sides grew even steeper, some rising at angles of fifty degrees or more. A stiff wind blew through the pass, whipping snow from the limbs and howling through the hatches.

Keyman gave Boomer the order to halt. Mingola and Halitov would dismount and head up the road for a little recon around the turn. That enemy observation post had obviously been established to provide intelligence to a larger force. Van Buren expected an ambush, and Keyman was glad that the need for speed hadn't outweighed the need to move cautiously.

Before Halitov climbed out of the turret, Keyman offered his hand. "No funny business out there, all right?"

"Do not worry, Sergeant. I am Halitov."

"Yes you are."

"Hey, Russian?" Zuck called.

"No, I am American now. Like you."

"Yeah, okay. I was just going to say be careful."

Halitov chuckled and raised his brows. "Sergeant, I think he loves me."

THE LIEUTENANT HAD told Mingola to just run around the corner, check out the road, then haul ass back. They weren't wasting any time with commo wire like they had when they'd set up one of their own listening/observation posts. And because the enemy was most certainly near, they weren't taking any risks with portable communications either. Not even cell phones. They were heading out swiftly and silently, cut off and completely alone.

Mingola kept telling himself that the whole the thing wasn't a big deal, that he had reconnoitered enemy positions before, that he shouldn't worry.

But the moment he set foot on the snow, he felt his heart heave, his breath vanish. He stood there for a few seconds, the enormity of the war hitting him so hard that he nearly lost his balance. Suddenly, he grew very attached to the heat emanating from the tank, to the road wheels that provided some cover should dismounts begin to take potshots at him. It was all he could do to drag himself away, run up to Keyman's tank, and raise his chin at Halitov, who stood there with his M4 rifle, smiling like he had just gotten good head.

"I am Halitov."

"No shit. I'm God. Follow me."

Mingola darted to the side of the road, then moved up toward the trees, slowing as the snow rose to his shins. He figured if he didn't keep moving he might not go through with it. Sheer momentum equaled courage.

"You are fast," the big Russian said from behind.

"You are slow."

"My dick is heavy!"

Mingola didn't answer as he crossed from one stand of trees to the next, then squatted to catch his breath. Halitov came up next to him and lowered himself onto his haunches. The Russian pulled out his NVGs and peered across the hillside.

"Put those away," Mingola said, slapping at the goggles. "We're not close enough yet."

"I'm not looking at the road," said the loader, shaking a finger. "There could be troops here."

Rolling his eyes, Mingola pushed up and started off again, mumbling, "There could be troops everywhere." Bile burned the back of his throat. That's what you got for eating MREs and then running around like an idiot.

Three stands of trees later, he crouched for another break, and Halitov once more surveyed the hillside.

"Just a little farther and we can see up the road," reported the loader.

"You really like this shit, don't you?"

"I am here to fight."

"That's not funny anymore."

The Russian's blue eyes widened, nearly glowing in the darkness. "Sergeant, it is no joke."

"Well, I'm sure the North Koreans will help you out." Mingola shivered, almost violently.

"You must eat more. You are too skinny."

"Yeah, whatever."

They hustled off, zigzagging between more trees and reaching a long ridge overlooking the highway. Halitov dropped onto his belly, crawled to the crest, positioning himself beside a tree, then lifted his NVGs.

Mingola came up next to him and raised his own goggles.

"Do you see it?" asked Halitov, his tone full of dread.

After blinking twice, Mingola peered through his goggles. A sheet of patchy gloom came in and out of focus. He lowered the goggles. Blinked. Looked around. The tree was a gray blob.

Damn it. Not now.

The come-and-go blurriness that he had been hiding from Hansen and the rest of the crew was rearing its ugly head. It was just stress. That's all it was. Stress from the moment. It had absolutely nothing to do with the old head injury. Nothing at all.

"What do you think?" asked Halitov.

Mingola raised his goggles once more and pretended to see. Then he banged on the lens. "Something's wrong. It's fucked up."

"Here," said Halitov, shoving his own NVGs into Mingola's hand. "Use mine."

With a bitter swallow, Mingola took the goggles and squinted. "Well, look at that," he said, wishing he could.

CHAPTER

TWELVE

BACK IN RUSSIA, Halitov's father had taught him a simple trick: you could tell if a man was lying by reading his body language. The way he used his hands and shifted his head—sometimes even the way he blinked—could betray him. However, Halitov did not need the trick to know that Sergeant Mingola was, as he might say, full of shit.

The sergeant's goggles were perfect. And there could be only one reason why Mingola repeatedly asked for a more detailed description of the road.

"So what do you think?" the sergeant asked, obviously prying for more information.

Halitov reached over and slowly removed the goggles from Mingola's eyes. "Sergeant, what's wrong?"

"Nothing."

"You can't see it?"

"What're you talking about?"

"Here." Halitov thrust the goggles back into Mingola's hands. "Tell me exactly what you see."

"Listen, motherfucker . . ." Mingola rubbed his eyes vigorously, then glanced up. "I . . . shit, man."

"You have a medical problem?"

"I'm just tired."

"Did you forget your glasses?"

"I don't wear them."

"And you are the gunner on the lieutenant's tank? This is very bad."

"Listen, asshole. You tell me exactly what you see down there so I can report back to him. You got that?"

Halitov pursed his lips, thought a moment, then realized that the right thing to do was to inform Lieutenant Hansen. "We will go back together, and you will tell the lieutenant that you are . . . *tired*."

"Bullshit. Now tell me what you fuckin' see."

Halitov turned back toward the tree, focused his goggles on the road below. "I see a man who lies. A man who will risk his crew and the rest of the platoon because he will not tell the truth. I see no honor. And no courage. And no—"

"Aw, shut the fuck—"

MINGOLA WAS A second away from rearing back and striking the Russian when a sharp pain razored from ear to ear—and suddenly his vision cleared. He jerked back, slammed the goggles into his eyes.

Dozens of surface-laid antitank and antipersonnel mines were spread across the road, leading up to at least four big barricades of eleven-strand concertina wire. Mingola panned up, figuring that the whole obstacle had to be covered by direct and indirect fires, but he couldn't spot any vehicles. They were either too cleverly concealed or waiting around the bend to move up, once Team Cobra attempted to breach.

"Let's go. The lieutenant is waiting," said Halitov.

"Hey, asshole. We got mines and concertina wire. I see the whole thing. You get back to your track and keep your mouth shut. You hear me? I *will* fuck with you if you don't."

"Little man. Big mouth. What can you do to me?"

"I can make your life so miserable that you'll wish you were dead."

"You do not have that power."

"Do you want to test me?"

The big Russian thought it over a moment, then aimed at finger at Mingola. "I will tell Keyman when I get back."

"No, you won't."

Halitov hoisted a brow. "I am Halitov."

Mingola swore under his breath, then resigned himself to the inevitable. "Let's go, you big foreign fuck."

HANSEN LISTENED INTENTLY to Mingola's report, then immediately called back to Captain Van Buren. They had made contact with an enemy obstacle which presumably was part of an ambush site around the corner. Van Buren contacted FSO Yelas and requested that mortars pull off the road and emplace to provide immediate fires. Then the CO ordered the MECH and engineer platoons to stop, dismount, and go up and over the hill for a better look while the tanks of Blue Platoon moved up behind Red.

While that happened, Hansen kept vigil in his hatch, shuddering as the wind and snow continued to hammer. His cell phone rang; it was Keyman. "You idiot. You shouldn't be calling, man."

"This is important. Our new Russian buddy gave me some interesting news."

Hansen's stomach knotted. "What now?"

"Your gunner might have a vision problem."

"What?"

"I'm not saying he's a sloppy recon guy. I'm saying he might literally have a vision problem. Halitov thinks he couldn't see through the NVGs."

"You're kidding me."

"Wish I were. I mean, you thought he was messed up anyway, right? This ain't no surprise."

"I guess it's not. Thanks. I'll take care of it."

"Wait. One more thing. How you doing?"

Hansen cracked a grin. "What happened to you, dude? You got weird."

"I guess it sounds . . . I don't know . . . cheesy, but I'm trying to be more of a team player. You know, actually giving a shit about people?"

"Well, good for you. I appreciate your shit. And I'm fine." Hansen returned the phone to his pocket, then brought his NVGs to his eyes. Keyman had come a long way in a short time. Maybe they all had. "Hey, Deac, I want you back up top—right now."

"Aw, c'mon, LT. I've only been inside a couple of minutes. I hardly got warm."

"Get up there, you pussy," taunted Mingola. "You're not giving your body a chance to get right with the cold. Ancient man, he spent a lot of time outdoors. Got right with it. His body adapted because he—"

"Don't give me that History Channel crap. . . ."

Hansen slid down into his hatch, turned a stern look on Deac, whose smirk evaporated. He moved up toward his frozen perch. "All right. I'm going. I just want y'all to know that if I freeze to death up there, I won't blame it on you, LT. It's not your fault. Really."

"Give me a break, Deac."

Once the loader was out of sight, Hansen made a decision about how he would play it with Mingola.

"Sergeant?"

"What now, sir?"

"Wrong answer. You say, 'Yes, sir?' "

"Whatever. Yes, sir?"

"Do you have a vision problem?"

Mingola didn't answer.

"Sergeant, I want to know. Is there something wrong with your eyes?"

"No, sir. I have a problem with that Russian, sir."

Hansen narrowed his gaze. "So he's making up stories?"

"We just got into it out there, and he's trying to mess with me. That guy's a rogue, man. Wouldn't listen to what I told him. Then he gets mad. And now this."

"Well, once we get moving, you will no longer be my gunner. Deac? You're finally getting your chance behind the sight. You hear that?"

"Yes, sir! I'm good to fire the gun, sir!"

"Sergeant Mingola's not feeling too well."

"That Russian motherfucker is a liar. I told you—he doesn't like me. He's making it all up. I can prove my vision is perfect."

Hansen smirked. "Maybe it is, maybe it isn't. Maybe it's perfect now, but maybe it'll go bad later. You hear that word? *Maybe?* I hate that fucking word."

"Don't do this, sir. I swear to God I'm fine."

"Don't swear," Gatch said, ever the eavesdropper from his driver's station. "And don't lie. That's a double whammy. They'll be warming the fires in hell for you."

Mingola threw up his hands. "Fine. Whatever. I'll load."

"Awesome," said Deac. "And as loader, you can get up here and take over for me."

"Not so fast, Deac. Right now I need your good eyes up there," said Hansen.

"Shit. I never catch a break, do I?"

"Sir, you're making a big mistake," said Mingola. "I have way more experience than this guy."

"And that means nothing if you can't see what you're shooting at. Now if I were you, I wouldn't say another word, otherwise I might loan you out to the grunts."

Mingola snorted. "Yes, sir."

Hansen took a deep breath and began to feel light-headed. *Please, God. No more surprises. No more . . .*

AFTER ABOUT TEN minutes, platoon leaders Ryback and Harris finished assessing the situation and relayed their reports to Captain Van Buren. Hansen pricked up his ears and focused his attention on the company net: in addition to facing the obstacle, there were at least two tanks, two BMPs, and a platoon of dismounts positioned on the right side of and perpendicular to the road. The Dear

Leader in Pyongyang had directed these forces to die in place, and the men of Team Cobra would be happy to help them accomplish their mission. Those enemy troops had most likely been skipped over for resupply, and the officers and NCOs had probably left the grunts to do the fighting, while they fled to more "glamorous" battles or stole away to hide until hostilities ceased. Hopefully, their underlings would be as disorganized as they were cold, though cold and hungry men could still fight like maniacs if they thought victory would end their suffering.

The MECH platoon's forward observer abruptly called for smoke and mortar fires to suppress the dismounts and vehicles, while the rest of Ryback's people were preparing to put Javelin and machine gun fire on the enemy. Those Javelins would do their silver bullet number on the tanks and PCs, though Hansen secretly hoped that one or two vehicles would escape the MECHs, only to be pounded into oblivion by Red Platoon. That might not happen, but you could always hope. Destroying an enemy tank was just what Deac and Gatch needed to improve their morale; Mingola, however, was beyond help.

Hansen lifted his CVC helmet away from one ear and listened as the distant fires echoed like timpani and bass drums from the other side of the hill. At times, the pops and booms grew regular but then would quickly crackle into discord. Not long after the first detonations, Hansen got on the platoon net and said, "Red, this is Red One. The fight's on. Are we ready to move? Over."

All three of his tank commanders checked in and were good to go. Amazing. No headaches. Yet. . . .

"Red One, this is Black Six, over."

"Black Six, this is Red One. Go ahead."

"Red One, engineers will breach the obstacle from behind with a Bangalore torpedo, following which your tank plow and Blue's will proof the lane, over."

"Roger that. We'll have Red Three move up, over."

"Good. Blue Three is already on his way. Stand by to move on my order. Black Six, out."

Hansen radioed Neech, who said Blue Three had started to move up. Once both mine plows were at the head of the pack, the tank platoons would sit and wait as the grunts and engineers went about their business of killing the enemy—and stealing all the glory.

Still, the tankers' moment to shine would come. You didn't waltz into North Korea aboard an M1A1 Abrams Main Battle Tank and expect to be welcomed with open arms, unless, of course, you had already pummeled the enemy to their knees, and the people opening their arms were a minority of civilians who had dreamed all of their lives of defecting to the south.

As Hansen leaned back in his hatch, he imagined what was happening on the other side of the hill:

A pair of sappers from the engineer platoon was breaking out the five-foot sections of the Bangalore torpedo, connecting up to ten of the tubes and getting them ready to move, once the enemy dismounts were suppressed. The device dated back to World War II, and it was a damned bitch to lug around. Although it was considered effective against AT and AP mines, the torpedo sometimes did only a marginal job of cutting through modern, high tensile–strength barbed wire obstacles.

Good thing the North Koreans were still using some very old wire. The sappers would slide the Bangalore through the minefield before detonating, then the call would come in: "Fire in the hole!" An electric or nonelectric blasting cap would do the rest. If it worked as planned—the operative word being *if*—the charge would cut a three-to-four meter footpath through the obstacle, allowing the sappers to advance to the next section of wire. It would also trigger many of the other mines, thus helping out Red and Blue.

After nearly five minutes of heavy mortar fire rumbling from the hills, Ryback's voice came urgently over the company net: "Black Six, this is Renegade One, over."

"Go ahead, Renegade."

"Black, we believe a squad-size force of dismounts has

bypassed our line. They are headed east, over the foothills. Believe they have a few RPGs with them, over."

"Roger, that. Renegade. Red and Blue will prepare to intercept. Black Six, out."

"Deac, get down here," ordered Hansen. "We got dismounts on the way. Get on that coax."

"All right, ya'll," cried the loader turned gunner. "Watch the 'coon hunter in action!"

Mingola slid gingerly from his seat and traded places with Deac. Only a surgeon's scalpel could remove the sour expression on Mingola's face.

Hansen dismissed the guy with a shake of the head, then manned his fifty and began an aggressive search for those troops. Every time something flickered in the distance, he stiffened, thought he had someone. Snow swirled, trees rustled in the wind, but no one appeared along the glossy banks. His mouth grew dry, and the heaves threatened.

"Anything?" he asked Deac.

"Nothing yet, LT."

"They got a lot of cover," said Mingola. "They'll get off a shot before we even see them."

"Listen to the optimist over here," Deac said. "I say the wind's working against them."

"Shhh," Hansen ordered. He paused, took a breath, then another, then gasped. He held up his gloved hand. The shakes had definitely returned. And worse, his thoughts were locked on Mingola, the semiblind liar who now threatened the entire crew.

Damn it. I'd been doing so well, he thought. Why was it so easy to slip right back into the worrying, the fear, the paranoia?

And now his arms and legs felt heavy, as though gravity itself were short-circuiting. "Deac, you got anything?"

"Still nothing."

"Don't sound so fucking casual. One shot. That's all it'll take. One shot. Now, do you have anything?"

"No, sir! Continuing to scan, sir!"

"That's right. Gatch? How's our fuel?"

"Uh, we topped off before we left, sir. We're in very good shape."

"Everything else okay?"

"Yup."

"See, it's not me," said Mingola. "It has nothing to do with me. It's all about you. It's all about that little voice in your head that keeps telling you something's going to go wrong. And you think it's me. But it ain't."

Hansen tore away from his gun and barked, "I told you to shut your fuckin' mouth!"

"Troops!" yelled Deac.

Hansen was turning toward his extension when he screamed, "What're you waiting for? FIRE! FIRE!"

Deac cut loose on the coax, the traditional Z-pattern of ball-and-tracer fire turned to scribble-scrabble, as though he were drunk or testing a pen to see if it had ink. The technical term for such firing was *going ape shit*.

"To your right! To your right!" Hansen shouted. "RPG!"

"Okay!" answered Deac.

"You're missing him! You're missing him," screamed Hansen.

"Let me on that fuckin' gun!" Mingola yelled.

"Sit down, asshole!" Hansen said, then opened up on his fifty, releasing a red-hot ribbon that unfurled up the mountainside, toward an ominous silhouette.

"I DON'T GIVE a shit if it's overkill or not," Keyman was saying a half-second before he gave the order to fire.

The tank reverberated, and a HEAT round exploded over the hillside where the lieutenant's men had spotted the troops.

"Did we get them?" asked an impatient Boomer.

"Too much smoke. Let's fire again!" said Keyman.

"I don't have a target," said Zuck.

"And I don't care," answered Keyman.

"Fine. Nothing identified," Zuck said.

"Up!"

"Fire!"

"On the way."

Ka-boom! The main gun coughed up another round that punched the hill, rained snow, ice, and debris, then sent flames wafting through the smoke. Any troops caught nearby were dead. Any caught just out of range had just shit their pants.

"If it was alive, it ain't anymore," said Keyman.

"Would you like to shoot at nothing again?" asked Zuck. "I don't mind. It's easy to aim. . . ."

Keyman's middle finger itched, but he didn't flip his gunner the bird. Business now. Bullshit later. "Red One, this is Red Two, over."

"DEAC, HOLD YOUR fire! Hold your fire!" Hansen was hollering as smoke from that second HEAT round swept down over their turret.

Deac's hands lifted from his controls.

Hansen keyed his mike. "Red Two, this is Red One, you hold your fire, all right? Over."

"Roger that. I think we got 'em, though, huh? Over."

Hansen went into his hatch, figuring he'd survey the hill with his NVGs, but smoke still blanketed the entire area, and another wave of snow had come in as though God were shoveling off His driveway and dumping it on them. The images grew distorted, and he still believed that a few grunts could be hiding up there, if they had fanned out.

Abruptly, the back of his neck tingled. He swung toward Abbot's tank, which was now pulling up the platoon's rear since Neech had gone up front.

That tingle become a horrendous shudder. A troop with a heavy backpack came charging down the steep hill, just behind Abbot's tank.

With about three seconds to get off a shot before the guy was out of sight, Hansen reached for his pistol.

* * *

SERGEANT PARK HAD spotted the soldier, had shouted to Abbot, and was about to say that he couldn't get the coax into position when Abbot told Sparrow to back up.

Just as the tank clanked into gear, muffled gunfire came from outside.

"Who is that?" Abbot cried.

"It's the LT," said Sparrow. "He's in his hatch, shooting the guy!"

Shaking with the desire to find the troop, Abbot burst into his own hatch, Beretta drawn. He glanced over the rear deck, but he couldn't see the ground just behind the tank. He'd have to climb into the bustle rack. "Sparrow. Stop. Move forward!"

Abbot's head whipped back as the tank screeched, stopped, then started back toward the lieutenant's track. After a couple of meters, the enemy troop appeared behind them, lying prone and writhing in the snow.

"Jesus Christ," Abbot said, his breath escaping. "Jesus . . ." He took aim and fired a round at the guy, then another, which struck the troop's backpack.

And suddenly the guy exploded, legs and head flying though a wall of fire and smoke as Abbot turned away, gasping and cringing in shock.

The rest of the crew began screaming, asking what had happened and if he was all right. "I'm good. But that son of a bitch just blew up!"

"Red Four, this is Red One, over."

Abbot went down, grabbed the mike. "One, this is Four."

"What the hell was that?"

"I put a couple more rounds in that guy. He must've had an AT mine in his pack. The thing was fused and ready to go off. I made a lucky shot, I guess. Not so lucky if I would've been closer. Damn. . . ."

"Just glad you're okay. But you know, Blue One should've seen that fucker. They're too far back. Call Black Six and let him know."

"Roger that. And hey, don't stop watching my back. And I'll watch yours. Thanks!"

"You got a deal. Red One, out."

"The LT must be doing okay," said Paz, perking up from his loader's station.

"Maybe better than okay," Abbot said. "Especially when he just saved our asses."

"Sometimes he does bad things," Park said. "But he is good man. Good officer." The KATUSA nodded as though to confirm his own conclusion.

"But you know what, guys?" Paz asked. "We're really pushing our luck now. And that ain't good."

"Paz, I am ready to die," said Sparrow. "But then again, if I go to hell, my days will be spent listening to you bitch and moan about every mission."

"Hey, man, I'm just trying to be realistic, you know? Thought you understood what it means to keep it real, huh?"

"I do. You don't."

"All right, shitbirds, that's enough," said Abbot. "Your nerves are talking. We'll kiss and make up later. Right now I want all of you scanning. Every sense reaching out there. I want you to smell the bastards when they come up. That guy got too close, too fast. That will not happen again."

Although Abbot had spoken firmly, he knew he was asking for the impossible. Once you buttoned up, you had your blinders on and you depended upon your wingman to watch your ass. There was only so much he and the others could do to spot dismounts around their hull—which was why he followed up on the LT's order and got Blue Platoon to move forward.

Once Blue One settled into position closer behind him, Abbot went below. He brushed the heavy snow from his shoulders and lowered his hatch to open-protected. "Does anyone know what's taking so long?" The question was a joke, and he knew it would incite his men.

"What's taking so long? Are you kidding, Sergeant?" asked Romeo. "Those engineers are still standing around, talking about how they're going to do it. And the crunchies? They're still running around, trying to figure out from where they're going to do it."

Abbot smiled. "I mean, come on. Two tanks, two PCs, and some dismounts? That's a walk in the park for this platoon, right?"

"Let 'em take as long as they want," said Paz. "This ain't no surprise party. Just let 'em make sure of that."

The trouble was, the longer the MECH platoon and engineers took, the more time they all had to be cold, bored, worried, hungry, and stressed out. All at once.

Don't think, Abbot ordered himself, realizing he just had. Every time he went to the extension, he first saw Kim before anything else.

Yet this time she looked different, a little sad, and she reached out for him, but he couldn't touch her. He was still too far away.

Just a few seconds later, "Fire in the hole!" rattled over the company net. The Bangalore torpedo detonated, crackling violently like popcorn in an overheating microwave.

"Shouldn't be too long now," said Paz. "Unless the NKs got some other surprises waiting in the wings."

"I'm sure they do," said Abbot. "And we'll deal with them too. First Tank don't fuck around."

"No, Sergeant. We don't."

"Ha! We finally got a warrior among us."

Paz smiled, but the grin turned bitter. "That's 'cause I've made my peace, just like Sparrow. How 'bout you, Park? You ready to die?"

"Die?" The KATUSA's frown tightened. "I will not."

Paz nodded. "That's cool, dude. I like your attitude. I'll box that up and sell it at the flea market back home."

Park waved off the loader. "You crazy guy. Crazy."

"No, I'm just trying to have a little fun. We don't have much time left."

"PAZ!" cried Abbot. "Don't give me that depressing shit."

"Sorry, Sergeant."

"ALL RIGHT, RED Three. The engineers will guide you toward the breach site. The area is apparently secure, over."

Neech snorted over the irony and the lieutenant's use of the key term *apparently*, which translated as "trust no one and keep all fingers on the triggers." "Roger that, Red One. See you on the other side."

"Roger. Red One, out."

Neech ordered Wood to advance. The driver hesitated a moment before throwing the tank in gear.

"You got a hearing problem, Wood?"

"Nope. Just a dying problem."

"Oh, don't worry," said Choi. "We almost die all the time. It's no problem."

"Don't be scared, Wood," said Romeo. "We are so in our zone right now that nothing can touch us. Besides, breaching the wire, shoving a few mines aside . . . it's no big deal, really. Easier than what we've already done, okay?"

"Thanks, guys."

"You didn't know we cared, huh?" asked Neech.

"Well, it's hard to feel the love down here."

Romeo chuckled. "The love *should* be hard. At least that's what my girlfriends say."

"Listen to this guy," said Neech through a chuckle. "What your girlfriends always say is, 'Romeo, Romeo, wherefore art thy hard-on, Romeo?' "

"Wood, do you hear this?"

"Sounds like *wood* is your problem," said Wood.

Laughter did relieve the tension, but the puns were getting beyond bad, and Neech needed to get into his hatch as they rounded the bend and approached the first obstacle. "Okay, guys. Time to punch back in. Let's do this."

The Bangalore torpedo had cut the usual footpath into the first barrier of concertina wire and had triggered a number of mines, the road bearing the pockmarks to prove that.

With a heavy, sulfurlike stench still thick in the air, they lowered the plow and started toward the wire, coils torn apart and hanging like gray spaghetti—yet only Neech, a man obsessed with food—would make such a comparison.

He almost laughed at the engineers as they gave him the go-ahead. They might as well be saying, "This is the way—right through all these mines. Have a nice night."

Although a few tunes might have been in order to take their minds off the deadly task, Neech opted for silence this time. Not even conversation. Just pure, unadulterated concentration. Breaching the four barriers might prove to be the longest tank ride of their lives. And they got to go first. No guts, no glory. Blue Three would mop up whatever Red Three missed, which hopefully did not include Red Three's guts.

Meanwhile, the lieutenant and the others, along with the rest of Blue Platoon, waited for them while the mortars put more smoke on the barriers and the engineers lit off some pots of their own.

Between the falling snow, all the additional smoke, and Neech's nerves, it was a wonder that he could see anything. But he did. And so did Wood, who joined him as they spotted and called out mines ahead.

They cleared the first barrier with relative ease. Neech's shoulders grew a little straighter, and his chin lifted a little higher. There he was, a tank commander in his hatch.

But as soon as they neared the next barrier, he realized that snow had already buried mines that would've otherwise been visible. And that wasn't the only new challenge.

The concertina wire hadn't been cut as neatly, and they ran the risk of damaging the plow's lifting straps if they weren't careful.

Neech had wanted to bolt some wire catchers on the moldboards in front of the straps, but there had been too many other things to worry about, and he had forgotten to ask. They would have to plow and cringe, plow and cringe.

"Would someone remind me to breathe?" Romeo suddenly asked.

"Breathe," said Choi. "It's good habit."

"I don't know, Choi. Without you, man, I just couldn't go on. No way," said Romeo.

"I want to be your best friend," the KATUSA said.

"You got a deal."

"Hey, Romeo," called Wood. "Speaking of deals . . . you said this was no big one."

"No, I didn't."

"Yes, you did. But now you sound like you're shitting a brick. Why'd you lie to me, man?"

"I didn't lie."

"Shhh," Neech said quietly. "Nice and slow, Wood. Nice and—"

There were two reasons why Neech never finished his sentence:

A bell-like clang resounded from the plow, making him believe for a second that they had struck a mine way too hard or had collided with something else, perhaps a piece of the road itself.

Then came a blast so sudden and so near that it sent Neech cowering into his hatch.

"Oh my God!" cried Wood.

"What the fuck?" Romeo echoed.

Neech blinked. "Christ! Was that us?"

CHAPTER
THIRTEEN

WHEN YOU WERE lined up and waiting for one of your mine-plow tanks to breach an obstacle, the last thing you wanted to hear was an explosion.

So when that detonation met Hansen's ears and the black smoke rose and whipped like an ugly black tail, he began to panic. "Red Three, this is Red One, over."

"They must've hit a mine," said Mingola.

"Shut up!" Hansen yelled. "Red Three, this is Red One, over."

Deac glanced back from the gunner's station, his mouth falling open, his eyes lacking focus.

Even Hansen imagined the carnage: Neech lying across his hatch, one arm torn off, the other chewed apart, his face half gone, the tank bubbling with flames. Yes, the crew could, in many cases, survive hitting a mine, but there were often exceptions . . . and deaths.

Hansen was about to call Neech again when Abbot cut in: "Red One, this is Red Four, over."

"Go ahead, Four."

"Blue has lost contact with Blue Three, over."

"And I've lost contact with Red Three, over."

Shit. How could they have lost both tanks?

Then came another voice, one that made Hansen slump in relief. "Red One, this is Red Three. Blue Three has hit a mine! Blue has hit a mine, over."

Feeling at once guilty and relieved, Hansen responded, "Roger that. How severe is the damage, over?"

"Not sure. One side of the plow looks torn up. Wait. TC and gunner are in their hatches. They're waving. They're okay. The tank got hit hard, though, over."

"Roger. We'll send up some help. Continue to advance. Red One, out."

The mine-clearing blade was not mine-proof to be sure, and the North Koreans may have acquired some more sophisticated AT mines, ones equipped with antidisturbance devices or maybe even magnetic and/or seismic fuses that often defied torpedoes and MICLICs. While the mine plows could sometimes withstand as many as three hits before becoming disabled, Murphy's Law had cut that number by two.

As a result, Blue Three was out of the plowing business for the time being and could be out of the fight. Losing a tank would hurt the entire team, but they would make do. Forge on. And fight.

While Neech continued to the next barrier, Hansen turned up the company net and listened to the reports from Blue One, who told Van Buren that Blue Three's track had also been damaged during the explosion and that they were out of the fight. The crew would be loaned out to the MECH platoon. Van Buren would order that all sensitive items be removed from the tank, that the ammo be cross-loaded, and that the vehicle be padlocked motor-pool style, its position relayed for Task Force recovery and repair. Every tank would eventually return to the battle, and every soldier would fight, no matter how.

"Sucks for them, huh?" Deac asked. "But at least that crew will make a good fire team. Every soldier a rifleman."

"Yeah, and Neech and his crew could be next," said

Mingola. "That plow's a huge burden, and he's been lucky so far."

"Neech makes his own luck," Hansen said. "That man will breach these barriers. And he'll be a master gunner some day. You mark my words."

"What makes you so sure?"

Hansen arched his brows. "He's not doing it for himself."

KEYMAN WAS TRYING to explain to Webber, Smiley, and Morbid exactly why he had left the tank, but he couldn't put it into words. Yes, revenge had been part of it, and so had respect, but there had been something more, something he had wanted for most of his life but couldn't get.

Was it power? Love? He just wasn't sure. And that's why he kept chasing it. And that's why they kept staring at him until a nudge at his shoulder jarred him awake.

"LT's on the radio," said Zuck. "Time to go."

"Shit, I actually fell asleep."

"And you were snoring."

"And not a one of you dumb fucks woke me?"

"Just this dumb fuck. Get the radio."

Keyman nodded, rubbed his watery eyes. "Red One, this is Red Two, over."

"Red Two, move out. For the third time, over."

"Roger that. Sorry, we uh, we had a little mechanical problem, over."

"Anything serious, over?"

"Negative. We're good to go, over."

"Roger. Red One, out."

"Hey, Sergeant?" Boomer called. "I hope you didn't jinx us by saying that."

"Saying what? I didn't even mention the word *abort*, did I? No way."

That drew groans from the entire crew, above which Keyman cried, "Driver, move out!"

As they rolled through the first barrier marked by the

engineers' cones, Keyman took a peek through his NVGs, following the highway as it pushed out north between the mountains, then veered once more to the right. You could imagine that every foothill, cliff, crevice, and ravine held troops waiting to unload on you.

Or you could keep your head low and concentrate on reaching the objective: the high ground near Kaesong. You had the choice. Sure, remaining strong was what the crew needed. They were more important than all those feelings knotting Keyman's gut, but he couldn't just stop worrying, stop imagining that he would lose yet a second crew. Webber, Smiley, Morbid, Lamont . . . would it ever stop?

"I am Halitov! And I like North Korea!" the big Russian hollered, then he slapped the handles of his machine gun.

"I am Keyman. And I like it too!"

Halitov shook a fist, then thrust it toward Keyman. They banged fists, then resumed their scanning. Keyman began to relax as they started through the second barrier.

Ahead, the smoke occasionally parted like curtains, and perhaps five hundred meters off lay the remains of the tanks and PCs, fire-filled carcasses surrounded by handfuls of smaller fires, their smoke columns all leaning in the same direction. "Sorry, dudes. Doesn't look like the grunts left us any armor."

"I'll get over it," said Zuck.

Keyman snickered. "I'm sure you will."

"But not me," said Halitov, pounding his chest. "Because I am here to fight!"

"You say that one more time, and I swear to God, man, I'm going—"

"To what?" Halitov asked Zuck.

"Oh, just shut up."

They cleared the second barrier, then the third without incident. They passed through the fourth and final one as though coasting toward the motor pool after a routine training run.

Still, Keyman was wary for anything the engineers

might have missed. Sometimes the enemy liked to leave a few mines well beyond the last obstacle, and those booby traps would literally catch you with your guard down. Worse still, the snow had become the enemy's best ally, and some of the drifts appeared suspiciously high.

"Hey, Boomer, keep right," Keyman ordered, hoping the NKs were as unimaginative as he thought. If they had emplaced a few mines, perhaps they had positioned them in the middle of the road.

Or perhaps they had strung them across the entire area, creating one last barrier that the engineers and scouts had not discovered.

The thought chilled him.

But he had joined the Army to be out in the cold and in the shit. He had trained for the big show. Lights, camera, fire! Time to focus on the war, not the worries. Getting stressed out was the LT's job, anyway, right?

But hell, the idea that Hansen might have a nervous breakdown was yet another source of worry.

"Hey, Sergeant?"

"What is it, Boomer?"

"We're coming up on a pretty big hill. Picked up two, maybe three inches of snow in the past half hour."

"So what? They said Korea was no place for tanks? Let's prove them wrong."

"Oh, I'm not bitching about it. But I do want to slow down. At least a little. If I really wanted to go skiing, I would've gone to Aspen."

"Hey, do you know what real estate goes for up there?" asked Mingola.

"Nobody cares," said Keyman. "Boomer, you slow down. But not too much. In Boomer we trust."

"Oh, that ain't fair. Don't be making those kinds of comparisons." Boomer laughed. "I can't take the pressure! I'm just a simple homey from the hood."

Keyman spat some chew over the side, then took in a long breath through his nose. Damn, he was scared. More scared than he had ever been before. He had jammed his finger into a light socket, and there was no one around to kill the power.

But damn, he felt so alive.

"ARE YOU LISTENING to me, driver? Stay in his fuckin' tracks!"

Gatch had veered perhaps a meter out of Keyman's track trails and already the lieutenant was having a coronary. "Sorry, sir. I'm getting in them now."

Just when Gatch's faith in Hansen had been restored, the man had returned to his paranoia and impatient criticism of everything the crew did. Maybe he was manic-depressive? He was roller-coasting from the highs to the lows the way Gatch's father used to—especially after he had lost a job. His dad would be screaming at and punching Gatch one second, then hugging him the next. You never knew what to expect, and Gatch's mom had grown too tired to cope. Leaving Dad was the best thing she had ever done. For herself. For him. She had taken charge.

As Gatch should now.

They couldn't ride up into the mountains with a stressed-out maniac in command. Someone had to speak up. Mingola was on Hansen's shit list. Deac was too busy—and too excited—by becoming the tank's gunner. It was up to Gatch.

Though he couldn't close his eyes, he stared through the images coming in via his night vision screen. And there was Jesus, climbing off his Harley and waving from the side of the road. Gatch pulled over, opened his hatch, and climbed down from the tank.

"Yo, what up, dog?" Jesus asked.

"Shouldn't you already know?"

"Yeah, right. You want words."

"If I piss him off, he'll just get madder."

"Maybe he's okay the way he is. Maybe you need him just like this."

Gatch shook his head. "I don't believe it. He'll get us all killed."

"Or not."

"Tell me what to say."

" 'Yes, sir.' 'No, sir.' That's all."

Gatch threw up his hands. "You got nothing else? Nothing at all?"

Jesus's eyes widened, and for a moment the beach and breakers shone in his irises. "What do you got for me?"

"What do you want?"

"Faith."

"Yeah, but you want me to just sit there and believe he'll do the right thing? You see how he is!"

"That's right. First Samuel, sixteen seven. Remember? You read it just a few days ago. 'I look beyond the outward appearance to see his heart'."

Gatch closed his eyes. "All right. I'm going to leave it in your hands."

"You're full of shit."

"Hey, you're not supposed to curse."

"It's your head. I can do whatever I want. I'm God, right?"

"Okay, I won't say anything."

"He's talking to himself again," said Deac.

With a hard blink, Gatch was back in the seat, driving the tank. Comforting hands braced his shoulders, and his vision had never seemed clearer.

"Gatch, how's our fuel?" the lieutenant asked.

"Little more than three quarters, sir."

"Good."

"Sir, everything else is in the green. This is like that night when we aced the gunnery. Top Tank. We're going to do it again. Hooah!"

"You got it going on, huh, Gatch?"

"Roger, sir. We all do."

"So now he's gung ho?" asked Mingola with a groan.

"That's right. And I'm not stopping him," said Hansen. "Hooah—you motherfuckers!"

* * *

THE HUMMING ENGINE and clanking tracks lulled
Hansen and his men into silence as they rolled deeper into
North Korea.

Then, about ten minutes after Gatch's little pep talk, a
strange tingling worked into Hansen's neck and crawled up
his face. Would he pass out again? No. He didn't feel light-
headed. He felt an otherworldly calm, like he had dialed
the wrong number on his cell and had connected with the
afterlife.

He looked at Deac and Mingola. They glowed like
ghosts. What was happening to him?

A breath. A blink. A look back to Deac, who was no
longer there. Sergeant Lee glanced back from the gunner's
station. "We are okay. You and me."

"LT, Red Two is slowing down as we approach the hill.
You want me to maintain this position or tighten up?"

That was Gatch, but his voice sounded distant, echoing
through a giant conduit.

"Lieutenant?"

"Uh, yeah, tighten up a little." Hansen caught his
breath and got on the platoon net. "Red, this is Red One.
We have some hills coming up. Be ready for them. Red
One, out."

"Red One, this is Black Six, over."

"Go ahead, Black Six."

"Red, we have lost contact with TF scouts. Could be terrain or weather. Maintain current speed, but keep a watch-
ful eye, son, over."

"Roger that, Black Six."

"Soon as we regain contact with the scouts, I'll forward
their report. In the meantime, we've got FA putting some
fires out there for us. Look for 'em. Black Six, out."

Hansen told Keyman to watch his ass, which the sergeant said he was already doing.

The road swung off to the left, taking them along some
of the steepest hillsides yet, with a tremendous cliff to their

right that would send a tank plummeting a few hundred feet to its explosive demise. A dismounted enemy attack launched from those hills to the left would have to be carefully planned. The men would need to either rappel down or pick their way so slowly and so carefully that they would probably get shot before they reached the road. Of course, there might be a few makeshift machine gun nests or better prepared concrete pillboxes and, perhaps, the occasional AT team set up, but hordes of dismounts rushing their tanks seemed less likely.

But you never knew.

Way off in the distance, through the falling snow, came the shimmer of lights, a carpet of gleaming pinpricks: Kaesong.

An intense barrage of field artillery added larger gems to the carpet, and through the NVGs Hansen picked up the multiple flashes of white across a green-tinted skyline that seemed part of some CNN news report. He had to remind himself that he actually was in his hatch as it was all happening in real time, right in front of him. He had thought the surreal feeling would go away with combat experience, but it just didn't. And it was just beautiful.

Until someone died.

He lowered the NVGs and went down to check his map. The platoon would advance about half a kilometer farther, then move into battle positions to hold the high ground. From there they would wait as the forces defending Kaesong were softened by those artillery fires. Then, with the aid of follow-on forces, they would proceed down to seize the objective. A textbook advance. A rather nasty MOUT fight to follow.

"Uh, sir?" Gatch called. "Red Two is pulling way ahead of us."

"I can see that. Give her the gas."

"We're starting to slip. I have to slow down."

"He's starting to turn around the corner. Don't lose sight of him!"

"I'm trying, sir."

Keyman's lead had grown to nearly fifty meters, and he disappeared behind the hill.

"Red Two, this is Red One. You are out of sight. Slow down. I say again, slow down."

KEYMAN HAD THOUGHT they were making good time, and Boomer, who had been bitching about the hills, had them rolling at a good clip now. When you were good, you were no damned good. "Boomer, slow down, man. We're too far ahead."

"Okay, but wait. I think we got a problem. Oil pressure's dropping fast."

A series of clanks and bangs erupted from the engine, as though they had fed the beast spicy fajitas instead of fuel.

"No, no, no, no, no," cried Boomer.

Next came the creak of metal grinding on metal accompanied by the stench of burned petroleum and grease, along with the lovely scents of singed rubber and wire insulation rising from the rear deck. Plumes of black smoke poured from the tank.

Keyman shook a fist at the heavens. *"Are you kidding me?"*

Boomer pulled to the side of the road, and the engine rumbled, seized up, died.

"Boomer?" Keyman called through clenched teeth.

"Yes, Sergeant?"

"How are you?"

"I'm fine, Sergeant. How are you?"

"Oh, fine, fine. Some weather, huh?"

"Yes, Sergeant."

Keyman bit his lip, cursed. "I shouldn't have said *abort.*"

"Yeah," said Boomer. "She's really blown this time."

"Yeah?"

Boomer's voice lowered in resignation. "Yeah. . . ."

Keyman craned his neck, saw the lieutenant's track coming around the turn. "Red One, this is Red Two, over."

"Two, this is One. I see you. And I don't believe it."

Keyman got defensive. That wasn't the best reaction, but he was too pissed off to think clearly. "Hey, ain't my fault! My driver thinks we've blown our engine."

"You assholes told me you were good to go!"

"Well, we didn't abort. But we didn't know we were given a piece of shit!" Keyman fought back the urge to tell off Hansen, let him have it with the main gun. Expend all ammo.

"Red Two, we're going to keep moving. I'll call Black Six. See what he wants to do. In the meantime, see what you can do. Red One, out."

As the lieutenant's track passed, he called over to Keyman, his tone a notch more civilized. "Hey, if you get loaned to the grunts, I'll see you in Kaesong."

Keyman just nodded, turned back to his limp dick of a tank, and shook his head.

Boomer came across the turret went back toward the bitch plate. "I'm sorry, Sergeant."

"Hey, man. It fuckin' happens. What're you going to do? Throw yourself off a cliff?" He gazed longingly into the shadowy depths across the road.

"I came here to fight!" cried Halitov from his hatch. "Not fix engine!"

"I know, buddy. I know."

Abbot's tank slowed as it passed Keyman's, and the sergeant lifted his voice above the roar of his perfectly-fucking-fine engine. "You really think it's blown?"

"With my luck?"

"Sorry, man. See you down there."

"Yeah."

Then came Neech's track, lumbering up with its big mine plow. Even with all that extra weight, the bastard still had no problems. That was the real miracle. "I could be a wiseass right now," hollered Neech. "But I won't! Good luck, man!"

"You too!"

He veered around Keyman's dead tank, then throttled up and chased after Abbot.

Blue Platoon had once more fallen pretty far behind, though Keyman figured Blue Two, the lead tank, would come thundering up in a minute or two. Those guys wouldn't be as kind as the LT, Abbot, and Neech had. They would taunt his ass, make him feel like an idiot because he was missing his chance to fight the offensive. Keyman would shine up his middle finger in preparation for their arrival.

"Boomer, did you fix this piece of shit yet or what?" he asked, trying to make himself feel better.

"Yes, Sergeant," the driver answered, his voice tight with exertion as he worked on removing the bitch plate. "I've installed the coat hanger, tape, and bike pedals. We just need someone with strong legs. Maybe the Russian?"

"We come a long way to sit on our guns," said Halitov.

Keyman sighed loudly—just as two massive explosions rumbled like earthquakes from far above. "What the fuck now?" he asked, shoving back his CVC helmet. He, along with the others, gaped at the hillside to their left.

"I think we're in trouble. . . ." Boomer sang, his voice going sour as it drifted off.

For a second, Keyman couldn't see a damned thing. He heard the quaking all right. Then he grabbed his NVGs.

Halitov began yelling something in Russian, while Boomer just muttered, "Now I *really* think we're in trouble. . . ."

A wall of tank-sized boulders, smaller rocks, and snow was barreling down the hill, a wall fifteen or twenty meters wide, a wall that would sweep over them in a matter of seconds. The NVGs fell from Keyman's hand.

"That shit's going to hit," cried Boomer.

Halitov grabbed Keyman's arm. "We have to run!"

"No, get below!" he ordered. "Boomer, come on. No time. In the loader's hatch!"

"You don't have to tell me twice." The husky driver scurried across the hull and turret, then vanished below, slamming the hatch after him.

With his heart hammering his ribs, Keyman ducked and was about to slam his hatch shut.

The rumbling grew loader. The tank began to shake violently. He couldn't help himself. He stole a last look.

"Oh my God."

They said tanks were cages of courage, but sometimes . . . they were just coffins.

"Shut the goddamned hatch!" screamed Zuck.

Keyman did—just as the first boulder slammed into their tank with a massive boom.

HANSEN HEARD THE explosions, but he first assumed that FA fires were falling short. He was about to call Van Buren to see what the hell was happening.

But then the hillside behind the tank grew alive, and a glimpse through his goggles had him screaming for Gatch to speed up. "Red, this is Red One. Landslide to our left. Rocks coming down! Red Four, speed up if you can, over."

Abbot's tank sat about twenty meters back, and the platoon sergeant was about to narrow the gap when the first few boulders—rocks the size of Range Rovers—came tumbling into the road, along with a wave of snow. Some stopped dead in the path, while others rolled right off the cliff like giant bowling balls dropped down a flight of steps.

Seeing that he couldn't move forward and that the slide would continue to pound him, Abbot ordered his driver to back up, and Neech, whose tank rolled about fifteen meters behind, did likewise.

"Gatch, stop! Stop!"

"Okay, LT."

"Red, SITREP, over."

He wanted them to answer, to say they were okay, but it seemed the entire mountain was coming down.

SMALL ROCKS AND chunks of ice pelted Abbot's tank, but he remained in his hatch, guiding Sparrow back along the road. Abbot might have been the platoon veteran and been delayed by rocks that had fallen onto the many mountain roads in South Korea, but even he had never been caught in a slide as it happened.

"They rigged this whole fuckin' hillside," Paz said. "Rigged the whole thing to come down on top of us! Command detonated to bury us alive!"

"Shut up, Paz! Sparrow keep moving!" Abbot waved to Neech, who was also backing up as more rocks and boulders collected on the road ahead, cutting them off from the lieutenant. A rising cloud of dust and snow grew well behind Neech's tank, in the area where they had left Keyman, and that drove Abbot below to the radio. He would answer the lieutenant's call, but first he wanted to hear from Keyman. "Red Two, this is Red Four, over?"

"Red Four, this is Red One. I want a SITREP, over."

"Roger that, One. Stand by. Trying to make contact with Red Two. Believe there's another slide near his location, over."

"Roger that. I'll notify Black Six, out."

"Keep moving back, Sparrow."

"And I thought we were on the offensive," the driver grunted.

Abbot cursed through a sigh. "The ball's been intercepted."

KEYMAN CLUTCHED HIS seat as the rock slide continued to pound the living shit out of them. Incoming fire was one thing, and they had all grown used to its sound, but this . . .

All four were squeezed into the turret, dice in a cup, the temperature inside dropping rapidly.

Bang! Another rock. *Boom-boom.* Yet another caroming off. Keyman's eyes felt like they would bulge right out of his head, then roll across the turret floor like aft caps.

"We should have run," muttered Halitov.

"Better we stay here and get buried," said Zuck with a

poisonous grin. "Think of all the money we're saving the taxpayers. Some military funerals are really expensive."

Boomer had his eyes closed. "It's in your hands. All in your hands. . . ."

Something hit the rear deck with a terrible clang, rocked the tank, and Keyman braced himself before being slammed into the wall.

"Talk about getting hit while you're down," said Zuck. "And I thought I'd seen it all."

"Shhh. Listen," said Keyman. "I think it stopped."

An odd sound, like sand being poured from a wheelbarrow, filtered through the hatches. A faint, almost imperceptible rumble slowly died off. The turret creaked like an old U-boat making an abrupt dive, then settled in with more dust sounds.

"I have to pee," said Halitov, tucking one knee behind the other.

Keyman put a finger to his lips, then he went up, tried to open his hatch, but it wouldn't give. "Halitov?"

The loader was already moving toward his hatch.

"Shit. Think about the math here," began Zuck. "We blew our engine right below a command detonated rock slide? What are the goddamned odds of that? I mean God has to be pissed at us—or at least one of us—to pull off something like this."

"Do not talk about pee," said Halitov as he tried his hatch. "Sergeant? Mine is stuck too. But I think I can open with some help."

"Zuck?" called Keyman.

"I got it," said Boomer. He and Halitov squeezed into position, and after several hard pushes the hatch creaked open, sending a shower of snow into the turret. The men swore and flinched, their faces covered. Halitov shivered, brushed himself off, then went up first.

"How bad is it?" Keyman asked.

The loader returned to the turret. "You will not believe. I have digital camera. I take pictures."

"Let me see," said Zuck, rising.

"You wait." Keyman shoved past the gunner and rose into the hatch. One look stole his breath.

The tail end of the tank had been smashed in by two massive boulders, one of which was still lodged in its side. The ammo and other gear that had been stowed in their bus- • tle rack lay strewn across the road. The main gun tube had been knocked askew, then bent down by more rocks. The radio's long antenna had been snapped off like a toothpick.

Four or five more wedge-shaped rocks lay across the front deck, the rest of the tank buried up to the hull by all the snow, ice, and dirt that had been dislodged. The loader's machine gun had somehow survived the onslaught, though Keyman figured it too, had been damaged—the problems just weren't obvious yet.

Damn, when it came to obstacles, you couldn't fault the North Koreans. Their makeshift rock drop was a beautiful one, with Keyman's tank buried to prove it. Even the TF scouts, who had been busy checking for mines along the road and had found none, wouldn't have thought to look for avalanche charges. Now the engineers would labor several hours to blow a path for the rest of the team and free the tank.

The whole operation had turned into a giant shitcicle, and they were all going to take a lick.

Keyman fished out his cell phone, speed-dialed the lieutenant, hoping the man was in his hatch—otherwise he'd get voice mail. What kind of a message do you leave after you've just been buried alive, or nearly so? *"Uh, this is Red Two, requesting a shovel, over?"*

A message flashed on the phone's screen: NETWORK BUSY.

"Fuckin' figures," he groaned.

"Hey, let us out," said Zuck. "The Russian's going to pee in this turret, I'm telling you."

"Just hold on. The ground's still unstable, I'm sure." Keyman thumbed his cell, redialed. *Eureka.*

"Son of a bitch, what's going on back there?" Hansen asked.

"Not even a hello?"

"Talk to me, asshole."

"We got fuckin' buried in a rock slide, man. Crew's okay. Tank is gone—I mean just rocks all over it. The whole road is blocked too."

"Shit, they blew another one up here. That means Abbot and Neech are blocked on both sides, and I'm cut off from everyone else. Hold on."

Keyman waited. The lieutenant muttered something, screamed a curse.

Automatic weapons fire rattled in the distance. Sounded closer. Drummed again. Closer still.

It wasn't their own.

"Lieutenant, what's going on?"

More gunfire.

Keyman's gaze turned to the hillside. No troops yet—but they would be coming. "Lieutenant, you there? Lieutenant?"

CHAPTER
FOURTEEN

THEY HAD RPGS, Molotovs, rifles, pistols, grenades, knives . . .

And a fanatical indoctrination that motivated them to sacrifice everything for the homeland.

There were about a hundred of them. To start. They were sidestepping and sliding and even tumbling down the hill toward Hansen's tank. They were not soldiers but young boys, most likely members of the Red Youth Guard, part of the Worker-Peasant Red Guard militia, a force numbering nearly four million countrywide. They had no uniforms, and some even lacked warm clothing and were fighting on frostbitten feet. That didn't seem to bother them.

"Got a shitload of boys coming down the hill," Hansen told Keyman. "I'm out!" He pocketed his phone, started down into the turret. "Gatch, get us the fuck out of here!"

"We're just leaving?" asked Mingola.

"We're putting some distance between us," said Hansen. "We still got that one AP round, don't we?"

Mingola kneed open the ammo door. "Roger that."

"Load that bitch."

"She's heading for the breach," answered Mingola.

Bad eyes or not, at least he was Johnny on the spot.

"Deac, ready on that fuckin' gun. We're going to paint this mountain red."

"Hooah!" yelled the hillbilly.

"AP round loaded. Loader ready," Mingola reported.

Small arms fire dinged off the hull as they raced forward. At about a hundred meters off, Hansen ordered Gatch to stop and turn the tank ninety degrees, the front deck facing the cliff.

At the same time, Hansen swung the gun tube over the side, putting Deac on the target: the entire hillside, which was now swarming with those young militia.

With his gaze fixed on his extension, Hansen cried, "Deac, ready to shoot those bastards?"

"Identified," answered Deac.

"Up!"

"Fire!"

"On the way!"

The AP round streaked off . . .

And punched a deep hole in the hill like a spear impaling a mountain of mashed potatoes.

"Shit!" screamed Hansen. "No detonation! A goddamned dud! What the fuck?"

"Ain't my fault!" Mingola retorted.

A small explosion tore up the ground a few meters from one of their road wheels.

"RPGs coming in," hollered Deac.

Hansen turned to Mingola. "Load HEAT!" Then he got on his fifty and let fly some ten-round bursts.

"HEAT loaded, loader ready."

Hansen released his trigger.

"Troops identified," said Deac.

"Up!"

"Fire!"

"On the way!"

While the HEAT round would take out far fewer troops

than the AP, it would still do some serious killing by shattering rocks that would in turn kill and wound. That was an old artillery trick. The explosion sent boys hurtling through the air, tore off limbs, sent showers of fire and blood across the snow.

But there were dozens more still coming, and the deaths of their comrades drove them even harder. Several slid down on their asses, firing until they lost balance and broke into rolls. Others literally ran down the hill, trying to keep their balance but dropping like rag dolls, rifles tumbling as they collided with trees.

"Mingola, up top! On your gun! Deac, coax troops! Gatch, get ready to move again!" Hansen reached for the mike. He was trembling so hard that he could barely hold it. "Black Six, this is Red One, over."

"Go ahead, One. What's going on up there?"

"Uh, two, uh, rock slides. I'm forward and cut off from the rest of my platoon. Red Three and Red Four are caught between the two obstacles. Red Two is still stuck in the rear. We got several companies or more of militia coming down the hill, over."

"Roger that. Get me the grid and we'll get some mortars up there, over."

"Negative, negative. We are way too close. Request CAS support, over."

"Red, I'll put in that request. Weather's an issue, as always. In the meantime, MECH will dismount at Red Four's position and move forward to assist, over."

"Roger that. We'll take all the help we can get, over."

"That's right, son. But until you get it, you'll fight and fight hard. Black Six, out."

ALTHOUGH MINGOLA KNEW to lay the loader's M240 machine gun for deflection, knew to fire twenty-to-thirty-round bursts, and knew to use tracer impact to adjust rounds on the target, that didn't mean shit if you couldn't see the bad guys.

Fuck it. The weapon wasn't known for its accuracy anyway. And given the number of troops out there, the chances were high that he'd hit a few.

So he hugged the big metal gun, its vibration coursing through his bones, and continued firing blithely into the blur.

"Won't be long now, Dix," he cried between bursts. "And Carey, you told me so. And you too, Goosey. Remember when we had them pinned up on that ridge? Now that was beautiful. Beats the clusterfuck I'm in now. You seeing this shit? You seeing it? Caught dead to rights in the defile. Cliff on one side, motherfuckers on the other. I'll be there soon."

That wasn't Mingola's depression speaking; he knew what he knew. When you spend so much time knocking on death's door, you begin to hear noises on the other side, and that, of course, makes you believe that at any moment someone's going to answer, a man with black lips, sharpened teeth, and hair permanently on fire. "Hello, there, Sergeant Mingola. You are very, very late. We've kept a place warming for you."

No big deal. He was on borrowed time, anyway. He should've died with his buddies when that mine had gone off. Now utterly resigned to his fate, he made a decision to fight hard-core, the way he knew how. He'd show this crew what he and the old boys were made of. Oh, yes, he would show them.

"But careful now," he grunted aloud. "That muzzle's getting real hot. Don't melt it off, you dipshit."

Rat-tat-tat . . . Rat-tat-tat . . .

KEYMAN WAS GETTING way ahead of himself.

The moment he had spotted the first troops cutting jagged paths down the hillside, the old synapses had begun firing and misfiring like that antique driven by the Beverly Hillbillies.

He had figured that he and the rest of the crew could remove the tank's machine guns, convert them into mobile lead throwers, then grab their two M4 rifles and form one hell of a fire team who would advance north to assist the rest of the platoon.

But naturally, the best laid plans of mice and men had been fucked up by Murphy and the North Koreans.

Okay, while they didn't have time to convert the big guns (and that loader's weapon might be damaged anyway), they still had the rifles and their pistols. Also, a lot of the gear they carried Keyman had customized himself via his own money and several orders placed to a company called BlackHawk Products Group. They had drop leg and assault holsters, Omega tactical vests with mag pouches and A.L.I.C.E. clips, CQB rigger belts, and the three-day assault backpacks jammed with enough emergency rations, first aid, and survival gear to last them at least a week in an escape-and-evasion scenario. In addition, they'd grab the combat lifesaver bag. Shit, if you had to dismount and fight like a crunchie, you might as well do it in style. And so they would, with some of the finest gear money could buy. "All right, you ugly bastards, grab everything you can. We're getting the hell out of here and heading north to link up with the rest of the platoon."

"We do that, we ain't coming back," said Zuck.

Keyman snorted. "You think we should go down the road, crying for help from Blue Platoon?"

"No, I think we should fall back until we have more support. The CO will send Renegade up here. Let's wait for them."

"Maybe he won't," said Keyman. "Maybe they're getting hammered too."

"You are coward!" yelled Halitov, leering at Zuck. "Are you here to fight or not?"

Zuck closed his eyes and sighed. "I thought we could fight smart and hard. But fuck it. Just hard then. Let's do it."

"Wait a minute, Sergeant," said Boomer. "We're all here to fight, but Zuck's right. Let's be smart about this. We dismount, link up with Three and Four, then call the LT, let him know what's happening. Abbot can let the CO know where we are. There'll be a lot guys running around out there. Don't want to catch a friendly bullet, know what I'm saying?"

"Yup. Sounds like a plan," said Keyman, drawing his sidearm. "Let's get going. Can't say I'll miss this fuckin' tank." He banged the wall. "Piece of shit!"

He was out of the turret first, climbed down across the hatch, then fell off. Bang, he landed on his side with a gut-clenching thud. *Son of a bitch!*

"Sergeant, you all right?" called Boomer, who was coming out after him.

Keyman sat up. "How come Rambo never fell on his ass?"

"Good boots? I don't know."

"Well, you'd better move yours. They're coming down."

Boomer glanced up over his shoulder, saw the silhouettes shifting among the trees. "Oh, boy."

Next came Halitov, who rose like a statue, unzipped his fly, then sighed as he drew a steaming arc over the gun tube.

"Jesus, Russian, you'll get shot pissing in the open like that," said Zuck as he shifted past the loader.

Halitov glanced up at the advancing enemy, then he drummed a fist on his chest and pointed up the hill. "I piss on you!"

When the Russian finished, he ensured that the radios were "zeroized" so they contained no crypto fills. Then he quickly assembled a little surprise for the enemy and snapped a few pictures with his little camera so they'd all have bragging rights. That done, he joined them on the opposite side of the road, trailing two wires.

They huddled behind two rocks resting near the edge of the cliff and waited as the troops eased down the hill, a few slipping and sliding from tree to snow-covered tree. Boomer kept watch over one flank, while Zuck focused on the other.

Keyman lowered his goggles. "They're all just kids. Militia out here."

"You feel bad for them?" asked Halitov.

"I feel bad they got turned into robots. But I'll still kill them. You ready?"

Halitov nodded. Two Claymore mines sat on the turret, aimed directly for the hill. Halitov controlled one, Keyman the other.

"We have an expression in English," Keyman began. "Curiosity killed the cat. Have you heard it?"

"No. But I understand. We have similar saying in Russian. A man who puts his face in woman's crotch may smell something bad."

"Are you serious? Dude, that's a funny saying."

"I know. But I lied. It is not Russian saying. I just think of this."

"You're a weird fucker too, huh?"

"This going to be a cultural exchange or what?" asked Zuck. "I thought Mr. Cockbreath was here to fight. I thought you were too."

Halitov shook his head. "He is coward."

"No," Keyman said. "Just impatient. And a little scared like all of us. He'll learn. Trust me. I was there."

"Okay."

"But what makes you so fucking fearless?"

"I want to be hero."

"That's it?"

"Yes."

Keyman hid his grin. "Okay. Here come the first few. Let 'em get real close. Oh, yeah, baby. Come right in. Stick your faces right in there—and you'll smell something bad—at least for a second."

Six or seven figures dressed in tattered parkas and carrying AK-47s mounted some of the boulders near the tank. They drew closer as another dozen descended within range of the mines. *Yeehaw!* At least ten more were on their heels. For a few seconds, the wind howled through the defile, then the place grew quiet again, giving way to Keyman's pulse thumping in his ears. *Relax.*

Halitov nodded, resumed surveillance through his NVGs.

"Oh, look at this party," Keyman said, losing his breath in anticipation. He was almost drooling.

"Okay, one's shouting," said Halitov from behind his goggles. "They must see the mines."

"Ready?" Keyman asked. "On three. One, two, three!"

The Claymores went off, a pair of thunderclaps inside the tight bag of the passage. "Surprise. . . ."

As the booms and shrieks of men being dismembered where they stood echoed across the road, Keyman signaled the crew to take off. They weren't sticking around for this week's episode of Gore TV. They had things to do, more people to kill, farther up the road.

DOZENS AND DOZENS of young men toppled into a juice-maker of coax, .50 caliber, and 7.62 mm fire from the weapons on board Abbot's and Neech's tanks. The bloody bodies were piling along the roadside, appendages jutting up here and there like little red trees. Others lay sprawled against the white, as though they had been making snow angels before choking on their own fluids.

As one squad dropped, another replaced it, and the butchery kept on and on, growing more brutal, more horrifying, and ironically more impressive to Abbot because they just threw themselves into the fray, as though deaf, dumb, and blind to the carnage. Mindless attackers. Absolutely mindless, their brains so utterly washed that you couldn't find a speck of fear or any other original thought inside. Unaffected, they watched their brothers die, then joined them. What did it take to get men to die so willingly? Remind them they had nothing to lose? And were they really that patriotic? Or were they more afraid of their commanding officers than of the enemy? They were at once pathetic . . . and chilling.

Because the road offered no good battle positions in which to shield their hulls, and the cliff kept them wary of straying too far, Abbot and Neech had positioned their tanks back to back, like a couple of wild west heroes caught in a ring of Indians. For the time being, they leveled their attackers before any could near their tanks.

But now the boys were driving more fiercely down the hill. A few even clutched AT mines to their chests and were going to slam themselves into the tanks, but Abbot and Neech cut them down at the roadside. Twice the mines went off, taking with them all the boys standing too close. Still more of them had attached shape charges to the ends of long poles. They wanted to get in close and jab those explosives into the tanks' tracks in an attempt to immobilize them. So far, none had survived the unrelenting barrage spewing from the American guns.

Abbot reached for the mike. "Red Three, this is Four. How's your ammo, over?"

"I'm about half into my fifty. Less than half left for the coax. Same goes for Choi's two-forty, over."

"Roger that. I'm about the same, over."

"I'll fire the main gun at these fuckers if I have to, over."

"Me, too. But hang in there." He switched to the company net. "Black Six, this is Red Four, over."

"Go ahead, Red Four."

"Any news on that CAS you promised us, over?"

"I put in the request. Weather's still a factor, but they're seeing what they can do. Still no confirmation yet, but we now have a dismounted force attacking the company trains to the rear, over."

Abbot swore under his breath. Now that the company team was being attacked from the rear, the chances of them getting help in the form of air support—or any other form for that matter—were fading fast. He had heard the lieutenant reject the suggestion to put mortar fire on the hillside, but Abbot felt certain that he had good grid coordinates and that the risk to himself and Neech would be minimal. Time to grab those mortars before another PL did—or before they came under attack themselves. "Roger that, Black Six. Request fires on the hill, grid coordinates to follow."

Yes, he was overstepping his bounds, and he did consider calling Hansen to assure him that they would be okay. But fuck it. They were under attack and he had to act.

Captain Van Buren and FSO Yelas would get the job done, all right. But would the mortars be enough, and would they arrive in time? Well, he wouldn't know unless he tried. He read off the coordinates and was setting down the mike when—*boom!*

A whoosh and a powerful explosion ripped across the turret, sending flames and debris tumbling down through the open loader's hatch.

Paz was still up there, manning his machine gun. He didn't move as flaming fragments tumbled past him.

"That was RPG," screamed Park, jerking back from his scope.

"Paz?"

Abbot reached up, grabbed Paz's hip. The man wasn't moving. Groaning with exertion, Abbot pulled the loader from the hatch and fell back with him into the turret.

"Oh, no . . ." said Park, gagging.

Abbot held his breath, forced another look.

Poor Paz's arms were gone. His CVC helmet tilted back, revealing that he had no face, only a blackish-red oozing mask. His skin was still smoking. And the smell . . . *Oh my God.*

"Fuck this shit," said Sparrow. "Sergeant, can I move?"

"Move!" Abbot echoed.

Sparrow threw them in gear, sent them barreling forward.

Another something—RPG probably—slammed into the hull, knocking Abbot and Romeo to the floor.

"Sparrow, what the fuck?" cried Abbot.

"They're blitzing now, man. Guys everywhere! Maybe a few companies. Pretty well armed. Some RPGs. Guys in the road now. Whoa! Just knocked too down!"

"Park, get back on the fuckin' coax," Abbot ordered, picking himself up, then clambering into his seat. He manned his fifty as Sparrow took them up the road, away from Neech and toward an oncoming wall of troops.

"Red Four, this is Three," called Neech. "Don't leave me, man!"

"Don't worry, Three, we're not. Just taking—"

"Two more RPG," hollered Park.

A one-two punch struck the road wheels and sprocket. After a loud creaking, they rattled to a stop.

"Sparrow?"

"That's it!" answered the driver.

Another RPG struck somewhere to the rear, possibly the bustle rack.

"More RPG!" Park reported, then he let loose a battle cry and leaned into his controls, the coax wailing in accompaniment.

Abbot grabbed the mike, raised his voice. "Red Three, maneuver as best you can to avoid that RPG fire, over."

"Roger that!"

Park squeezed off coax fire in remarkably precise bursts, shifting effortlessly from target to target in one of his most violent killing sprees. Abbot let his fifty do the talking, punching big holes in a few guys to their right flank. So many militiamen swarmed down the hill and spread across the road that he couldn't be sure which ones were carrying RPGs. They all looked the same, and an aching feeling rose in his gut.

"Red Four, this is Red Three. I've taken two hits from RPG fire. Loader's weapon is gone, over."

"Roger that, Three. Keep evading and fighting. Mortars should be here soon."

Oops, maybe Hansen had heard that. *Oh, well.* Then again, the lieutenant had probably listened to the request in the first place. He still hadn't said anything, though. He must be as busy as they were.

"Oh, Sergeant," Park said, wearing his tightest grimace. "Paz is still making very bad smell. Very bad."

"I know," Abbot said, his eyes burning, voice cracking. "But we ain't dumping him. Fucking nut knew he'd go. Brave son of a bitch took them all on. And so will we! Boys, KILL 'EM ALL! KILL 'EM ALL!"

With a curse and a rustle of boots, Sparrow dropped into the turret, all lean and mean, a pistol in his hand, a brother ready to get it on. Abbot smiled inwardly. The driver would bitchslap those NK motherfuckers if he had to. "What? We ain't going anywhere. And I ain't sitting in that hole without a chance to fight. Give me one of the rifles."

Abbot shoved the M4 into the driver's hands. "Knock yourself out, Mr. President."

Sparrow holstered his pistol and returned to the loader's hatch, where his rifle announced that he was in the fight.

Abbot squeezed off a few more bursts, tracers lighting the road, his gut aching even more.

They would, at any moment, get overrun because far too many kids were punching through their wall of fire. As he hosed down the next squad of attackers, he reached out for Kim, who took his hand and caressed it, placed it on her cheek, and whispered, "It's okay."

Park beat a fist on his Cadillacs. "We must do something more!"

Abbot wrenched away from the vision. *Do something.* Where were those fucking mortars?

Okay. Think. Maybe the main gun would stall them just a little longer. "Sparrow, back down here. Load fuckin' HEAT!"

WOOD WAS CRYING, and Neech wanted to go out there, rip open the driver's hatch, and smack the kid back to reality. The tank was still mobile, but the kid wasn't responding to commands.

"Goddamn it, Wood! Take us back to the fuckin' boulders. Get us right back there! At least they can't surround us!"

But the tank wasn't moving.

"Wood!"

Neech went ballistic. In the middle of all that incoming, he drew his pistol, climbed out of his hatch, then kicked away piles of brass casings as he climbed down to the driver's hatch. Small-arms fire whistled and rang all over the place, but he was so pissed off that he barely noticed. He lifted and swung aside the hatch, then recoiled as gunfire stitched within a few inches of his knees. He craned his head toward the hill. "Fuck you!" Then he shot a look down into the diver's hole.

Wood faced him with swollen eyes.

"You goddamned pussy! You will drive this fucking tank right now!"

The driver's face creased and reddened.

"Wood, goddamn it!"

"We're going to die!"

"Drive this fucking tank! Now!"

"Yes, Sergeant!"

The kid threw the tank in gear, throttled up hard, just as Neech holstered his pistol.

"Wait!"

Famous last words.

Neech lost his balance, fell back off the hull and rolled overboard amid a shower of more brass.

With a sharp thud he hit the snow, sensing the ice below, his breath torn from his lungs. He rolled.

Strangely enough . . .

The ground disappeared below him.

And then, as he dropped through midair, he realized they had been way too close to the cliff.

The cliff! Goddamn it, what a fucking stupid way to die!

Another boom. And he stopped. Lay there. Where was his breath? He gasped. Thank God (the guy whose name he had just taken in vain. . . . *Sorry*). There. Breathing now. He was on his belly. Pushed himself up onto hands and knees, flickered open his eyes. Where the fuck was he?

Lightning bolts of pain ripped through his elbows, and the wind came so harshly that he could barely see. But he saw enough. A chill gripped his entire body.

He had fallen about a meter or so and was on a jagged ledge below the road, a ledge maybe three feet wide and about twice as long. Any more momentum and he would have missed the it. Oh, he would have eventually hit the mountainside, where he would have tumbled like an extreme skier whose ego and adrenaline addiction had finally reached critical mass. Maybe he would have survived. As a quadriplegic. With a tube to breathe through and others for shitting and pissing.

Another chill seized him.

Carefully, he pulled himself up, making sure he had good purchase, one foot firmly planted on the snow-covered rock, the other tucking in close to the hillside, where a slight indentation caught the front of his boot. His chin barely cleared the road, yet between two rocks and a lump of ice he could see what was happening up top.

Shit, his arm felt warm and funny. Then a stab of pain. He'd either been shot again or had torn the bandage during his fall. The arm had been feeling better. But not now. It really ached, and he had to climb.

Or maybe he shouldn't. What he saw out there made him want to cower against the rock.

Wood was driving the tank, all right, heading straight toward the hill and into a massive swarm of dismounts numbering at least a hundred, maybe more.

He mowed down about ten guys, but three had managed to leap onto the hull and were climbing across the bustle rack, heading straight for the loader's open hatch.

At the same time, a bunch of assholes with shape charges on their long poles were moving in toward the tracks and road wheels, getting ready to disable the tank.

Romeo was too busy raking the shit out of the guys on the hill to see what was happening.

Choi, who must have heard the bad guys in the bustle rack, got in the loader's hatch, did a jack-in-the-box while wielding his M4, and—*bang bang*—he blasted two motherfuckers in the face.

But the third got him by one-handing his AK and delivering a brushstroke of fire across the turret and into the KATUSA's chest.

"Popeye" Choi, the South Korean who loved fried chicken, the man who had talked sense into Neech when he had been freaking out over Batman's death, shook like a doll, then fell back, lifeless, across the turret.

Neech screamed, tried to pull himself up over the edge. The arm screamed back. He threw up his leg. No use. With the bad arm he couldn't get enough leverage.

He was fucking stuck. Stuck in a private seat to watch his entire crew die before his eyes.

Shape charges went off, and a cloud of smoke began to swallow the tank—but not before Neech saw one kid pry open the driver's hatch and drop a grenade into the hole. Another was about to do likewise down the loader's hatch when Romeo burst up, shot him in the head with his pistol, swung around, shot two more guys. He cursed in Spanish, his voice hollow and strained.

And then he was gone in all that white.

More gunfire. A scream. Romeo's? A sick roar from the militia boys.

They had killed a tank and its crew.

"Oh, dear Jesus. Dear God," Neech said, swallowing, trembling, about to vomit. He shivered through his breath, fought off the heaves. Drew the sidearm at his hip.

Suddenly, after a few shouts in Korean, a squad-sized force began running east down the road, back toward Keyman's tank.

Neech reached into his pocket for his cell phone, pulled it out. The screen was cracked, the battery broken off. He tried to get it working. Nothing.

He realized only then that he didn't hear Abbot's tank any more. Didn't hear anything except the wind, the shuffle of troops, the cries in Korean, and his heartbeat.

Were they all dead? Was he the only one left?

A minute passed. He tried once more to fix the phone. Light flashed briefly on the busted screen, but the battery wasn't making good contact. He fiddled some more, his hands shaking.

Footfalls sounded nearby. He tensed, drew his weapon, shoved his head against the cliff and stole a peek.

Miracle. It was Keyman, doing the hunched over boogie

dance down the road, keeping to the hillside but veering around the smoking silhouette of Neech's tank.

The militia had no doubt left a few squads behind, but they hadn't seen Keyman yet. They were too busy sitting on their asses near the trees and smoking cigarettes, while a few of them stood near the burning tank for warmth.

Oh, man, it was beautiful. Keyman and his crew took down those guys near Neech's tank with the whispering violence of SpecOp warriors—and they were just a bunch of DATS, dumb ass tankers who weren't supposed to know their asses from their elbows. They rocked.

With the tank inspected, they were getting ready to move on, and Neech was beside himself with frustration.

Keyman paused, panned around with his NVGs, probably searching for him. Neech had to get their attention without alerting the other guys on the hill.

How? Wave? Scream? Throw a goddamned pebble?

Shit.

And so Neech watched them vanish one by one into the ditch alongside the hill, leaving him alone.

He fell back onto the rock, then slid to his rump. He sat there another two minutes, feeling sorry for himself and fighting back the tears as he thought of his crew, replayed each of their deaths, flinching in sympathetic pain. He couldn't believe they were really gone. And now living felt like punishment.

But for what? What the hell had he done to deserve this? He had come back strong from Batman's death, driven his crew to new heights, guided the platoon through obstacles, contributed to the company team's efforts the best he knew how.

And this was his reward? What else did God want from him? What else? What the hell was he supposed to do now?

He could just wait it all out. And then, if the team secured the road, he would be rescued.

Yet how would he explain winding up on the cliff? They would say he had pulled a Keyman: he had abandoned his crew, but instead of going after the assholes that had threatened his tank like Keyman had, they would think Neech had run off to hide like a coward. He would never live it down. He would be disgraced.

Fuck that shit. He'd go out like a man. Fuck the pain in his arm. He was getting off the fucking ledge. Now.

With clenched teeth he hauled his ass over the ledge, rolled onto the road, the rushed up to his feet, leveling his pistol. "All right you godless sons of bitches! Are you ready to get fucked up?"

Was it an act of suicide?

That depended upon your point of view. He was attacking the enemy. The odds of victory were slim to none. He knew beyond a shadow of a doubt that he would die. But he was just doing his job. Like his crew had. Like every soldier should, with a weapon in his grip and a curse on his lips.

He was an army tanker. First Tank. 1st Battalion, 72nd Armored Regiment. Crusaders!

And he would let those assholes know it.

He paraded across the road, chest thrust out, pistol leveled at the troops who were now coming out from behind the trees, a few laughing.

Neech stopped. Glanced over his shoulder. Pins and needles spidered across his arm.

The sky opened up, mortars exploding all over the hill with hellacious thunder, light flickering. *Boom!* A nearby concussion knocked him onto his rump.

The militia boys were running, screaming, dying, as a dumbfounded Neech scrambled to his feet.

Boom! Boom! Boom! Boom!

He saw an opportunity, seized it. Bolted up the road.

He wasn't running from the enemy. He was running to link up with his brothers.

It would be better to die in their company, in the company of great men at arms. *Hooah!*

CHAPTER
FIFTEEN

AN RPG IGNITED the last of the ammo in Abbot's bustle rack. Rounds began to cook off in a cacophony of small bursts that rang through the turret.

Meanwhile, Park's hungry coax could no longer be fed. He released his last burst and shouted something in Korean that even Abbot did not understand.

Sparrow, who had ducked inside as the rocket had whistled toward them, returned to the loader's hatch, jamming a fresh magazine into his rifle, his last. He was a maniac, going up there with the ammo still doing a Jiffy Pop number, but he didn't give a shit. At least the open hatch would shield him a little.

Within a minute, Abbot's fifty would be dry. *Oh, well.* They had dressed the tank in hot brass for her final departure. . . .

But then, glory hallelujah, the mortars arrived! Not in the nick of time, but he wouldn't bitch. They were falling far up the mountainside, into the zones Abbot and his men couldn't reach with their main and machine guns.

Park shifted out of his gunner's seat. "I want to go up top."

"Sit down."

The gunner reached for his pistol.

Abbot gasped.

But Park simply freed the weapon, brought it to his chest. "Please, Sergeant. My country. My fight. Let me do my duty."

Abbot dropped a palm on the gunner's shoulder. "Wait."

After a quick scan of the hillside, still rumbling with mortar fires and draped in wind-whipped clouds of smoke, Abbot targeted a few more militia guys and unloaded his fifty until it clicked empty. Had he hit them? He couldn't tell. He nodded at Park. "Sparrow? Get down here. Let Park up top."

The driver didn't answer, didn't move.

"Sparrow?" Abbot shifted to the loader's hatch and squeezed up. The lean black man lay unconscious on his back, blood dripping from his neck. "He's been hit!" Abbot checked for a pulse, got a weak one. "But he's still alive!"

While Abbot struggled to lower Sparrow into the turret, Park went for the combat lifesaver bag.

Abbot nearly broke his back wrestling the driver below and propping him up in the loader's seat. He removed the young man's helmet, then instinctively tucked the driver's head into the crook of his arm and held him for a moment.

Sparrow couldn't die. Not before he became president of the United States. It wasn't his time.

But now there was only the expectation that the driver would die. Sparrow was a son, a dying son, and there was no greater pain than losing a child. Abbot's chest felt so tight that he could barely breathe, and it seemed every muscle in his body was rapidly shrinking.

Park dropped the lifesaver bag at Sparrow's feet and began to rifle through it.

"Do what you can," Abbot said.

While the KATUSA got to work, Abbot went into the hatch, taking up Sparrow's rifle. He gritted his teeth. Time for payback.

Despite the heavy mortar fire, a few squads of those Youth Guard troops had made it onto the road, and at least three individuals were running forward to get good shots with their RPGs while a squad to Abbot's left was hitting the tank with small arms to keep him buttoned up.

Okay. His tactical experience kicked into high gear. He had analyzed the situation and needed to use what he had. *Okay. Okay . . .*

He went below. Park was applying a big trauma bandage to a wound behind Sparrow's ear. Damn, there wasn't time. "Park, stop what you're doing."

"But he is bleeding very bad!"

"He won't make it! Stop what you're doing and load sabot!"

The KATUSA rose, kneed open the ammo door, and withdrew a round from its tube. Seconds later he cried, "Sabot loaded, loader ready!"

Abbot lowered the gun tube to fully horizontal. The round itself might not hit the boys with the RPGs, but when fired, the sabot's petals would separate from the penetrator and cartwheel through the air, becoming lethal instruments themselves. Like all experienced TCs, Abbot was well aware of the safety hazards associated with firing sabot rounds in the vicinity of friendly dismounts.

The key word here was *friendly.*

Which these guys weren't.

Clenching his teeth, Abbot fired the main gun from his position. As the aft cap clattered across the turret floor, a flash and smoke tail began dissipating over the troops' heads.

And damn, the penetrator must have actually hit one guy, who had simply vanished. The petals had decapitated another, his head still tumbling across the road. Another guy who had miraculously survived screamed and broke off, running toward a stand of trees about six meters up the hill, joined by a few other troops.

"Load HEAT!" Abbot cried.

Park slammed the next round home into the breach block. "HEAT loaded."

Abbot had them now. Once again the round would strike high because he couldn't depress the gun tube low enough; however, the detonation would create a mini-avalanche amid all the shrapnel.

He fired. Didn't wait to glimpse the results. "Keep loading HEAT till they're all fucking gone!"

"Yes, Sergeant! We will kill them all!"

There was no question about Park's loyalties. He had made peace with himself . . . so he could go to war.

The round was loaded.

Abbot fired at the hill again, suddenly traversed the turret. Heat loaded. *Fire!*

The gun boomed, and the tank jerked back.

Two RPGs hissed in from somewhere above and exploded in succession across the forward deck.

Then came another, sending a shower of flaming debris down into the open hatches. Abbot paused, cursed, slammed his hatch shut, while Park did likewise with the loader's.

He traversed the turret again. God, they were trapped—but they would fight even after the main gun ammo ran out. Those young men with cobras' eyes and hearts even blacker would come, and Abbot and Park would go hand-to-hand. They would go out kicking, screaming, spitting.

"Someone firing from along cliff!" Park cried. "Someone firing! Maybe dismounts from MECHs!"

Abbot raised his head, gaped through his hatch's vision blocks.

Muzzle flashes. He pricked up his ears. Heard the distinctive pop of AK-47s. "Shit, just more bad guys."

"Then why they shoot across?"

Another look confirmed that whoever was out there was targeting the militia. "Damn, I don't know who they are, but we ain't stopping them."

KEYMAN WRENCHED FREE the empty banana clip, jammed a fresh one home, and went back to work, giving the North Korean boys a taste of their own ammunition.

He and his crew had "borrowed" a half dozen AK-47s and rucks full of spare magazines from those other guys back at Neech's tank, and now they were happy to return them to the NKs, ammo first, rifles later.

Keyman glanced sidelong at his war companion. Oh, yeah. The guy was Halitov. And goddamn it, he was definitely here to fight. It felt damned good to be with him. Halitov was as serious as a brain surgeon, doing a little brain surgery of his own on the enemy. *Bang!* Another headshot. Keyman grinned. "Keep it up, you fucking Russian. Whack those motherfuckers! You are the baddest motherfucker out here! Shoot! Shoot! Shoot!"

"Yes, Sergeant!"

Zuck and Boomer had paired up and positioned themselves about twenty yards farther up the road, closer to Abbot's tank. The platoon sergeant was clearly on his last legs, firing HEAT rounds to keep those kids from getting too close. So far the ploy was working, but it hadn't stopped a few of those RPGs, and it wouldn't be long before some asshole with brass balls decided to sneak up on them.

And that's what Keyman and his crew of newly minted crunchies needed to prevent.

Too bad Abbot wasn't up top. Keyman would give him a ring on his cell; they could cavalierly bullshit about sports and the weather as though they were driving on the freeway instead of sitting in a defile, in a snowstorm, in a kill zone, in North Korea, in the middle of a goddamned war with an enemy who was forcing them to expend all of their ammunition.

"Okay, let's move again," Keyman said, his crunchie senses tingling. Still, you didn't need super-powers to realize that muzzle flashes betrayed your position.

He and Halitov skulked off along the edge of the cliff, coming within a meter of the drop-off, the damned snow collecting in his eyelashes and playing havoc with his pace. He slipped twice, then a third time, his breath gone for a second as his boot reached the very edge, a few rocks tumbling into emptiness and falling so far that he never heard them hit bottom. *Whoa. Way too close.*

Just ahead lay a little impression, the cliff edge sloping off more gradually. Halitov saw it, dove to his belly, and Keyman slid in beside him.

"What happened to Neech?" asked the Russian as he reloaded.

Keyman began reloading himself. "Shit, you imagine they dragged him out of there? Took him as a POW?"

"I don't want to imagine. Maybe he ran."

"You mean he left his crew? Bullshit. He's here to fight too."

"I hope so."

"Hey, look at those two fuckers!"

A pair of troops came hustling down from the hill, RPGs slung over their shoulders. They crossed to the back of Abbot's tank, where a few rounds were still cooking off.

Zuck and Boomer, who had moved up as well, blasted them, and one guy dropped, but the other took a round, staggered to his knees, then lifted his RPG and fired at the back of Abbot's tank before dropping face-first in spasms to the snow.

KA-BOOM! The M1A1's turret blow-off panels flew off, venting the explosion away from the guys inside.

But then the TC's hatch popped open, releasing a puff of heavy white smoke. The Halon fire-suppression system had gone off, and Abbot and his men needed to get the hell out of there. No time to mask up. They'd hold their breaths and bail. "Give 'em cover!" Keyman ordered Zuck and Boomer.

The gunner and driver began laying down a fierce wave of suppressing fire.

At the same time, two RPGs screamed in from the mountains.

Keyman's men ceased fire a half-second before the explosions engulfed them. It all happened in the blink of an eye. In a single breath.

Mr. Chip-on-his-shoulder Zuck, the mirror image of the

old Keyman, and Mr. Miracle-worker/tank-driver Boomer, the most clever and fearless driver Keyman had ever known, had been swept off the earth, ashes to ashes, dust to dust.

He wanted to shout their names. Opened his mouth. Looked at where they had been. Flaming appendages lay everywhere, with a headless torso appearing through the smoke. No time to register the shock or gag from the odor.

Abbot was climbing out of his hatch while small-arms fire chinked and sparked around him as though he were part of some bizarre Christmas display. He leaned over and began hauling Sparrow out of the hatch, smoke still wafting around them. If the platoon sergeant had not taken at least three or four rounds, it would be a miracle. At the same time, Park rose into the loader's hatch and began picking off troops with his rifle.

"Let's go," Keyman shouted, eyes wide on Halitov.

They dashed across the road, gunfire tracking and tossing up divots of ice into their path until they reached the tank, ducked behind the road wheels.

Then, ever so slowly, Keyman mounted the hull, but when he got up top, he found Park slumped in the hatch, blood pooling beneath him. Abbot lay face down on the turret, with Sparrow next to him. Neither moved.

"Sergeant!"

Still taking heavy fire, Keyman crawled over to Abbot, took the man's hand.

The platoon sergeant stirred, gave a weak smile. "Get 'em, Key. Go get 'em."

"Not without you."

"Fuck me. I'm happy right here. Couldn't end any better. Get the fuck out of here. They'll blitz any minute when they realize it's just you assholes."

A shadow appeared from the corner of Keyman's eye. He whipped his head around . . .

And there was Neech, climbing up the turret. "Let's get him down."

"Hey, fucker. We found your tank. Where the hell were you?"

"Long story," Neech answered, his tone hard, defensive. "Come on."

Keyman shot him a dirty look. "You get Sparrow. I got him. Halitov, you big prick, get up here and get Park! No, wait. You stay down there and cover us. Okay, let's do it!"

Halitov wormed his way around the back of the tank, then he dropped to his gut beneath the track, tucking himself in close before firing at the troops behind the nearest trees.

Keyman reached for Abbot, who was no longer moving, his eyes shut. No carotid pulse.

You were the best, old man. . . .

In truth, Abbot had died back when his wife had been killed. And if there was any justice at all, then he was with her now. Always.

Keyman dragged the platoon sergeant off the turret, across the hull, and then gingerly set him on the snow. It took a Herculean effort to accomplish that, and where he found the strength he didn't know, but it was there, his pain dulled by shock.

"Goddamn motherfucker!" Neech screamed, rolling off the turret and slamming hard onto the icy road. His leg twisted at an improbable angle. Broken, no doubt.

But that was the least of his worries.

Keyman crawled over to the moaning TC. "Aw, shit man, they got you in the jugular."

Neech began panting, blood squirting between his fingers. Keyman spotted two more holes in Neech's Nomex, near his right shoulder.

"I know it fuckin' hurts, man, I know," Keyman said.

Neech's eyes grew emphatic, and he flinched hard through all the pain. "You'll . . . tell . . . my dad. Won't you?"

"I, uh . . ." Keyman could barely face the man.

But that didn't matter. Everywhere he looked there was death.

They were all going to die.

And Keyman couldn't bear it. The tears flowed freely, and his lips began to tremble. "Fuck you, asshole!" he whispered. "Fuck you."

"Tell him."

Keyman bit his lip. The Koreans, the gunfire, the cold, the snow . . . they meant nothing. He was breaking down, ready to collapse into a deep sob.

But he fought it by imagining himself standing there, speaking to Neech's dad, telling him what a brave soldier his son had been. He couldn't deny this poor guy that much. He just couldn't. He needed to live. Needed to do that. Goddamn it, he would hang on!

"Don't worry, buddy. I'll tell him. I'll tell him everything."

Neech smiled, then his eyes went vacant.

A collective roar came from the mountain, followed by a single, familiar shout: "I AM HALITOV, YOU MOTHERFUCKERS! I AM HERE TO FIGHT!"

Halitov released volley after volley, but then a pair of RPGs howled in and hit the far side of the turret.

Keyman tucked his head into his chest, and the bursts rang out so loudly that his eardrums felt as though they had been ripped from his head. He and the others had replaced their CVC helmets with the ones worn by crunchies, and you heard it all when you donned those.

His ears kept ringing, but above that din, a little voice inside rose and told him to get the fuck out of there. Get past the guilt. They could recover the bodies later. But he had to live for Neech. For everyone. And living meant leaving.

"Halitov! Let's go!" He seized his rifle and took off running up the road, the smoke from the RPGs camouflaging his exit.

He threw a look over his shoulder. No big Russian pulling up the rear. "Halitov?"

Aw, shit. With a palpitating heart he charged back, neared the tank, staggered forward, stopped.

There wasn't much left of the Russian who had come to fight.

Were Halitov gazing upon the scene from that great motor pool in the sky, he would be doing so with great pride. He had been destined to die in a blaze of glory, and both the fires and the fame were now his. He was a tanker. A warrior. And those who had fought with him would never forget.

Eerie shouts in Korean echoed from the mountainside.

Oh, God. Keyman was the last man standing. No, not a man, a little boy alone in the woods, breathless and shaking.

What was he doing? *Run! Run!* He sprinted across the snow, about to wipe out with every step.

Ahead lay a wall of shadows: the rock slide that had cut off the lieutenant. Keyman bounded for it, never once looking back. He reached down to where his cell phone should be clipped at his waist. It was gone.

ABBOT'S LAST REPORT echoed in Hansen's head: "Red One, we're dead in the road. One casualty. Lost contact with Red Two and Red Three. . . ."

And that was it. No one was answering. Should he call Captain Van Buren?

There shouldn't be any question. You lose contact with your platoon and you call the CO. No-brainer.

But Jesus Christ—to admit he had potentially lost his entire platoon?

He'd rather cap himself than do that. Besides, there was always hope.

But what were he and his men doing now? Behaving like cowards. They had returned fire for a while, then Hansen had ordered Gatch to take them up the road, away from the rock slide. He figured they should at least see what lay farther ahead, perhaps another obstacle or maybe even some BMPs, BTRs, tanks, what have you. The road had turned lazily to the north, and they had stopped, surveyed, reloaded, and waited. The gunfire behind grew more distant.

He tried contacting the rest of the platoon. Nothing. Again. And now he couldn't even receive transmissions via the company net. Terrain interference no doubt. *Wait a minute.* If he could raise the FSO, he could call in more mortars, maybe even call them in on his own position, have them fire airbursts with variable time "VT" fuses while they kept buttoned up. All those fragments would keep his tank clean of troops, at least for a little while. He had the FSO's cell phone number. He got up in his hatch, dialed. NETWORK BUSY. Shit.

Maybe the MECH FO team would come forward, and Hansen could relay his request though them.

Or maybe they'd all die first.

"This is the most fucked up mission I've ever seen," said Mingola. "The rest of the platoon is dead because our fearless asshole leaders didn't plan this properly. We should have had more scouts, immediate CAS support, and nonstop artillery fires all the way in."

"LT, permission to grease this whiny cocksucker right now?" asked Deac from behind his gunner's sight.

Hansen cleared his throat. "Permission granted."

Deac formed a pistol with his fingers, aimed it at Mingola. "Boom! You're dead. Now shut the fuck up!"

"Gatch, take us to the rock slide," ordered Hansen. "We're getting back in the fight."

"Hooah!" cried the driver, then took them around, heading down the road.

"This is bullshit," said Mingola. "There is no fight. It's us on the wrong side of a massacre."

"Get out," snapped Hansen.

"Excuse me?"

"I said get up into the hatch, climb down, and get the fuck off my tank."

Mingola's lips curled in a sarcastic grin. "Why don't you leave? I'm not the one having the nervous breakdown."

Somewhere deep in Hansen's heart, in a place he rarely visited, came a distinct crack, a crack he had heard only once before, when he had fired the main gun and killed Sergeant Lee. He threw open his holster, whipped out his pistol, aimed it at Mingola. "Get out."

The gunner folded his arms over his chest. "No."

"The safety's off. I'm going to kill you, then throw you over the side, you lying little motherfucker. I thought maybe you'd come through for us. But you're a selfish prick. So get the fuck out. Fight your own war."

Mingola laughed. "This is bullshit. You won't fire that gun in here."

"Deac, get him up into the hatch, so I can shoot him."

"You got it, LT." Deac removed himself from the gunner's seat and went toward Mingola, big paws extended.

The skeleton in Nomex lifted his bony fingers. "All right, all right."

"No, it's not," said Hansen. "Too late. Deac, get him the fuck out of here."

"LT, you serious?"

"I said, GET HIM THE FUCK OFF MY TANK! RIGHT FUCKING NOW!" Hansen's cheeks burned, and he had spat through his words.

"Yes, sir." Deac took Mingola by the shoulders. "I can beat the shit out of you until you pass out. Or you could just go. Which way you want it?"

Mingola leaned around Deac, putting bug eyes on Hansen. "Lieutenant, you really mean this?"

"You got ten seconds," said Hansen, his innards tightening even more.

"Hansen, you're a sick motherfucker, you know that? I'm going to make it back there, and your career will be over. You understand, you fucking butter-bar piece of shit?"

Hansen began counting backward from ten.

Mingola climbed into the hatch. Deac followed and closed the hatch, then they listened to Mingola climb down into the bustle rack.

"Sir, he's only got a pistol. Not even a ruck," said Deac.

"I know. You're back to loading."

"Sir, this is crazy."

"I SAID, YOU'RE BACK TO FUCKING LOADING, YOU REDNECK ASSHOLE! YOU WILL LISTEN TO ME—OR I WILL SHOOT YOU IN THE FUCKING HEART!"

"LT?" Gatch called. "Don't worry, man. We're here and ready to go. If Mingola makes it back, we'll just say he went AWOL. It's three against one. He lied to us about being okay. You did the right thing, sir. And we're good to go! We got Jesus on our side, and no one can stop us."

"No, Gatch, I didn't do the right thing. But I thought it would make me feel better. I still feel like shit."

"It's all right, LT. We'll all be okay."

"Yeah, we will," Deac said.

Hansen didn't believe that. He was spiraling downward, no end in sight. The shudders kept coming, along with the strange noises, the voices, the feeling that he had failed and now it was time to pay for his mistakes.

"Okay, coming toward the slide," said Gatch. "Got muzzle flashes on the hill. Troops! Troops!"

KEYMAN SLIPPED INTO a narrow crack between two boulders, then, hunched over, pushed himself deeper inside while glimpsing the defile ahead. The welcome hum of an M1A1's engine grew louder, along with an unwelcome flurry of shouts in Korean and gunfire. He dropped to his belly, crawled to the edge of the boulder on his right, then reached around for his NVGs.

He could barely see straight. He had lost his tank, lost his crew. For the second time. But he wasn't to blame, and every one of them had fought hard, fought valiantly.

A couple of blinks to clear his eyes. Then . . . there they were. Those bastards in the hills.

Hansen's tank appeared from the gloom, rolling straight for him. The LT must have figured he'd back up to the rocks, use them as partial cover to make his last stand.

What they could use now were more mortars, but there was no one but Hansen to call them in. Would he?

Maybe, maybe not. The tank turned a little, and Keyman zoomed in with the NVGs. "What the fuck?"

"DEAC, COAX THOSE bastards," cried Hansen. Damn, he was manic, depressed one second, feeling a burst of adrenaline the next. "Gatch, get us as close to the cliff as you can, then tuck us up tight to the rocks. I'll swing the turret around. We can't shoot high, but we'll shoot what we can."

"Yes, sir!"

Gatch increased throttle. Deac began firing at the troops along the mountainside, and Hansen traversed the turret, keeping them on the targets. Then he got on his fifty and went to work, suddenly feeling a huge pang of regret in kicking Mingola off the tank. What had he done? That was insane!

"How many you think, Deac?" he asked.

"I don't know. Couple squads. They probably sent the rest of those assholes back toward Blue Platoon. Who knows?"

"Who cares," said Gatch, nudging them into the rocks. "Just please kill them. Okay, LT? Are you liking this spot?"

Hansen stole a quick glimpse through his open-protected hatch. "Good Gatch. Be ready to haul when I call."

A slight rustling noise came from the turret, and Hansen shot a look over his shoulder, then up toward his hatch. "What the hell was that?"

"HEY, ASSHOLE? OVER here," Keyman stage-whispered.

Mingola, who had just climbed down from Hansen's turret, leaned over and scrambled toward the rocks and boulders.

"What were you doing up there?"

The gunner shifted in beside Keyman, the rumbling tank and rock slide shielding them both. They spoke in a rapid fire, lifting their voices above the echoing guns. "The fucking lieutenant kicked me out."

"He what?"

"He kicked me out. But I stayed up there. Figured I'd hitch a ride toward the rocks. Maybe get picked up. What the hell happened to you?"

Keyman just looked at him.

"Are you kidding me?"

Keyman turned away.

"Oh my God. You're the only one left?"

"Yeah."

"Jesus Christ! This is it, then. We all die in this fucking hellhole."

"Not me."

"Oh, really? You got a plan?"

"If the LT stays with his tank, he'll die like everyone else. We have to let 'em know we're out here. Have him ditch the tank. We'll fall back, set up a perimeter, and wait for CAS or follow-on forces."

"He'll never do it. He's fucking nuts. He'll die in there."

"Not if I can help it."

Just then Keyman bolted from behind the boulder, ready to rush up the tank's forward slope.

But the whoosh of incoming RPG fire sent him diving for cover.

THREE, MAYBE FOUR explosions shook the tank, armor groaning, and Gatch expected that at any second the lieutenant would order him to pull out of there.

"Deac, whack those bastards who shot us!" hollered Hansen.

"I can't reach them!"

"Figure it out! Fire on the turret. Mingola, get me the extinguisher!"

"He's not here," Deac told the lieutenant.

"Then you get it!"

"You want me to get it or shoot those bastards!"

"Fuck! I'll get it myself!"

"Sir, you want me to get us out of here?" Gatch asked.

"Fuck no! We're Red One! Were here to fight!"

And here to die, Gatch thought, struggling to trust in the lieutenant. Struggling even more to trust in God.

He closed his eyes, searched for Jesus. Heard the

Harley, saw Jesus roar up and lift off his helmet. He cocked a brow. "Have faith."

"Sorry, dude. I can't!"

"Holy shit!" screamed Deac. "They're coming down the hill with big poles and charges. We should get out of here!"

"No, we're staying!" ordered Hansen.

"I'm sorry, LT. I'm sorry, God. But we're not." Gatch threw the tank in reverse and pulled away from the rocks.

"Gatch, what're you doing?" cried the LT.

Though Gatch could barely keep his trembling hands on the T-bar, he guided them away from the slide. He had turned his back on God, on the LT, and on his own career.

Because he was too damned scared to do anything else.

THAT GATCH WAS right wasn't the point. That he had disobeyed a direct order made Hansen so furious that he was about to go up top, rip the driver out of his seat, and beat the living shit out of him.

But he didn't. He kept firing viciously at the oncoming troops, dozens of them who just kept coming, kept dying, didn't give up. Ever. Some came so close that the fifty-caliber rounds literally lifted them from the snow and hurled them across the road.

Gatch mowed down a few militia, turning them into tank grease as they backed away from the rocks, but then another wave came.

And these new guys weren't militia but North Korean Army regulars, better equipped and better trained, perhaps a recon squad who had linked up with the Youth Guard to join the battle.

"Gatch, take us back to the rocks, goddamn it!"

"Negative, sir!"

"Gatch, I swear to God, man!"

"Sir, I don't want to die!"

"Gatch, I'm telling you. Take us back to the rocks. We're going to dismount and get the fuck out of here!"

"If you don't listen to him, I'm coming down there," said Deac. "I will do it, you fuckin' midget!"

"Shut up, asshole!" Gatch slammed on the brakes, then started back for the rock slide, passing into an incredible wave of incoming small-arms fire, perhaps fifty or more shooters positioned along the mountainside. It was déjà vu—another gauntlet with them caught in the middle.

Hansen swung the turret, got on his fifty, brought down four guys who looked like scrawny, barefoot pole-vaulters trying to get near the road wheels with their shaped charges.

As the tank neared the slide, Hansen sensed that more militia and recon guys were coming down the hill, and he was right. A whole line of them formed a side-winding snake whose skin flickered with muzzles flashes.

"LT, you seeing what I'm seeing?" Deac asked, his voice low and shivery.

"Yeah, I do."

Although it wasn't IAW—in accordance with—the Geneva Convention, and was an act of total desperation perpetrated by only the most cold-blooded killers, Hansen decided to do it.

There were just too many troops, and he couldn't reach the FSO on his cell phone for those airbursts.

He had no choice.

One of the six-barreled M250 grenade launchers mounted on the side of the turret was already pointed in the direction of the mountainside. "All right, boys," Hansen cried. "You watch this! They want to fuck with us? Fine! Now they say hello to Willie Pete! Grenade launcher!"

All hatches were already closed. Hansen held the launcher's READY/SWITCH to READY. "Okay, here they go!"

Three white phosphorous smoke grenades burst from their barrels, struck the mountain, and exploded, sending showers of burning material all over any troops within a 160-degree arc and within about fifty meters, though the wind would mess with those numbers. That was inconsequential. The effects would be devastating enough.

"Dear God, forgive us for what we do," Gatch said with a gasp.

As long as there was oxygen, the chemicals would keep burning, and water wouldn't help. Even a speck on the skin would sizzle all the way through to the bone and keep on going. The pain would be unimaginable, the effect on morale complete.

There it was. Hansen had just sentenced those men to slow, excruciating deaths, and he had just become—some would argue—a war criminal.

A peek through his extension was almost too much. Guys were running in and out of the smoke, flapping their arms like birds, some clutching their hips, faces, abdomens. They screamed, cried, tried to put out their burning skin with snow, with gloves, with each other. Some shrieked, faces twisted in the most horrible kind of agony. A few even shot their comrades to put them out of their misery.

And what did Hansen do as the tank rumbled along toward the next cluster of troops?

He fired again! Three more grenades hurtled toward the enemy, burst in blinding balls, tiny novae that lit up the entire mountainside like "deathday" candles atop a giant white cake. The troops scattered like roaches from the lethal spray, though most didn't make it. They were consumed by the light, their deaths thankfully unseen.

"LT, man, oh my God. I can even smell them now," said Deac, beginning to dry-heave.

But Hansen did not hear the loader. A serial killer had crawled inside him, was directing his thoughts, his body, his soul. All he could think about was killing the next troop, every sense focused on that. He feared that if didn't keep fueling his rampage—if he let up for just a second— then his worst fears would come true.

CHAPTER
SIXTEEN

WHAT KEYMAN WITNESSED through his goggles was so ghastly that even he, a confessed warmonger, had to look away and swallow the bile rising in his throat.

But then that twisted side of his personality took hold, and he lifted his goggles and glimpsed the shrieking souls, young men who were burning alive. He whispered a curse, as sickened as he was amazed. Jack Hansen was a fuckin' Nazi out there, an executioner without conscience. *Holy shit.* But it had to be done. No question about it.

"I told you he's insane," said Mingola. "Fuckin' Willie Petered them all. The Crispy Critter Society will have him court-martialed for that."

"Fuck them," said Keyman. "There ain't no fuckin' rules. Not out here. We kill 'em any way we can. Now, soon as he gets close, you cover me while I get up near the tank. I want Gatch to know we're out here."

"What? No cell?"

"Where's yours?"

"Didn't pay the bill. Shit. You know what? Let's go. Those grunts from Renegade are probably close."

"You stay here and cover. Otherwise, when we get back, you'll be carrying your nuts in a paper bag. You read me, asshole?"

Before Mingola could answer, the tank rushed up, and Keyman shoved his rifle into the gunner's hands, then sprang to his feet, threw himself up onto the forward slope, and rapped on the driver's hatch vision blocks.

A few NK assholes fired three-round bursts from above. He ducked and cried, "Mingola, you cocksucker! Cover me!"

But the skinny runt was gone.

"You son of a bitch!" Keyman wrenched up his pistol, took a few shots, just as Gatch pushed up and slid aside the driver's hatch.

"Keyman? What the fuck?"

"Tell Lieutenant Dickhead I'm out here. Tell him to disable the tank and meet me back in the rocks. You stay here, you're going to die."

"He knows that. He was talking about the same thing. Where's everyone else?"

"It's just me and Mingola!"

"Mingola? That asshole? I thought—"

"Shut up! Come on!"

With that, Keyman slid off the forward slope, then started toward the rocks.

His leg jerked. Air blasted from his lungs. Then a sharp pain ripped up his calf and hip. He put his left foot down. And fell. The leg felt damp.

At that second an RPG struck the tank, even as Gatch was closing his hatch. Keyman rolled away from the blast, slamming into a boulder.

Behind him, Gatch let out a blood-curdling scream, then went silent.

HANSEN REPEATED THE man's name. "Gatch?"

The driver would not answer.

"They got him!" cried Deac. "He's fucking dead!"

The loader started toward his hatch, but Hansen seized his arm. "Stay down."

"Hey, assholes," Gatch whispered through the intercom, his voice freezing Hansen and Deac. "I'm fuckin' hurt bad. But I ain't with Jesus yet. Keyman's out there with Mingola. Everyone else is . . . gone. They're waiting for you. Get the fuck out of here."

"You're coming too!" said Deac, choking up.

"You know, I wanted to be holy. But not like this."

"Don't joke, you little prick," cried Deac.

"I'm not. I hope I'm right enough with God. That's all." Gatch coughed, made a gurgling sound.

"Gatch?" Deac called.

Just a hum through the intercom.

"GATCH? TALK!"

Hansen closed his eyes.

"LT, we have to go!" urged Deac. "Fuck getting permission. I'll get the backplates in the breach, then get the grenades and zeroize the SINCGARS. We'll disable the tank and get Gatch. That's it."

In a combat zone you shouldn't take time to mull things over. You shouldn't take time to feel.

But Hansen had just learned that he had lost his entire platoon. Only one TC left. Now his driver was probably dead. The mission was over. They had failed, had been defeated. Red Platoon was no more.

Hansen leaned forward, opened his eyes, and thought he was going to throw up.

But then the turret walls collapsed, and the floor rose to swallow him.

BACK INSIDE THE crevice between the rocks, Keyman wrenched off his belt, fashioned a makeshift tourniquet around his leg. At least he had a clean entry and exit wound, though both hurt like motherfuckers. He glanced up, couldn't understand why no one was leaving the tank.

But then Deac rose into the loader's hatch. "Key? Gatch's hurt! And the fuckin' lieutenant passed out!"

"Shut up, asshole! I'm hit, too. Do something to bring the LT around!"

Gunfire drove Deac below.

A shuffle to the rear. It was Mingola crawling forward.

"Where the fuck where you?"

"Dude . . ."

"I said, where the fuck where you?"

"Dude, I . . . I can't see."

"Oh, Jesus fuck! Well, I got shot, you little turd!"

"I would've shot you, asshole. I can't fuckin' see!" He blinked hard. "I can't!"

"Give me that fuckin' rifle." Keyman yanked away the weapon. He got up on one leg, then began hobbling toward the tank.

"Where you going?"

"Thought you couldn't see?"

"It's blurry. Comes and goes. Where you going?"

Ignoring Mingola, he reached the tank, crawled up and across the still-hot slope, drawing a few rounds from the trees somewhere above. He reached into the driver's hatch and put a hand on Gatch's neck. Cold.

Poor guy. Keyman had secretly admired the driver. He'd had a big mouth but the guts to back it up. He could even get himself laid, no small feat given the mistakes God had made on his face. The Army had lost a great tanker.

"Keyman?" Deac called. "I need help! I tried whacking the LT's chest. No good. I can't find any of that smelling salts shit. He won't wake up!"

"You checked the lifesaver bag?"

"Yeah! Can't find it!"

At that, Mingola burst from the rocks, ran up to the tank, and scaled the forward slope like he was born to it. "Hey, dipshit," he called to Deac. "Let's go. Grab that pull handle on the back of his Nomex, the one under the Velcro flap behind his neck. We'll use it to haul him out."

"Can you see?" Keyman asked the gunner.

"Coming and going now. But I don't need eyes for this. I want Hansen to make it—so I can burn him when we get back."

"Fuck you, you little runt. You get up there and bring him down. Now!"

"What about Gatch?" called Deac.

Keyman's voice dropped. "He's gone. We'll have to come back for his body. I'll cover you assholes. Get it done!" Keyman slid down, off the tank, then limped back to the rocks.

Another shot boomed, and his good leg gave out. *Fuck!* He'd been hit again, fell to the snow, pushed himself into the crevice, thought of checking the wound, but couldn't. He had to cover Deac and Mingola. The second wound felt very wet. He set his jaw, groaning. Even the slightest movement sent needles up and down his hip.

Dizzy now with pain, he grabbed a few magazines from his assault pack, dropped them by one knee, slid against the rock for support, then lifted the rifle, ready to fire into the trees directly opposite the tank. A silhouette shifted between the trunks but was gone before he could fire.

The leg burned now. At least the fresh wound made the other one feel better, but what kind of dumbass logic was that? Hey, when you were shot up and desperate . . .

Meanwhile, Mingola, who lay flat on his belly, reached down into the loader's hatch, ready to receive the lieutenant.

That he and Deac would need to haul an unconscious Hansen out of the tank while taking heavy fire was just par for the fucked-up course. Murphy was hovering over the whole scene, laughing his ass off while these pathetic mortals fought to defy him.

Mingola got Hansen into the hatch, then, with Deac pushing from inside, dragged him out and across the turret.

At that moment, gunfire from the mountain died off. And for a few seconds, Keyman wondered what the hell was happening.

If Murphy had anything to say about it, then an antitank team was getting ready to fire at them. The end would come swiftly.

But then Keyman heard them, the militia, spread out among the trees, shouting in Korean, almost in a song, a strange song obviously meant to taunt them. First a few voices. Then dozens. Then a few words in English: "Fuck you, American! Fuck you!"

They were having fun watching Mingola and Deac trying to get Hansen down from the tank. Not one of them even fired. They had joined old Murphy, and it was the strangest thing Keyman had ever seen, and the moment that Hansen was safely on the snow and behind the tank, he opened fire, emptying a clip before rolling back into the crevice. "Fuck me? FUCK YOU!" he shouted back.

Oh, shit. He'd woken them up all right. No more taunting with the words. They were back to lead, rounds chiseling at the rocks, debris flying in all directions.

Deac and Mingola carried Hansen toward the boulders and were about to set him down when three RPGs struck successive blows, all directed at the tank.

However, the shrapnel was flying high, and Deac must have caught a piece in the back because down he went, his face creased for a second before going limp. He hadn't made a sound.

Mingola fell himself, but he kept dragging Hansen, pulled him into the crevice as Keyman shifted out of the way. "Are you hit?"

"I don't think so."

"Get him all the way back."

"He's fuckin' heavy!"

"Like I give a shit? Do it!"

Holding his breath against the pain, Keyman pushed himself forward, came up beside Deac, nudged him, checked for a pulse. The snow beneath the loader was drenched red. "I'm glad he didn't see this," Keyman whispered in Deac's ear. "I know he liked you. And I know you and Gatch are the motherfuckers who put lipstick on me. I'll meet you in heaven—or in hell—for payback."

Keyman had never mentioned the incident to them because really, it had been his own damned fault, drinking too much on Christmas Eve, making an ass out of himself, passing out, and inviting a prank by Hansen's crew. Keyman had figured that one day, when the timing was right, he'd spring it on them, tell them that he knew, that Webber had broken down and finally told him what they had done. He would never get that chance, not in this lifetime anyway.

Three rounds tore into Deac's torso, robbing any doubt of his passing. With a grimace, Keyman took his cue. He dove back for the crevice, then elbowed his way inside. Both legs were throbbing now.

The shouting behind him sounded closer. The NKs were coming down to follow and finish them.

And the situation was not exactly in hand. Mingola could run, but he was mostly blind.

Keyman could shoot, but he couldn't run.

And Jack Hansen couldn't do jack shit. In fact, Mingola would have to carry him. But then who would carry Keyman?

"Aw, fuck," he said aloud, continuing on through the rocks. "I wanted to die in a big fuckin' tank battle, and you give me this? Crawling like a roach? Come on . . ."

WAS IT A dream? Hansen was strapped to a spinning disc and a squinting Mingola was throwing knives at him. A prickling sensation erupted in his arms, his legs; then suddenly the ground spun; he sat up, leaned over, and opened his eyes.

His cheeks sank. *Oh, no.* He puked. Coughed. Dragged a sleeve across his mouth. Looked around.

He was seated on the snow, big rocks to his right, something far uglier to his left: Mingola. The gunner sat on his haunches, grinning crookedly. "Some fuckin' PL you are."

Hansen grabbed him by the neck, dug icy fingers into the guy's flesh.

"Hey, motherfucker!" the gunner gasped. "I dragged your passed-out butt off the tank and saved you!"

After a few hard blinks, Hansen relaxed his hand, released Mingola. *Oh my God.* He had momentarily passed out again. "Where's Deac?"

Mingola shook his head. "And Gatch too."

Hansen's hand went reflexively for his eyes. He was nanoseconds from tears when a shuffling sound from behind startled him.

Keyman crawled up, threw out his arms and just lay there, panting.

Hansen rolled over, went to him. "Jesus Christ, Key, you're hit."

The TC looked up, his face half-covered with snow, the rest equally pale. "We have to go. They're coming."

"That's right. But where do we go?" asked Mingola, bearing his trailer-park teeth. "We're fucked!"

"Wait? Listen," said Hansen. The faintest thumping of rotors sounded between the gusts of wind. "Finally, that fuckin' CAS."

"Just in time," Keyman said bitterly. He rolled onto his side, clutching his hip. "First aid in my pack. Get me a bandage or something. This fuckin' hurts."

"It's all right, Key. We'll patch you up. Just not now. Mingola, help get him across my shoulders. You take his rifle and his pack. You cover us as we go. We'll stick close to the mountain. Maybe the guys way up top won't see us."

"And I definitely won't see them," said the gunner.

"Again?" Hansen asked.

Mingola nodded.

"Fuck. You just stay right behind me."

"Yeah. I will. I can see pretty good right now, considering this fuckin' weather, but I don't think it'll last."

"Just leave me, LT," Keyman said. "Give me the rifle. I'll hold them off and buy you some time."

"No." Hansen lifted Keyman to a seated position, then, with Mingola's help, hoisted the TC across his shoulders. Keyman couldn't help but moan as Hansen shifted to balance the weight.

"You're fucking killing me," the TC said, nearly out of breath. "Leave me here."

"I can't."

"Why?"

"*I can't.*" Hansen staggered away from the rocks. "Mingola?"

"Right here."

"Stay close, man."

Now it was all about the boots. Keep them moving. Hang on tight to Keyman. Listen to make sure Mingola was keeping up. Listen for those choppers. . . .

And those troops shuffling down from behind.

He hadn't thought to ask if they had disabled the tank. Screw that. He couldn't worry about it now. Worry about getting away, linking up with anybody who didn't want to shoot them.

The snow, which had been coming in waves, tapering off for several minutes, then falling much more heavily, was now really coming down, and Hansen muttered, "Thank you, God."

They shifted about ten meters down the road, working along the ditch that ran parallel to and abutted the mountainside. He asked Mingola what it looked like behind them.

"Can't see shit."

"Does that mean you really can't see, or that the snow—"

"I'm talking about the snow."

"All right. Key, how far back is Abbot's tank?"

"Ten, fifteen minutes, maybe. They probably got a squad or two still there."

"Fuck 'em."

"Yeah."

Hansen refused to let his mind wander to those dangerous thoughts. He felt so guilty for passing out, so responsible for the loss of his platoon, so overwhelmed by it all that he was ready, really ready, to take that bullet, end the pain.

But Keyman didn't deserve that. And even the asshole Mingola didn't. He would do everything he could to save them. Call it reckless courage, but reckless only in regard to his own life. He was expendable, as long as he got them back. And really, there wasn't any time to feel bad. Action, reaction. And ride the adrenaline.

"LT, if we make it, I'm telling the CO what happened. What you did," said Mingola.

Hansen snorted. "Are you asking me to shoot you?"

"If you don't shoot him, I will," said Keyman.

"I'm serious," the gunner said, hardening his tone.

"You dragged me out of the tank to tell me this?" asked Hansen.

"That's right. Oh, shit. It's getting dark again. Real blurry. Slow down."

"That's karma," said Keyman. "Biting you right in the ass, you little fucker."

"LT, slow down!"

"Stop screaming, you asshole!" cried Keyman.

"Both of you shut up," ordered Hansen.

After three more steps, gunfire cracked from just above, puffs of snow forming lines a few meters to Hansen's right. "Mingola, move it!"

Hansen quickened his pace, unable to glance back, the rounds booming loudly now, drowning out everything, even his own breath hanging thickly in the air. Keyman moaned, kept saying, "You got it. You got it. You got it."

The boots, the boots. All about the boots. Moving steadily. Machines. Don't slip. Don't fall. Don't worry about the gunfire. Just move. Action, reaction.

And Hansen did, the pace now a near-jog that had Keyman gasping as his wounded legs bounced across Hansen's shoulder and back.

Time for an asshole check. "Mingola?"

The gunner didn't answer.

A few more rounds echoed, then it was just his boots thumping against the hiss of falling snow.

"He must have fallen back there, maybe got shot," said Keyman.

"I'm putting you down for a minute," Hansen said, shifting closer to the mountain. He lowered himself to one knee, then slowly slid Keyman off his back. "Here's my Beretta. Last mag, so take care. I'll be right back."

"I don't believe this. You're going after that fucking coward blind piece of shit?"

"I know, it's insane, right?" Hansen winked and took off.

Without Keyman's added weight, he could race along the ditch, even occasionally slide and jump over the smaller drifts.

Sure, a weight had been lifted, but what he carried inside . . . *Shit.* No one would understand.

"Who's that?" said Mingola, sitting against a rock and waving the rifle in Hansen's general direction.

"Hold your fire. It's me, asshole."

Mingola slumped and started to cry.

"Aw, come on. Thought you'd be happy to see me. Get up. Let's go."

"I can't see anything now."

"Give me that AK."

The gunner offered the rifle, and Hansen snatched it away. "Grab onto my back."

"I thought you'd leave me."

"No one—even an asshole—gets left behind. And don't worry. Spill your guts to the CO. I don't give a shit."

"I won't."

"That's too bad. Because I will. Move out."

Hansen kept a solid, if not blistering, pace. Mingola tugged hard on the back of Hansen's Nomex, but he kept coming. They reached Keyman without drawing a single shot. Then again, the temperature had dropped several degrees and anyone outside was freezing his ass off, just like them.

As Mingola was helping Hansen get Keyman onto his back, several volleys of automatic weapons fire rained down from a long ridge to their left, followed by another volley coming from across the road, near the cliffs: a goddamned crossfire.

Mingola grunted and dropped to the snow, just as Hansen turned to watch, Keyman draped across his shoulders. The gunner lay face down, unmoving. "Aw, fuck, they got him."

"Go!" cried Keyman.

"Mingola?"

"He's gone!" Keyman snapped, then he elbowed Hansen in the back. "Run."

Hansen did. But you wouldn't call it running.

More gunfire.

His leg gave out. He dropped to one knee. But he didn't fall, shifted Keyman, regained his balance.

Bang! A round nicked him in the side. Nicked him? Maybe not. Maybe he'd been hit hard. He felt weak. Then came a stinging pain that tightened his gut. But he couldn't give up.

More gunfire. *Just keep going.*

Keyman was back to whispering: "You got it. You got it."

Another wave of gunfire. And then, from the blinding clouds of snow appeared the outline of Abbot's tank. Some cover right there. Maybe bad guys right there too. He couldn't consider that. Just had to get out of the fire.

His arm jerked. *Fuck.* Shot again. *Bang!* Another round hit him in the ass. He trudged on three more steps, four, five. "Key? I'm sorry, man."

Hansen dropped to his knees, then, unable to bear Keyman's weight any longer, he released the TC and fell forward into the snow. His cheeks should sting. They didn't. He was growing numb, pleasantly numb.

"LT?" Keyman crawled around, pushed Hansen onto his side. They lay there now, facing each other, as another volley of automatic fire cut through their trail.

Hansen grinned weakly, then reached down for the pocket watch, for Karen.

"What're you smiling for, you dumbass?" asked Keyman. "They got you good."

"It's okay. I just want you to know . . . I'm not a coward. I'm not."

Keyman shivered. "No, sir." His eyes grew wide. "NO, SIR!"

CHAPTER
SEVENTEEN

KEYMAN DECIDED THAT he wouldn't play dead, hoping the troops would pass by. When those fuckers came down from the mountain, he would ambush them, empty Hansen's pistol, then get shot and go out like a man. Hansen would have done the same thing, if he hadn't lapsed into unconscious. God, the lieutenant was bleeding badly, but he still had a pulse.

For a few seconds, as the gunfire began to taper off, Keyman thought of crawling away. Call it human preservation, selfishness, or just plain being scared to die. What would it be like? Was he right with Jesus, as Gatch had been talking about all the time? Or was there just nothing? All that religion just bullshit, people trying to feel good about leading pathetic little lives, believing it all meant something when they were just spinning their wheels. Damn, that would suck. There had to be more. Just had to be. He asked God to give him a sign.

And holy shit, God did. Brought those damned choppers even closer, still in the distance, but loud enough to know they were well within range. Keyman lifted his head.

With a clatter of distant thunder, the mountainside surrendered to an onslaught of Hellfire missiles that raked the living crap out of the place. The explosions were so intense that Keyman threw himself over Hansen and just lay there for several minutes, covering his ears and listening to the bombardment. With every burst, he prayed the next wouldn't get any closer, prayed the shrapnel wouldn't blast down and kill them. Wouldn't that be the ultimate kick in the ass?

And then, the booming faded. New sounds: gunfire. Recognizable. Yeah. M16 fire. Growing near.

He opened his mouth, wanted to scream. His lips were frozen and cracked, his voice straining. "Over here."

Like they had heard that. They couldn't hear shit. And even more irony? They would advance, leaving Keyman and Hansen to bleed or freeze to death, whichever came first.

Footfalls. Fast. Near.

Keyman rolled away from Hansen, raised the pistol—but it slipped from his weak grip and hit the snow. *Shit!* He suddenly faced a frightened boy, a little Red Youth Guard shit, clutching a rifle. The kid had come running down the mountain and had stumbled upon them.

Junior had a decision to make.

Keyman had already made his. "Shoot me, you godless motherfucker. Shoot me now."

The kid, whose face was as red as a maraschino cherry, lifted his rifle, looked up. His narrow eyes appeared from the deep folds, and his mouth opened.

Keyman jolted as rounds tore into the kid's chest, his thin shirt flapping, arms beating as he fell back, boom, dead.

More footfalls. Keyman felt too weak to turn his head and find the pistol. "All right, you little fuckers. Just shoot us and get it over with."

A troop from Renegade Platoon, a young replacement guy with a few gold teeth, hunkered down, looking seriously dumbfounded. "Hey? Sergeant? Sergeant Key?"

"Yeah, that's me."

"They call you Keyman. I know who you are. Damn, with all this snow we would've missed you—if it wasn't for that kid."

Keyman glanced at the dead North Korean. "Dumb luck I guess."

"Or a miracle," said the grunt.

"You're right. A miracle. How 'bout one more? Can we bum a ride?"

HANSEN REGAINED CONSCIOUSNESS while being whisked to Seoul via a MEDEVAC chopper. He lay on a backboard, in a litter basket, and was attended to by a much too peppy medic who kept grinning and lifting his thumb. Hansen's ass felt really sore, but the damned IV in his arm hurt even more. Figured.

The damned chopper was loud. You couldn't hear yourself think. He glanced across the bay, where Keyman lay in another litter basket. The TC caught sight of him and just stared. No expression. A zombie. Hansen assumed that he looked the same.

Now there was plenty of time to think. Plenty of time to wander back to those dangerous thoughts. Plenty of time to beat himself up over what had happened.

What *had* happened? He couldn't comprehend it all, could barely believe that everyone save for himself and Keyman had died. Everyone.

Abbot, Park, Paz, and Sparrow.

Neech, Romeo, Choi, and Wood.

Halitov, Boomer, Zuckerman . . .

And dear God, Gatch, Deac, and Mingola.

Not to mention his old roommate, Gary Gutterson. Fifteen warriors had given their lives. Maybe they weren't the bravest souls or the most patriotic. Maybe they weren't the sharpest warriors. But they had believed in each other, as Hansen had believed in them.

Or had he? Had he spent too much time worrying? Too much time ridiculing them? Had he really been a good platoon leader, a proud officer? Had he truly done his duty?

A FEW DAYS later, while Hansen and Keyman were recuperating at the 121st General Hospital, located on Yongsan Garrison's south post, Hansen learned what had happened to the rest of Team Cobra.

They had continued to fight with reinforcements from the battalion. Abbot's tank, with the FSO's BFIST as wingman, had provided direct fire support to the engineers, who had come up to blast the road clear. CAS and artillery had begun prepping the rest of the route, and then, with more follow-on forces, the team had gone on to take Kaesong within a day.

However, they hadn't rolled on to the North Korean capital in Pyongyang. Higher had decided to let the ROKs conduct a forward passage of lines so that they could seize Pyongyang for political reasons. And that operation was currently underway, with Combined Forces Command standing by in case the ROKs' best laid plans went suddenly south.

Scuttlebutt had it that the Dear Leader in Pyongyang would either surrender or commit suicide. Apparently the bookies in Vegas were going nuts over the whole thing.

On a side note, no one had ever asked Hansen why he had fired his smoke grenades at those troops. Maybe that would come later. Or probably not at all. He had rehearsed his answer: "I fired them in order to protect my vehicle and my men."

Who up the chain of command would argue?

Hansen had a chance to watch some CNN news coverage, and he even spotted a few guys from Blue Platoon rumbling down the streets of Kaesong, standing tall in their hatches.

"That should've been us," said Keyman, leaning over his bed to spit in his little chew cup. "Right there.

Should've been us." He had tied a bandanna bearing the Harley-Davidson logo around his bald head. He looked more biker than tanker; ironically, he had never ridden on a motorcycle before, but the bandanna was the best the nurses could find. "At least it ain't pink," he had joked. "Fuckin' Gatch would've loved it."

That reminder left them silent.

Hansen winced as he tried to roll onto his side. He and Keyman had been shot up good, but they hadn't sustained any permanent injuries.

Physical ones, anyway.

ON THE DAY they would leave the hospital and fly out of Korea, Hansen finished his breakfast and said, "You ready to talk?"

Keyman rolled his eyes. "I told you. I just don't want to go there right now."

"But they were my men. You were there. I have to know. You can't keep it from me."

Keyman rolled over, his back to Hansen. "Why's it so fucking important? They died like men. That's all."

"I was thinking that if we talked about it now, we could just . . . I don't know . . . leave some of it here."

Keyman rolled over and ripped off his bandanna. "Dude, I lost two fuckin' crews. Not one. *Two!* And I watched those fuckin' guys die. Fuckin' Abbot right there, that sweet old man telling me it couldn't be any better. He knew he was going. He knew it. Fuckin' Neech begging me to tell his dad how he died. Fuckin' begging me, for God's sake. And he's looking at me and holding his neck, and the fuckin' blood is everywhere." Keyman slammed back into his bed, burying his face in the pillow.

Hansen fell back on his own bed, draped an arm over his eyes. So he had been kidding himself.

No one got left behind. Ever.

Now the people in Hansen's world assumed two forms: flesh and blood . . . and ghost.

"Lieutenant?" Keyman called.

"Yeah?"

"I, uh—"

"It's okay, man. That's enough."

"Thanks. Do you think you could help me contact Neech's dad? I want to tell him myself. I made a promise to Neech."

Hansen's eyes burned. "You'll, uh, you'll keep that promise."

BEING IN WHEELCHAIRS made taking the flight from Osan Air Base to Tokyo even more miserable, but they managed. From Tokyo they hitched a ride aboard a big, old C-17 bound for Hickam Air Force Base in Oahu. Once there, they would spend the next two months at Tripler Army Medical Center in Honolulu, the largest facility of its kind in the entire Pacific basin. They would receive physical therapy and be interviewed by the armor school leadership for lessons learned. After their release, they would get two weeks leave to go home, then they would return to First Tank in Korea. Replacements would have assumed their old jobs, so Hansen figured he might be a candidate for scout or mortar platoon leader or work the battalion staff as an assistant S3 (operations officer). Keyman would either become a company master gunner or work on the battalion staff too, in the S3 section.

Although the C-17 put down in the middle of the night, they, along with about fifty other service personnel, were greeted by a small crowd who applauded as they disembarked. While that wasn't unusual, most of the men and women Hansen had spoken to on board the plane did not have family or relatives who lived in Hawaii.

He asked the private handling his wheelchair to roll him up to one kind-faced woman in her fifties who was handing out bags stuffed with fast-food hamburgers and fries, along with care packages of toiletries. "Excuse me, ma'am?"

"Oh, you didn't get one? Here." She shoved a bag into his lap. "Take one of these too." The toiletries.

"No, I'm just wondering. Do you guys know any of us?"

"Nope. Not a soul." She stopped what she was doing, leaned over, and placed a hand on Hansen's cheek. "We're just here to make sure you're taken care of. Thank you for what you did. Thank you."

Hansen never felt more proud to be an American.

She went on to explain that local civic and church groups were prescreened and allowed on the base, along with the usual employees and dependants, as well as people from all the other bases on Oahu, including Schofield Barracks, Camp Smith, Fort Shafter, Kaneohe Base, and the U.S. Navy Base, Pearl Harbor. Everyone wanted to make sure the boys coming back received a proper welcome. Hansen thanked her, and she smiled and returned to her work.

"Hey, I thought your woman was supposed to be here," Keyman said as he was rolled up by a specialist.

"Me too." Hansen glanced around the terminal. The last time he had spoken to Karen she had sounded thrilled by his return. And while he had insisted that his parents not waste all that money catching the first flight to Hawaii (they would arrive the next day), he hadn't argued with Karen, since, well, she was already here.

But maybe, like some women do, she had finally realized that the sacrifices were too much.

Dear Jack . . .

"Jack? Jack?"

He spotted her through the crowd, all brown eyes and dark hair swinging behind her as she wove toward him. She had flowers. Damn, that was embarrassing!

As she neared them, Keyman muttered, "Nice tits."

"Shut up, asshole," said Hansen.

"Oh my God, Jack!" She dumped the flowers in his lap, grabbed his head, and planted one so deep that his groin tingled.

"Oh, that's hot. Yeah," said Keyman.

Karen pulled away, glanced over. "Wait a minute. I thought you guys hated each other."

They had. Several lifetimes ago. Karen assumed they were the same people.

If she only knew . . .

"What I hate about him," Keyman began. "Is that he got a gorgeous woman like you to date him. And what he hates about me is my good looks."

Hansen chuckled. "Yeah, I hate this guy."

Keyman nodded and took Karen by the wrist. "Hey, sweetheart, you got a sister?"

"She wouldn't subject her to that kind of punishment," Hansen said.

Karen moved back and grinned. "Look at you two. Traded in your tanks for wheelchairs."

"And hopefully we'll trade these in for something with tracks again," said Keyman.

She grew sober and nodded. "Right now, it's good you're home."

THE NEXT AFTERNOON, Keyman was able to track down Neech's father. They spoke briefly on the phone, and Keyman could barely collect himself. "That's right, sir. I was with your son. I'd love to get together. Yes, sir. Thank you, sir."

Keyman hung up the phone. And the son of bitch broke down. Hansen tried to hang on himself. And failed.

LATER ON, AT a public awards ceremony set up in one of Hickam's colossal hangers, Hansen and Keyman were rolled up onto a dais to join about a dozen other Army personnel who had also fought in Korea. Military brass and dignitaries present included the commander, U.S. Army Pacific (USARPAC), the commander of Hickam AF Base, the commander of Tripler Medical Center, and the governor of Hawaii.

The PACOM commander, a four-star admiral with a white crew cut who took spit and polish to a new level, spoke eloquently to the crowd of family and friends, and while Hansen beamed at Karen and his parents, the admiral read the citations: "Attention to orders. For extraordinarily meritorious service and valor during major combat operations in Korea, the commander, Combined Forces Command, awards the Purple Heart and the Silver Star to Second Lieutenant Jack Hansen. Staff Sergeant Timothy Key is awarded the Purple Heart and the Bronze Star with 'V' device for valor. Lieutenant Hansen and Sergeant Key led the way for CFC ground combat forces counterattacking into North Korea. As their tank platoon neared Kaesong, they encountered a series of ambushes and dismounted guerrilla attacks from enemy forces. Though the sole remaining survivors, Lieutenant Hansen and Sergeant Key continued to fight dismounted until reinforcements arrived. Their persistence in conducting the attack allowed ROK and U.S. forces to achieve their mission of seizing Kaesong and eventually led to the defeat of North Korean forces. Their warrior spirit and dedication to duty are in the finest traditions of military service. Their actions bring great credit to their unit, the United States Army, and the United States of America."

The admiral pinned on Hansen's medals, then leaned over and did likewise with Keyman's. Out in the audience sat Keyman's father and brother, who wept openly.

Hansen wished he could have been standing for the ceremony, but receiving the medals made him feel incredibly tall.

Still, the heart and star weren't just for him. They were for all of them. The ones for whom he stood.

For gallantry in action.

He pressed the medals to his chest and lowered his head . . .

As the audience applauded.

BATTLE MAPS KEY

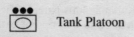 Tank Platoon

Mechanized Infantry Platoon

Engineer Platoon

120mm Mortar Platoon

Engineer Float Bridge Company

Observation post; usually occupied by forward observers and/or scouts

Enemy artillery observer element

Enemy tank

Enemy armored personnel carrier

Concertina wire obstacle

Enemy antitank mine

Enemy antipersonnel mine

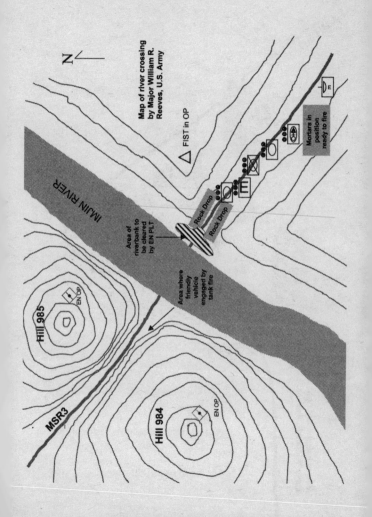

Map of river crossing by Major William R. Reeves, U.S. Army

IMJIN RIVER

△ FIST in OP

Mortars in position ready to fire

Rock Drop

Rock Drop

Area of riverbank to be cleared by EN PLT

Area where friendly vehicle engaged by tank fire

Hill 985

EN OP

Hill 984

EN OP

MSR3

N

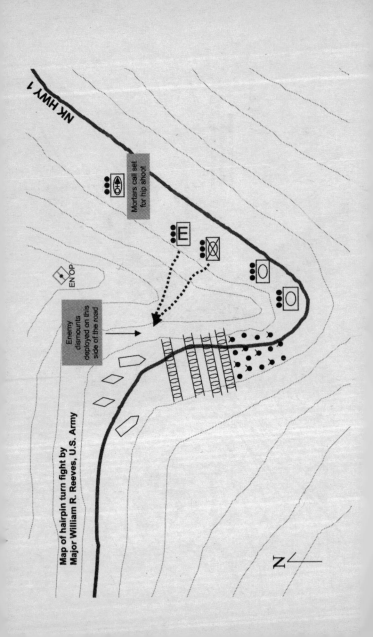

NK HWY 1

Mortars call set for hip shoot

E

EN OP

Enemy dismounts deployed on this side of the road

Map of hairpin turn fight by Major William R. Reeves, U.S. Army

N

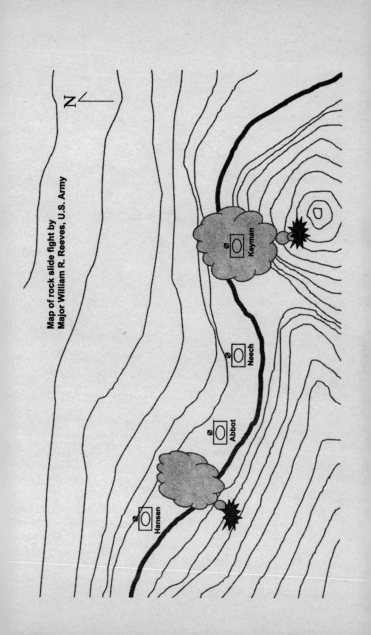

Map of rock slide fight by
Major William R. Reeves, U.S. Army

GLOSSARY

Compiled by
*Shawn T.O. Priest, Major William R. Reeves, U.S. Army,
and Captain Keith Wilson, U.S. Army*

A

AA avenue of approach; assembly area

AAR after-action review

ABF attack by fire (position)

abatis an obstacle created by felling trees or poles in an interlocking pattern across a road or path facing toward an approaching enemy; can be reinforced with wire, mines, and direct and indirect fires

ACE armored combat earthmover

ACR armored cavalry regiment

active air defense direct defensive action taken to destroy attacking enemy aircraft or missiles

ADA air defense artillery

adashi Korean: uncle, GI slang for any adult Korean male

ajima Korean: *aunt,* GI slang for any adult Korean female

A/L administrative/logistics

A.L.I.C.E. all-purpose lightweight carrying equipment

ammo ammunition

AO area of operation

AOI area of interest
AOR area of responsibility
AP antipersonnel
APC armored personnel carrier
APFSDS-T armor-piercing, fin-stabilized, discarding sabot–tracer (ammunition); a high-velocity inert projectile of depleted uranium
ARTEP Army Training and Evaluation Program
ASAP as soon as possible
ASLT POS assault position (abbreviation on overlays)
AT antitank
ATGM antitank guided missile
ATK POS attack position (abbreviation on overlays)
AVLB armored vehicle launched bridge
AXP ambulance transfer point

B

Bangalore torpedo Sections of pipe filled with C4 explosive that are assembled in combat, pushed under/through obstacles, and detonated by timed or electrical fuses. Used primarily by dismounted engineers to clear a path through wire and mines.
BAS battalion aid station
BDA battle damage assessment
BDE brigade
BFIST The M7 Bradley Fire Support Team Vehicle is the latest combat vehicle provided to armor, mechanized infantry, and armored cavalry FIST teams. A highly modified Bradley Fighting Vehicle, it contains an assortment of radios, computers, optics, and other accessories for target location and fire support coordination on the modern battlefield.
BFV Bradley (infantry) fighting vehicle, equipped with 25 mm cannon and TOW launcher, battle-proven in both Gulf Wars.
BHL battle handover line
BII basic issue items

blivet a rubber storage bag, transportable by air or ground, that holds 500 gallons of fuel or water, used at forward resupply points

BMNT begin morning nautical twilight; time of day when enough light is available to identify the general outlines of ground objects

BMP *Boyeveya Machina Pyekhota;* Russian-designed infantry personnel carrier; used by the North Korean People's Army

BN battalion

BP battle position

BRDM Russian-designed four wheel drive amphibious light reconnaissance vehicle; used by the NKPA

BSA brigade support area

BSFV Bradley Stinger (missile) fighting vehicle, modified to fire the Stinger for anti-aircraft defense

BTR Soviet-designed wheeled APC used by NKPA

C

CA civil affairs

cal caliber

CAM chemical agent monitor

CAS close air support

CASEVAC casualty evacuation

CAV air cavalry (slang)

CBT combat

CBU cluster bomb unit

CCA close combat attack; attack helicopter aviation in support of ground combat operations

CCIR commander's critical information requirements; composed of EEFI, FFIR, and PIR

CCP casualty collection point; pre-established point to consolidate casualties and prepare for evacuation

CDR commander

CEV combat engineer vehicle

CFC Combined Forces Command

CFL coordinated fire line; a line beyond which conventional fire support may fire at any time within the zone established by higher headquarters without additional coordination

CFV cavalry fighting vehicle

CIP combat identification panel

Claymore a command-detonated directional fragmentation mine

CMD command

cml chemical

CMO civil-military operations

CO commanding officer; company

CO TM company team; company-sized combat element that includes attachments such as engineers, aviation, air defense, etc.

coax coaxially mounted (machine gun)

COLT combat observation and lasing team

CP command post; check point

CQB close quarters battle

CS combat support

CSM command sergeant major

CSS combat service support

CTCP combat trains command post

CVC combat vehicle crewman

CWS commander's weapon station, from which he can engage targets with the main gun, coax, or the M2HB .50 cal machine gun

D

DA Department of the Army

DD, DoD Department of Defense

DIV CG division commanding general

DMZ demilitarized zone; space created to neutralize certain areas from military occupation and activity

DOA direction of attack (abbreviation on overlays)

DP decision point

DPICM dual-purpose improved conventional munitions

DS direct support

DS/R direct support/reinforcing
DTG date-time group

E

EA engagement area
ECWS extreme cold weather system
EEFI essential elements of friendly information; critical aspects of a friendly operation that, if known by the enemy, would compromise, lead to failure, or limit success of the operation
EENT end evening nautical twilight; there is no further sunlight visible
ELINT electronic intelligence
EPLRS enhanced position locating and reporting system
EPW enemy prisoner of war
ETAC enlisted terminal attack controller; enlisted Air Force personnel assigned to provide close air support/terminal guidance control for exercise and contingency operations, on a permanent and continuous basis
EW electronic warfare

F

1SG first sergeant
FA field artillery
FAAD forward area air defense
FARP forward arming and refueling point: A temporary site where helicopters land during combat operations to refuel and reload gun, rocket, and missile ammunition. The fuel storage and pumping system can be used to fuel ground vehicles in contingency situations.
FASCAM family of scatterable mines
FDC fire direction center
FEBA forward edge of the battle area; foremost limits of area in which ground combat units are deployed
FFIR friendly force information requirement; information the commander and his staff need about the forces available for an operation
FIST fire support team

FIST-V fire support team vehicle

FLE forward logistics element

FLOT forward line of own troops; a line that indicates the most forward positions of friendly forces at a specific time

FM frequency modulation (radio); field manual

FO forward observer

FPF final protective fires

FRAGO fragmentary order

FROKA First Republic of Korea Army; mission is to defend the eastern section of the DMZ. The VII ROK Corps defends the eastern coastal invasion route, and the VIII ROK Corps is responsible for the coastal defense of Kangwon Province.

FS fire support

FSCL fire support coordination line

FSE fire support element

FSO fire support officer; special staff officer responsible for helping to integrate all mortar, FA, naval gunfire, and CAS fires into the maneuver commander's combined arms plan

FSSG fire support sergeant

FTCP field trains command post

G

GEMSS ground-emplaced mine scattering system

GPS global positioning system; gunner's primary sight

GS general support

GSR ground surveillance radar; efficient system for tracking enemy troop and vehicle movement in near-zero visibility

H

HE high explosive

HEAT high explosive antitank (ammunition)

HEMTT heavy expanded mobility tactical truck; provides transport capabilities for resupply of combat vehicles and weapons systems

HHC headquarters and headquarters company

HMMWV high-mobility multipurpose wheeled vehicle (Hummvee); the able replacement for the military Jeep

HPT high-payoff target; a target whose loss to the threat will contribute to the success of an operation

HQ headquarters

HUMINT human intelligence

HVT high-value target; assets that the threat commander requires for the successful completion of a specific action

I

IAW in accordance with

ICM improved conventional munitions

ID identification

IED improvised explosives device

IFF identification, friend or foe

IFV infantry fighting vehicle

IN infantry

IN (M) mechanized infantry

IPB intelligence preparation of the battlefield

IR infrared; intelligence requirements

IVIS intervehicular information system

J

JAAT joint air attack team

Javelin a shoulder fired, fire and forget antitank weapon capable of killing any modern armored vehicle

JCATF joint civil affairs task force

JDAM Joint Direct Attack Munition; a GPS guidance package attached to conventional bombs giving aircraft a highly accurate, all-weather, autonomous precision bombing capability

JPOTF joint psychological operations task force

JSA joint security area: The central location in the western portion of the DMZ where diplomatic meetings occur between the two Koreas and other international mediators. It also lies along a main avenue of approach between the two nations.

K

KATUSA Korean Augmentee to the United States Army; an ROK soldier attached to U.S. units to augment manpower and provide cultural and linguistic knowledge to formations; a program that has been in place since the beginning of the Korean War.

KIA killed in action

klick one kilometer

KNP Korean National Police; the ROK paramilitary police force

KSG Korean Security Guard; ROK contractors charged with guarding the gates and walls of U.S. Army camps in the ROK

L

LBE load-bearing equipment

LBV load-bearing vest

LD line of departure; a line used to coordinate the departure of attack elements

LNO liaison officer

LOA limit of advance; a terrain feature beyond which attacking forces will not advance

LOC line of communications

LOGPAC logistics package

LOM line of movement

LP/OP listening post/observation post

LRF laser range-finder

LRP logistic release point

LT lieutenant (2LT, Second Lieutenant; 1LT, First lieutenant)

LTC lieutenant colonel

LTG lieutenant general

M

M4 The shorter, carbine version of the popular M16 series of rifles. Replaced the M3 "grease gun" as a tank crew dismount weapon

MACOM U.S. Army Major Command

MAJ major
MANPADS man-portable air defense system
MBA main battle area
mech mechanized
MEDEVAC medical evacuation
METL mission-essential task list
METT-TC mission, enemy, terrain (and weather), troops, time available, and civilian considerations (factors in situational analysis)
MG major general
MICLIC mine-clearing line charge
Molotov cocktail crude incendiary weapon which consists of a glass bottle filled with flammable liquid
MOPMS Modular Pack Mine System; a man-portable box containing antitank and antipersonnel mines that can be initiated by remote control, scattering the mines in a semicircular pattern
MOPP mission-oriented protective posture; consists of seven levels of preparation for chemical or biological attack, MOPP READY being the least protected and MOPP 4 the most protected
MOUT Military Operations on Urbanized Terrain; fighting in cities
MPAT multipurpose antitank (ammunition)
MRE meals, ready to eat; also referred to by troops as meals rejected by everyone, brown bags, or bag nasties
MRS muzzle reference system; a system enabling tank crews to adjust the gun alignment quickly in combat to compensate for gun tube droop caused by the heat from firing
MSR main supply route
MST maintenance support team

N

N-Hour an unspecified time that commences notification and outload for rapid, no-notice deployment
NAAK nerve agent antidote kit
NAI named area of interest; point or area through which enemy activity is expected to occur

NBC nuclear, biological, chemical
NCO noncommissioned officer
NCOIC noncommissioned officer in charge
NCS net control station
NEO noncombatant evacuation operations
NFA no fire area; an area into which no direct or indirect fires or effects are allowed without specific authorization
NGO nongovernmental organization
NKPA North Korean Peoples Army; the North Korean army
NLT not later than
NOD night observation device
NVG night vision goggles

O

OAK-OC obstacles, avenues of approach, key terrain, observation and fields of fire, and cover and concealment (considerations in evaluating terrain as part of METT-T analysis)
OBJ objective
OIC officer in charge
OP observation post
OPCON operational control
OPD Officer Professional Development; mentoring sessions usually given to junior officers by more experienced middle or senior officers to educate them on subjects not taught at the military school house
OPLAN operation plan
OPORD operation order
OPSEC operations security
OPTEMP operational tempo

P

passive air defense all measures, other than active air defense, taken to minimize the effects of enemy air action
PC personnel carrier; slang for APC
PCC pre-combat check

PCI pre-combat inspection
PEWS platoon early warning system
PFC private first class
PIR priority intelligence requirements
PL phase line; platoon leader
PLL prescribed load list
PLT platoon
PMCS preventive maintenance checks and services
POL petroleum, oils, and lubricants
POS position
POSNAV position navigation (system)
PSG platoon sergeant
PSYOPS psychological operations
PVT private (buck)
PV2 private

R

R3P rearm, refuel, and resupply point
RAAM remote antiarmor mine
recon reconnaissance
REDCON readiness condition
REMBASS remotely emplaced battlefield area sensor system; a set of seismic/acoustic, magnetic, and infrared sensors
REMS remotely employed sensors
retrans retransmission
RFL restrictive fire line; line between two converging friendly forces that prohibits direct or indirect fires or effects of fires without prior coordination
ROE rules of engagement
ROK Republic of Korea
ROKA Republic of Korea Army
ROM refuel on the move
RP release point
RPG rocket-propelled grenade; a Soviet-designed shoulder-fired weapon; deadly to both personnel and armored vehicles
RTE route

S

S1 adjutant (U.S. Army)

S2 intelligence officer (U.S. Army)

S3 operations and training officer (U.S. Army)

S4 supply officer (U.S. Army)

SALUTE size, activity, location, unit identification, time, and equipment (format for report of enemy information); abbreviated format is SALT or size, activity, location, and time

SAM surface-to-air missile

SAW squad automatic weapon

SBF support by fire (position)

SFC sergeant first class

SGM sergeant major

SGT sergeant

SHORAD short-range air defense

SINCGARS single channel ground/airborne radio system

SITREP situation report

SITTEMP situational template

SOFA status of force agreement; an agreement that defines the legal position of a visiting military force deployed in the territory of a friendly state

SOI signal operation instructions; a code book for encrypting and decrypting coded messages

SOP standing operating procedure

SOSR suppression, obscuration, security, and reduction (actions executed during breaching operations)

SP start point

SPC specialist

SPOTREP spot report

SROKA Second Republic of Korea Army; is responsible for defending the rear area extending from the rear of the front area to the coastline, and consists of an army command, several corps commands, divisions, and brigades. The Second Army has operational command over all army reserve units, the Homeland Reserve Force, logistics, and training bases located in the six southernmost provinces.

SSG staff sergeant

STAFF smart target activated, fire and forget (ammunition)

STRYKER A new generation of wheeled APCs adopted by the U.S. Army to fill the gap between light and heavy forces. Capable of being rapidly airlifted to contingency areas on short notice. The Stryker APC bears a striking resemblance to the Russian-designed BRDM that is also used by the NKPA.

T

TAA tactical assembly area

TAC or TAC CP tactical command post

TACP tactical air control party; USAF personnel attached to maneuver units to conduct terminal control of close air support (CAS) where friendly and enemy ground units are in close proximity to each other

tac idle tactical idle (speed), keeping the engine at high RPMs for maximum efficiency of hydraulic systems and electrical output

TC tank commander

TCP traffic control post

TDC Tongduch'on; a city north of Seoul containing several of the U.S. Army's 2nd Infantry Division camps and the majority of the division's ground combat units

TF task force

TIS thermal imaging system

TM team

TOC tactical operations center

TOE table(s) of organization and equipment

TOW tube-launched, optically tracked, wire-guided (missile)

TRADOC U.S. Army Training and Doctrine Command

TROKA Third Republic of Korea Army: South Korea's largest and most diversified combat organization is responsible for guarding the most likely potential attack routes from North Korea to Seoul—the Munsan, Ch'orwon, and Tongduch'on corridors.

TRP target reference point
TSOP tactical standing operating procedure
TTP tactics, techniques, and procedures

U

UAV unmanned aerial vehicle
UMCP unit maintenance collection point
U.N. United Nations
UNC United Nations Command
USFK United States Forces, Korea

V

VTT North Korea-designed tracked APC; similar to the BMP-1

W

WARNO warning order
WIA wounded in action
WP white phosphorus, also called "Willie Pete"

X

X-Hour an unspecified time that commences unit notification for planning and deployment preparation in support of operations not involving rapid, no-notice deployment
XO executive officer

Z

Zulu (time reference) Greenwich Mean Time

ABOUT THE AUTHOR

Pete Callahan is the pseudonym for a popular author of fantasy; science fiction; medical drama; movie, television, and computer game tie-ins; and military action/adventure novels. His heavily researched work has been sold worldwide and translated into Spanish, German, French, and Japanese. Contact him at armoredcorps@aol.com.

Don't miss the first two books
in this series

PETE CALLAHAN

Armored Corps

West Point graduate Lieutenant Jack Hansen is
stationed near the 38th Parallel in South Korea with the
1st Tank Battalion. They haven't seen any action yet,
but that's about to change.

0-515-13932-7

Armored Corps:
Engage and Destroy

The battlefield changes in North Korea when the city of
Tongduch'on comes under attack. Now, Lieutenant
Jack Hansen and his platoon find themselves caught
in a brutal street-by-street battle for the city.

0-515-14016-3

Available wherever books are sold or at
penguin.com